**As she rose,
Isobel's gaze flitted toward the doorway,
and her eyes met his—
the mannerless, wicked, impudent brute
who'd humiliated her at the club.**

Behind him was a collection of the tallest, most beautiful beings she'd ever seen. The women were the height of most men, their features delicate and perfect. The men were giants, at least a foot taller than any other gentlemen in the room. Like the fighter himself, their muscles were pronounced beneath their dark blue coats, protruding like great river stones beneath a shallow creek.

She sucked a deep breath into her lungs. Where had these huge, beautiful creatures come from?

One corner of the fighter's lips lifted in a cocky grin and he tipped his head toward her.

Lord above, he's recognized me.

By Kathryn Caskie

TO SIN WITH A STRANGER
HOW TO PROPOSE TO A PRINCE
HOW TO ENGAGE AN EARL
HOW TO SEDUCE A DUKE

Coming Soon

THE MOST WICKED OF SINS

KATHRYN CASKIE

TO SIN WITH A STRANGER

AVON

An Imprint of HarperCollinsPublishers

AVON BOOKS
An Imprint of HarperCollins*Publishers*
10 East 53rd Street
New York, New York 10022-5299

Copyright © 2008 by Kathryn Caskie
Excerpts from *Tempted By the Night* copyright © 2008 by Elizabeth Boyle; *Secret Desires of a Gentleman* copyright © 2008 by Laura Lee Guhrke; *All I Want for Christmas Is a Vampire* copyright © 2008 by Kerrelyn Sparks; *To Sin With a Stranger; The Most Wicked of Sins* copyright © 2008, 2009 by Kathryn Caskie
ISBN 978-0-06-149100-9
www.avonromance.com

First Avon Books paperback printing: December 2008

Printed in the U.S.A.

10 9 8 7 6 5 4 3 2 1

For Jenny Bent, Lucia Macro,
Sophia Nash, and Franzeca Drouin.
Without you, this book
would not have been possible.

Acknowledgments

There are so many people to whom I owe my great thanks for helping me bring this story to fruition. (I am certain to forget someone, so I will thank that person first. Thanks. Couldn't have done it without you.)

Dr. Peter Higgs, curator of the Elgin Marbles collection at the British Museum in London, as well as his very knowledgeable staff in the museum's Greek and Roman Antiquities Department.

My amazing editor, Lucia Macro, who loved the idea of the series as much as I did, supported me when I needed it most, and even scored a stunning red cover for *To Sin With a Stranger*.

My agent, Jenny Bent, who believed in me and kept me writing through the hard times.

Sophia Nash, my friend and fellow Avon Books author, who called me nearly every day to cheer me on to the finish line.

My online buddies from the Avon Romance Blog and Romance Novel TV, who searched out and found the visual inspiration for all seven heroes of the Seven Deadly Sins series: Kim Castillo, Gannon Carr, P.J. Ausdenmore, Crystal Broyles, Keira Soleore, Buffie Johnson, Marisa O'Neill, Kati Dancy, and Jenny Teo. You all have the best taste!

And finally, Franzeca Drouin, my incredible research assistant, who even managed to locate a drawing and description of the coal shed where Lord Elgin stored his Greek marbles. Is there anything you can't do?

Thank you all.

To Sin With a Stranger

His Grace, William ········ m. ········ Her Grace, Patience
The Duke of Sinclair   The Duchess of Sinclair
(1754–)   (1768–1795)

Sterling Sinclair   Lady Siusan   Lord Grant
Marquess of Blackburn   (1790–)   (1791–)
(1788–)

···· m. ····

Isobel Carington

(To Sin With a Stranger)

Sinclair Family Tree

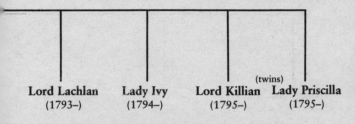

Lord Lachlan
(1793–)

Lady Ivy
(1794–)

Lord Killian
(1795–)

(twins)
Lady Priscilla
(1795–)

Prologue

The source of your problem is your blessing.
Unknown

March 1816
Castle Sinclair, Scotland

He's gone completely mad.

Sterling Sinclair shoved his rain-sodden ebony hair from his eyes, then charged across the great hall to collect his sister. He snatched up her hand and pulled her away from the portmanteau she had hurriedly packed and managed to drag down from her bedchamber. "Leave it, Ivy. We must go—now. You've no need anyway for gowns and baubles this night."

She brushed a copper lock of hair from her fa

and turned her pleading green eyes up at him. "Please, you can't ask me to leave my clothing here. I'll have nothing—*nothing*!" Ivy bent, struggling to reach the handle of the leather bag, but it was just out of her reach.

"You can." He tugged hard at her hand and started his stubborn sister toward the door. "Father will come to his senses by morn and send for us. He always does." Movement caught Sterling's notice then, and he turned to see his father standing at the top of the sweeping stone staircase. The old man's pale blue eyes flashed angrily in the light of the lamp he held in his hand.

"Did you not hear me?" the duke shouted down at them. "I said you *all* are to leave at once!"

From where they stood near the open timber-hewn door, Sterling could barely hear his father's words. Rain rode the roaring wind that tore through the doorway into the great hall, sending the old man's unkempt silver hair streaming behind him like a war banner of old.

Ivy tugged against Sterling's grip. "You came home too late to know, Sterling. It's not the whisky this time. For the first night in years, I vow, he's as dry as a peat brick." Ivy broke free of him then and raced back across the slippery stone floor for her precious belongings. Fretfully she peered up their father, who had started down the staircase. She looked over her shoulder at Sterling as she struggled to lift the heavy bag. "Help me! He won't bring us back this time. I fear he truly means to cast us out for good—and we'd deserve it—you especially."

The howling of the storm muted the curses the old duke showered on the two of them, like stinging pelts of hail.

Sterling trailed after Ivy. He reached his muscled arm over her shoulder and lifted the leather case by its belt. "It will not fit in the carriage, Ivy. There's seven of us as it is."

"It must, for I know we'll not return." When she stood and turned to follow him, Sterling saw that Ivy's cheeks were wet, with rain or tears he did not know.

Their brother Grant stood under the timber transom, his hand right hand cupped at his brow against the slants of rain. "Come now. The others have already boarded. We have to leave now before the road is naught but a mire." His gaze focused on the portmanteau as Sterling and Ivy neared. "Ah, bluidy hell. What is this—baggage? Don't even think it, Ivy." He strained his voice to be heard over the wind. "There's no room inside as it is, and Siusan and Priscilla—they've got nothing."

"Please," she beseeched Sterling and then Grant "I'll share what I have."

"No, you won't, but we'll take it anyway." Sterling passed the case to Grant. "Strap it to the perch if you can. If not, set it on her lap if it means so much to her to take it."

In the blur of the storm, he could not see the carriage, but the jingle of bits and the nervous whinnies of the horses reached through the darkness.

"Come now, Sterling!" came his brother Lachlan's resonant voice from the direction of the carriage. Sterling started for it, but he couldn't leave just yet. Not without saying his piece.

Cold rivulets of rain trickled under the collar of his coat and lawn shirt, where it traced his spine like an icy finger. It was as though his father prodded him out into the storm. Slowly he turned around and met his father's steely gaze.

Finally, Killian, the youngest of the Sinclair brothers, called out to him. "There's no reasoning with him, Sterling. Just give him some time. He'll change his mind. He always does."

Sterling did not heed his brother's advice and follow him to the carriage. Instead he strode back into the hall until he stood only a few paces from his father. Rain dripped from Sterling's kilt and puddled on the floor. "Let my brothers and sisters stay." He held his voice firm. "I know you fault me, and perhaps rightly so, for what we have all become." He remained silent for a moment then, waiting for his father to at least agree that his blame was well placed, but the duke said nothing. "Banish me alone. Let it be known I died and that Grant is now your heir if that will appease you—but let them stay."

The old man's eyes widened, and he did not blink for some moments. "I am not addled, Sterling. I am well aware that I am fully responsible for the spoiled, wicked, and irresponsible adults my children have become."

Sterling was startled by his father's unexpected admission, and had his wide stance not braced him, his footing would have faltered.

"I retreated to my whisky when your mother died, leaving the seven of you to your own devices . . ." The duke's eyes seemed to soften then, for just a moment, before his back stiffened and his voice sharpened into a steel blade. ". . . to embrace your weaknesses, your sins." He raised the candelabra higher then, as if to let Sterling see his eyes and understand the depth of his anger. "I will not have the name of Sinclair be made a mockery of by my children. I will not allow it."

Sterling bit back the callous retort poised on ' tongue and instead straightened his back to d' up to his full, commanding height. He wou' allow his father to reduce him to the boy ing his father's attention so badly that h do anything, say anything, no matter how horrid, to possess it. "And so you cast us out into the night."

"I have thought deeply about this, but there is no other way. Tonight you will all leave Scotland for London, where no one knows of your wayward histories. There you will each earn the respect the Sinclair name deserves—or never come back to your home"—he smiled coldly—"never again to taste the *riches* of being a Sinclair."

Sterling flinched at that comment.

"Ah, I thought that might snare your attention, my greedy son. I shan't leave you penniless. I have had my man of affairs arrange for a modest house for all of you to share. I have also provided him with a small portion for the lot of you—enough to put food on the table, but little more, for four years. Each of you will have to earn your own way in life. If you wish to return, you must first earn my respect."

Sterling shook his head slowly, and a hardened smile pulled at his lips. "You are our father. I can't believe you would do this to your own children."

"I was remiss in being your father for so many years. I should have disciplined you all when I first heard that your selfish behavior and antics earned my children the title the Seven Deadly Sins. Obviously I did not teach you when you were young what honor and respect mean. So you will learn it now."

My God. Sterling swallowed deeply. Their father truly did mean to rid himself of them this time.

The duke's eyes flashed angrily. "Now, *go*! I cannot bear the sight of what you have become any longer." He turned his back on Sterling and followed the glow of his lamp up the staircase.

Sterling stared at his father in disbelief, until the duke disappeared through an arched doorway. He turned then, his boots pounding the stone floor as he crossed the great hall and went through the open door into the driving rain.

Och, their father was mad all right.

Chapter 1

Learn to live a life of honest poverty, if you must, and turn to more important matters than transporting gold to your grave.

Og Mandino

April 1816
The Sinclair residence
No. 1 Grosvenor Square, London

Sterling Sinclair, Marquess of Blackburn, peeled back the soiled lint dressing from his raw knuckles and dropped the bloodied bandage beside a chipped basin of steaming water.

"This is going to hurt, Sterling, but no so fierce as it will if you fight tonight." Lady Siusan, the second eldest of the seven Sinclairs, slowly straightened his stiff fingers over the bowl, then dipped a cloth into the water and squeezed it over his hand. She glanced up once more, then took up her thinnest embroidery needle and threaded it through his skin.

Sterling sucked a staggered breath between his lips.

"Oh God. I'm so sorry." She turned her gray eyes to his and gave a sympathetic cringe. Her fingers holding the needle trembled. "I'm being as gentle as I can."

Sterling chuckled. "Don't fret so. I'm just funnin' with you, Su. What sort of fighter can't handle a scrape or two? Give me your best stitch. Come on." He grinned at his sister, but his levity did little to calm her.

He'd split her silk stitches and his knuckles wide almost every day that week sparring at the Gentleman Jackson's saloon. But he was ready. He was sure of it. He could win this prize battle.

He had to.

Siusan raised his hand to her eyes, drawing his gaze to his wound. Watery blood oozed up through the seam of sewn skin. She shifted her eyes to his. "God Almighty, Sterling, I have to bandage this. I cannot leave it to weep."

"Bare knuckles for this bout. Makes for higher

wagers than gloved matches, you know." Sterling sighed with frustration and pulled his hand from her grip. "The bleeding will cease soon enough, so stop your fretting. I have to do it."

"No, you don't. We'll get by," she pleaded. "Just look at your hand. Go on!" She shook her forefinger at his knuckles. "All red, blue, and yellow. Why, it looks more like a ball of hammered mutton than a hand."

"I promised all of you that it's my first and last money bout, Su."

"But at what cost?" Siusan's lower lip quivered, and she suddenly became wholly focused on wringing the water from the cloth over the basin.

Sterling reached across the small table and squeezed her shoulder with his left, less mutton-like, hand. "Pugilism is naught but sport to me and ever will be, but we *need* the money. I had no choice but to accept this match."

"There is always a choice," she replied, but her voice quavered.

Just then, a huge figure filled the doorway, blocking out the whisper of candlelight that had reached the garret from the passage beyond. Siusan glanced up and exhaled in relief. She scrubbed the back of her hand over her eyes. "Grant, you tell him. Our stubborn brother here will not listen to me!"

"Tell him what? That I'm the better-looking brother?" Lord Grant Sinclair flashed his perfectly straight teeth at them. "I think he knows that, don't you, Sterling?" He ducked slightly, but the crown of his tousled mahogany locks brushed the top of the doorway as he stepped into Sterling's sparely furnished garret.

Three similar, yet less spacious garrets also sat beneath the roof of the uppermost level of the grand house, each filled by one of the Sinclair brothers. But this suited them well enough, they had all agreed, for if not comfort they would at least have some semblance of privacy.

The Sinclair sisters had taken what would have been the family bedchambers a floor below, but theirs were no better outfitted than their brothers' rooms. There simply was not enough money to properly furnish any but the most public of rooms.

"Grant, tell him that he cannot do this." Siusan poked her finger toward Sterling. "Look at his hands. Go on. Do you see? *Pulp*. They're little more than haggis stuffing."

"Och, they don't look as bad as all that." Grant sat down on the narrow pallet that served as Sterling's bed. "Give it up, Su. There's no way you can persuade him from fighting this eve. Once he's got his mind set there is no changing it."

Siusan dabbed a dry cloth over Sterling's hand once more, watching for the bleeding to stop. "We have enough to get by. You don't need to subject yourself to this brutal pummeling. Father gave us enough."

"Enough to *exist* . . . perhaps." Sterling stood from the pallet and examined his hand. "I can change that tonight."

Siusan growled as she dried her hands and tossed the cloth onto the table. "You knock some sense into him, Grant, since a punch is all he seems to understand." She caught up a handful of her blue satin skirt, then pushed up from the wooden chair and stalked across the bare floor. She whirled when she reached the doorway. "When you've changed his mind, you may find me in the parlor with Ivy and Priscilla."

"In the parlor, eh? What's the occasion?" Grant slapped his hands to his knees and stood shoulder to shoulder with Sterling.

"And is that Ivy's gown from the Fraser gala . . . last year?"

Siusan shrugged. "What if it is?"

"Quite grand, isn't it? In fact, I believe it might have been Ivy's last new gown." Sterling cast a wry glance at his brother. "Why, Grant, I think our sisters have got some grand guest coming to call."

Siusan lifted her chin and flicked her long sable hair over her shoulder. "As a matter of fact we do ... er ... may ... possibly. Ivy and I made the acquaintance of the grand Miss Irene Hillobean this afternoon and invited her to call this eve."

"And you think she'll come, do you?" Sterling tossed a doubtful gaze at Grant, who passed it along to Siusan.

She settled her hands upon her hips and scowled. "Doubt me if you like, but my sisters and I have the right of things. We will earn the respectability Father demands of us by establishing ourselves in London Society."

"You do that, sister." Sterling turned and gestured for Grant to wrap his neck cloth so that he would not mar it with blood. "But until Father forgives us all and finally deems us respectable, *I* will earn the bread that fills your bellies."

"Sterling, why not set this fighting notion aside and stay to greet Miss Hillobean?" Siusan moved a little closer to wait for his reply. "Who knows, a proper impression could be all that stands between the Sinclair family and entrée into London Society."

"It's not quite as easy as that, Su." Grant assisted Sterling with his waistcoat, then plucked up his coat from the bed and eased it over Sterling's shoulders. "Besides which, Sterling cannot forfeit the battle. We've got too much invested in the outcome."

Sterling's eyes widened as Siusan turned back toward them and prowled closer.

She approached Grant and turned her head up to glare into his eyes. "What did you say?"

Grant's gaze shot to Sterling.

"All right," Sterling admitted. "So I had Lachlan bet a few bob at White's. But it's for the good of us all. Why, when I take the battle, our winnings could be as much as ten times my victor's portion."

Siusan staggered back a step. "How much did you wager? How much of *our* precious allowance are you gambling away?"

"Not so much that you need to worry over it." Sterling reached out to calm her, but she stepped away.

Siusan shook her head. "God save you from your opponent's fist this night, Sterling. Because if you lose our money, *I* will kill you!" She whirled on her toes and stalked from the garret.

Grant chuckled. "Think she means it?"

"Och, I don't doubt it at all." Sterling rolled his shoulders, then tipped his neck to the right, then the left to loosen his muscles. "Are we ready then?"

"Aye, Killian has a hackney waiting on the square."

"A hackney? That's a bit rich, especially when we could be wagering the cost of the conveyance instead." Sterling bent and blew out the flame of the lone candle, then followed his brother from the tiny garret and down two flights of stairs into the parlor.

Sterling squinted his eyes against the brilliant light reflecting off the glistening crystal chandeliers as he peered at his sisters collected in the parlor. "Just how many candles have you lit in here?"

Lady Priscilla, the youngest of the Sinclair siblings, flashed him a gleaming, practiced smile as she settled herself upon the silk settee beside Siusan. "Enough to show the Sinclair family hasn't a care about money."

Siusan looked away from Sterling and slunk back against the tufted backrest, wrapping her arms tightly around herself.

Grant set his hand on Sterling's shoulder and peered at him most seriously. "Dear brother, you know full well our sisters cannot be expected to wait for their esteemed guest by the light of a single lamp. Why, Miss Hillobean might see the dark windows and then leave, thinking no one is at home." A grin began to twitch at his lips. "And then where will we be without a connection to proper London Society?"

Sterling chuckled softly, but could not help glancing upward, then around the room to tally the number of candles being wasted. There were four flickering atop the carved marble chimney-piece, two upon the tea table, a dozen tapers in the chandelier—

"Sterling! Stop." With a grimace pinching her perfect features, Ivy leaped to her feet and raced toward her brothers, her wavy red hair streaming behind her. "Don't be so miserly, Sterling. We aren't paupers . . . yet." She slapped a hand to her heart. "But I know how wastefulness vexes you, and so I vow to extinguish every candle in the parlor within five minutes of our guest's departure." Suddenly she became distracted. Her gaze drifted down his coat sleeve and fixed upon his bare hand. She snatched it up and then jerked her head around toward Grant. "Siusan said you promised to convince Sterling not to fight."

"I didn't promise anything," Grant protested, "especially the impossible." He nodded to the tea brewing in a gleaming sterling pot. "Besides, someone has to pay for *that*."

"Hyson tea gives the right impression," Priscilla interjected. "It, indeed everything in this lushly resplendent parlor, is part of the grand illusion that the Sinclairs are a family of means and re-spectability."

"As long as no one ventures upstairs and learns what we've truly been reduced to." Siusan shot a pointed look at Sterling and pursed her pink lips, then averted her gaze from him once more.

The front door slammed open, sending the brass knocker tapping, and Killian stomped into the parlor. In the bright light of the chandeliers, his raven hair reflected with the same dark blue as his angry eyes. "How long will you keep me waiting on the pavers? The hackney will leave if you delay any longer—unless you wish to pay him to wait."

"Don't be absurd. We're leaving now." Sterling bent and kissed each of his sisters on her cheek. "Wish us luck, dear ones, for if we are successful, we shall dine on roast beef on the morrow."

He turned to leave, just catching notice of a roll of eyes bouncing from one sister to another.

The Pugilistic Club
No. 13 New Bond Street

Though polished and cultured, Sterling Sinclair was a Viking of a man. And he'd prove it to all this very night. But by then it would be too late for the Fancy, who even now pushed and shoved, waving their guinea-filled purses for a chance to wager against the naïve Scottish marquess.

The corner of his lip twitched with anticipation as he stepped to the square crudely chalked on the floor. His opponent, the Irish champion, already glistened with the sweat of eagerness. Poor soul. He hadn't the faintest of notions what was about to happen.

No one did.

The seconds aligned their men across from each other on opposite sides of the square, and then took their own places as Gentleman John Jackson stepped onto the stage and signaled for the men to be stripped of their shirts. The seconds stepped away as Gentleman Jackson ensured that both men were fairly in position at the lines.

Sterling stared into the Irishman's eyes, then grinned and waggled his ebony eyebrows, earning a confused scowl. But this, of course, was exactly what he wanted, to break his opponent's concentration.

The Irishman bellowed a feral growl and then lunged for him. Sterling simply stepped aside. The Irishman was huge, a sweating, two-toothed boar of a man whose heft made him slow on his feet.

Sterling sighed. *Too bad.* This was hardly sport at all. He could sidestep the giant brute all night.

But he wouldn't.

Soon enough, at the moment of his choosing,

he'd let one or two punches land. It wouldn't do to make his own victory appear too easy.

The Irishman spun, the leather of his shoe sole smudging the chalk line. His face, already as scarlet as beet-root soup, contorted in a mask of concentration as he drew back his fist.

Sterling raised his fists, then bent his knees and braced for the blow. It was time. He didn't care for what he must do, but it was part of the betting game. He would take a punch, falter, and side wagers would mount.

The Irishman's massive fist hurled toward him. Sterling girded himself, turning his head at the last moment. He meant only to allow a graze this time, but the Irishman's solid fist met his jaw with a jarring thud.

Dizziness assailed Sterling's senses as copper-tasting warmth surged into his mouth. He shook his head, sending a fan of red droplets toward the crowd, then spat a mouthful of blood on the floor.

He raised his head and glared at the Irishman. *Bugger it. That's all.* One blow was more than enough this night. The Season had just begun, after all, and they'd not yet received invitation to any esteemed events, but he knew that a bruised and battered face would not draw the ladies.

It was Sterling's turn now, one he would choose carefully. He listed a bit, for effect, and the crowd groaned as if worried its entertainment was already at an end.

But it wasn't.

It was just about to begin.

The Irishman was grinning at Sterling, gloating over the ease of thrashing the fine lord.

Now was the time.

He staggered forward like a drunken sot, then dropped his head to his chest. Even with his pale gray eyes cast toward the floor, he could see the Irishman lower his fists momentarily, already chewing on the fat of victory.

Somehow he thought he heard Grant calling out, "Leave the stage. Leave!" But that didn't make sense at all.

Now was the time.

Now.

Sterling snapped his head up and drew back his fist. Suddenly a trim-waisted miss was standing between him and his barrel-chested opponent.

Bluidy hell! He jerked his fist back, somehow his stitched knuckles missing her delicate nose. The draw of air from the swift recoil of his punch sucked a few fine tendrils of her golden hair across her face for a moment.

He hadn't seen her approach. She just suddenly appeared, madly waving a fanned bundle of print pamphlets above her head.

The woman's startled cinnamon-hued eyes blinked rapidly and she gasped, slapping the handful of pamphlets to her chest.

A trickle of blood dripped from the corner of Sterling's swollen lip and splashed upon his chest as he stared down at the insane beauty. What could be so damned important that she would throw herself in harm's way by lunging between two modern gladiators in the midst of a prize-fight?

"Your wife, my lord?" His Irish sparring mate grinned and snorted. The crowd cinching around them roared.

Sterling stepped closer, unfolded his fist, and swept the tips of his fingers gently across the young beauty's soft cheek. "Nay." He lifted the corner of his busted lip, breaking the skin anew. "Well, not *yet* anyway." The gathering of gentlemen laughed even louder.

"How dare you, sirrah!" The miss gave his hand a stinging slap, then jerked around and faced the raucous gathering of gentlemen.

Sterling set his hands on his lean hips and waited with interest for what she would say to the Englishmen, who were already grumbling about her interruption of their evening's sport and wager.

The woman glanced warily over her shoulder at Sterling. Her breath came fast, shallow. Aye, she feared him, though she was taking great pains to conceal it. At least that showed she had some common sense.

Sterling's ebony-topped head and muscled shoulders rose above every other gentleman in the room.

As did his three brothers'.

In truth, as he compared his brothers to the delicately polished members of the *ton*, the Sinclairs almost appeared another race entirely. They were a far larger, stronger version of the pale gentlemen standing in a heaving, clamoring ring with guineas poking out from between their untested hands.

But Sterling and his brothers and, aye, his sisters too, *were* different, and soon everyone would know it.

They were Scots, after all.

And more importantly still—they were *Sinclairs*.

The miss shook her pamphlets high above her pretty little head again. "How is it that you fine citizens see fit to throw away your hard-earned coin on a contest between ruffians, when your money could do so much good elsewhere?"

"It's quite simple, miss," replied a lean, knobby-kneed gentleman standing no more than a yard from her. "My money wasn't *hard-earned*. I've never worked a day in all my years." The crowd chuckled at that.

She straightened her spine and appeared, to Sterling, to grow in height by nearly a hand's width. She now stood nearly as tall as his sisters. "Then perhaps you do not know what it means to go hungry. To see your children die because you haven't the money to summon a physician."

"And you know of this, lass?" Sinclair folded his arms over his broad chest. "You're dressed well enough and don't appear in want of anything."

She whirled around. Her eyes flashed with annoyance. "I do not speak of myself, but of the widows and orphans of our soldiers."

"And you reckon that interrupting a fight, a night's entertainment, is the way to convince these gentlemen to dip into their bulging pockets for your cause?" Sterling coughed a laugh. "Lassie, if that's your daft notion, then you'd best leave."

Gentleman Jackson nodded to a stocky matched pair of low-browed grunts. "Escort the lady to the street, please." He turned and looked at the buxom redhead who was busily refilling patrons' glasses. "Maggie, see her to the corner so she can find a hackney."

The men closed down upon the young woman, then gently, yet firmly, grasped her upper arms and marched her toward the door. She turned her head and met Sterling's eyes with a furious glare. "You've not seen the last of me, Scotsman!" she warned.

"Do you promise, dearie?" Sterling called back. He watched her thrash fiercely against the men dragging her from the club. "Ah, don't struggle, miss," he called out to her. "You're apt to make more money for your *cause* on the street corner anyway."

The crowd erupted with laughter and gibes as the woman was escorted through the doorway.

Sterling sucked his swollen lips inside his mouth, watching the doors until Gentleman Jackson's men reappeared a few moments later. He was curiously relieved when they returned so quickly, without the young woman with the blazing doe eyes.

"Sterling." Grant was tugging at his arm, urging him back to the square. "The bout. Come on. It's time to end the game."

"Time to end it." Sterling shook his head, shook the image of her from his mind. Gentleman John Jackson set the pugilists to the chalk lines once more and signaled the battle to begin anew.

The Irishman heaved forward, but Sterling's stitched hand thrust up from below, delivering the blow he'd intended before the feisty miss had walked between them.

Eyes rolling white into his head, the Irishman crashed to the floor. He did not make to approach the chalk lines or even to stand.

All eyes fixed on the Irishman's second, who nodded his head ruefully to Gentleman Jackson.

"The battle's over, Sterling!" Grant was beside him in an instant. "You are the victor." Grant opened his leather pouch and began wrapping a lint bandage around Sterling's bloodied knuckles.

Killian was muttering something about the side wagers as scores of gentleman surged forward. Slapping Sterling's back, one after another pumped his hand hard in congratulations, proudly showing off Sterling's bloody prints on their gloves.

As the crowd subsided, Gentleman Jackson reached out for Sterling's left hand as though to shake it, but when their palms met, Sterling felt several coins press against his skin. He opened his hand and saw six guineas gleaming in his palm.

"Your portion of the winnings, lad. Just a token, mind you." He gestured to the patrons tossing coins to Killian, his smile as bright as the guineas he was pocketing. "As you evidently know, even in by-battles, the real money comes from the betting."

"Aye, so I've heard." Sterling looked down and ran his thumb over the cool coins, making them clank together in his hand.

So much money, with so little effort. They'd live like kings for a month or two on his portion alone.

How simple this was. Why, he could dress the leased house on Grosvenor Square, launch their success in London, and finance their bids for redemption—if he broke his promise to his brothers and sisters. If he fought a prizefight again.

As he peered past his hand, he noticed a pamphlet lying crumpled on the floor. He bent and picked it up, taking only the time to read the front before folding it and surreptitiously tucking it into his breeches. He looked down at the guineas in his hand, then unwound a bit of lint wrapping from his left fist, and tore it off with his teeth. Unrolling it widthwise, he settled the coins inside and tied it into a tight bundle.

Grant slapped him hard on the back. "Criminy, Sterling. Everyone is positively thunderstruck. The Scottish marquess landed the Irish champion. You did it!" He juggled four bulging bags of coins in his hands like a jester at a fête.

Sterling smiled, sending a fresh trickle of blood down his chin. "Lachlan's seeing to our winnings on our bets in White's book?"

"Aye. He left the moment the clover hit the floor." Grant laughed deeply, giddy to be holding so much money once again. "I can't believe it. All of this, from a single punch."

His youngest brother, Killian, drew alongside Sterling. "You look bluidy awful, Sterling, but och, it was worth it, wasn't it? Single Sinclair. That's what they've dubbed you. Did you hear?"

Sterling was still dazed. Images of the battle flashed in his head. Images of *her*.

Killian nudged Grant. "He's not looking so well."

Grant eased Sterling's shirt over his head, guiding his tired arms through the cambric sleeves. "I've got a hackney out front. Let's get you home and have Siusan look at that face of yours. Maybe have her add a few stitches to that Sterling sampler of hers—what do you reckon, *SINGLE SINCLAIR* right across your knuckles?" His brother laughed and made to guide him forward, but Sterling stopped.

"Go on ahead. I'll be right there. I just want to thank Gentleman Jackson . . . for this opportunity."

Sterling exhaled and smiled inwardly. Just as Sterling turned to search him out, Gentleman Jackson caught his arm and stopped him.

"I have a battle scheduled at Fives Court, next month."

"Aye." Sterling nodded. "I saw mention of it in the *Times*. Madrid and Dooney. Touted as the match of the century, is it not?"

"Would have been. Madrid's neck was broken in a battle two nights past. He's dead." Gentleman Jackson sucked in a great deep breath. "Dooney's a champion. When he takes a man down the odds are fair that he won't be walking again for a good long while . . . if ever. I will be honest with you. He's dangerous." Gentleman Jackson peered silently into Sterling's eyes.

"You're not inviting me to fight Dooney—after what you've just told me?"

"I know, I'm a madman for asking this, you being a marquess and all that, but I am asking. I'd like you to consider fighting in Madrid's place."

Sterling did not reply, but stared down into Jackson's eyes, dumbfounded.

"The victor's portion for this battle is a bloody fortune. And with the by-bets . . ." Gentleman Jackson closed his mouth, and then exhaled through his nose. "Look, I know the money mightn't mean much to a fine marquess, but I have a notion that the challenge, the sport, might. And you've got the natural talent. You're fast and light on your feet. Dooney won't be able to touch you." A faraway look muted the excitement that had been in his eyes only a moment before. "Reminds me of myself in days past, you do."

Sterling swallowed, his saliva still thick with

the blood of the fight. The money did have great appeal to him—but so did the ability to walk. "I—I don't ken what to say, Jackson."

Sterling glanced up, and over Gentleman Jackson's shoulder noticed a small group of club members eavesdropping on the conversation over the rims of their brandy glasses.

Gentleman Jackson turned his head and grimaced at the cluster of men. Cupping his hand around Sterling's upper arm, he walked him into the center of the smudged chalk square. "Now, now, you don't have to answer me now. Just consider it. You'd be the toast of Society. Every drawing room door would be open to you. Everyone of consequence will be in attendance at the fight." He clapped his shoulder. "Consider it, won't you? That's all I ask."

"I will." Sterling nodded, then shook Gentleman Jackson's hand and bade him good eve. For several moments he stood on the edge of the chalked square, trying to think about the offer Jackson had made him. Instead, visions of the golden-haired beauty invaded his thoughts with as much surprise as she herself did when she had climbed up onto the stage waving her pamphlets in the air and making her plea for donations to anyone who would listen.

He weighed the lint packet of coins in his palm, then closed his fingers around it and headed from the Pugilistic Club toward the hackney.

Consider it he would, but fighting a world champion known for inflicting lasting injury, and even death, well, that was madness, pure as it comes.

Chapter 2

*Many go fishing all their lives without knowing that
it is not the fish they are after.*

Thoreau

The next day
The Sinclair residence
Grosvenor Square

It was unusually early for Sterling to be about.
The day had yet to ripen and the noon meal
was still at least an hour from being served.
But he could not sleep. His jaw still ached and his
mind still dwelled on the battle the night before,
on that bold miss . . . and on the offer Gentleman
Jackson had made.

After the arduous task of dressing one-handed and without the assistance of the valet he'd had nearly all his life, he descended the stairs. His footfall was barely muted by the tattered and well-used runner, but he did not wish to awaken his slumbering brothers or sisters. It was not yet noon, and he needed time to be alone, to think. To consider.

He made for the contrasting comfort of the ornately adorned ground floor, the only place in the house that felt like home to him—that reminded him of the one place he truly belonged—Castle Sinclair.

Sterling cupped his left hand around the wear-polished newel post and swung around to step into the passage. Suddenly he found himself looking down at a balding head barely covered with a chaotic web of fine white hair. "Bluidy hell!"

"Oh, I do beg your pardon, my lord. I did not mean to startle you. No, I did not. I simply did not expect *anyone* to have risen so early in the . . . afternoon." Poplin was a short—by Sinclair standards anyway—heavily wrinkled manservant of dubious skill.

From what Sterling and his siblings had been able to ascertain from their father's agent, the services of Poplin and Mrs. Wimpole, an ancient, equally unskilled cook and maid-of-all-work, were somehow included in the three hundred and seventy-five pounds per annum they'd paid to lease the house.

The staff, as it was, was actually a blessing, for the pittance of a portion their father had deigned to provide during their banishment from Scotland was not sufficient to pay for any more than the Sinclair brood's most basic needs.

"My hearing is not what it once was, but I have tried to listen for any sound and open the door before the knocker slammed down—but they keep coming." Poplin's voice shook with fretfulness. "No sooner do I close the door than another footman is there . . . knocking . . . threatening to wake the family."

Sterling rubbed his left hand brusquely over his face. "I haven't the damnedest notion of what you are trying to tell me. Whose footmen? Gentleman Jackson's?"

"No, his man hasn't come at all. But dozens of others have come—from all over Town."

"What do you mean?"

Poplin beckoned for Sterling to follow, then began to shuffle toward the gilt fore-parlor. He winced as he opened the door, as quietly as he could, but the hinges squealed like one of the rats that scurried across the bare floor each night in Sterling's garret bedchamber.

"There they are." Poplin gestured to the white marble mantelpiece. It was covered with a veritable litter of calling cards and invitations.

"Damn me." Sterling strode forward and grabbed up a handful of cards, bracing the pile against his chest as he read one after the other from Lord and Lady This, and Sir That. Plutocrats all, with only one thing in common besides their wealth and influence—what they had written.

Every card referred to Sterling's upcoming battle of champions. Every card expressed how grateful the sender would be if only Sterling, and his family, would grace them with their presence at a dinner, a ball, a musicale; at the theater, a race, or a rout.

Sterling stared down at the mound of invitations before him, then turned and released the cards in his hand, letting them flutter down upon the highly polished surface of the tea table, like butterflies landing on a garden puddle.

It seemed his decision to fight at Fives Court had already been made for him.

He heard a creak in the floorboards and looked up, expecting to see Poplin approaching, but it was Siusan.

Her eyes were wide, but her eyebrows inched toward the bridge of her nose. "Wh-what are these?"

Sterling coughed a breathy laugh. "These, my dear, are what you and your sisters have sought since we arrived in Grosvenor Square from Scotland."

Siusan crept closer, then bent and snatched up an invitation and raised it to her eyes. "I can't quite believe it. Sterling, we've been invited to a ball."

"And everywhere else," he muttered. He waved his hands toward the mantel. "These, my darling sister, are our entrée into London Society."

A tremble of astonishment shook Siusan momentarily as she turned her slate-hued eyes to his. The hint of a smile twitched at the edge of her lips, and she reached out blindly for the arm of a gilt chair and dropped down upon its seat. "Dear God, Sterling, you've done it. I don't know how, but somehow you've opened up Society to us."

"So it seems." Sterling scratched the back of his neck, brushing down the wisps of hair that had begun to stand on end.

One week later
Almack's Assembly Rooms

Miss Isobel Carington stood at the perimeter of the dance floor sipping a tasteless tincture of lemon juice in a goblet of water. It did not, as she'd hoped, quell the queasiness she'd felt since she arrived; in fact, the weak lemonade made her feel like retching.

Hurriedly she deposited the goblet onto the passing salver of a distracted footman, and then sighed, nervously shifting from one foot to the other. Isobel knew she didn't belong there—didn't really belong anywhere—but grand Society events especially made her feel an absolute misfit.

At balls and galas like this one, Isobel was all too aware that she was but a politician's daughter in a glittering assembly room rich with nobility and the descendants of kings.

Still, she always accepted any invitation Minister Cornelius Carington's notoriety in the House of Commons garnered the two of them. She and her father were all that was left of their once happy family.

Everything was different for them, now that her mother had died. Her father spent full days and nights at Parliament, often failing to return home, all the while growing more and more embittered with life, and intolerant of others. She tried not to give her father reason to be disappointed in her, at least not more than her sex already had, but somehow she always managed to do just that.

Tonight, it seemed, would be no different. From the corner of her eye, she observed a gentleman trying to conceal that he was jabbing a finger toward her, while conversing with a gaggle of snickering matrons and their escorts. He raised his fist before the shortest of the ladies standing near and drew it back, then let it fly, jerking it away a scant second before it hit her nose. They all laughed.

Criminy. A tickle coursed up Isobel's throat as she realized that the gentleman was recounting her . . . exhibition . . . at the Pugilistic Club. Of course, that was it. Why she hadn't done anything the least bit scandalous since then.

Truth to tell, she had been rather amazed that her father hadn't already heard of her impulsive entry into the club to request money from the clodpates inside. Those men obviously had so much, they were willing to throw it away on two brutes pounding each other.

She glanced back at the gentleman, and as if his report was a pebble tossed into a pond, she watched the gossip spread into the crowd in ever-widening circles. It was only a matter of time before the story reached her father. "Oh, that wretched louse," she ground out beneath her breath as she quickly turned to scan the room for her father.

She had certainly fooled herself by thinking he mightn't hear of what she'd done. What a goose she had been!

Then she spied him near the doorway and began to glide toward him, not wishing to draw any more attention than she already had. Why, if she was quick about it, mayhap she could convince him that she had a pain in her head and they ought to leave. It was possible he would never hear about the incident with the fighter on the stage.

By the time she reached her father, his jowls were red and wobbling with anger—but amazingly he did not seem angry with her. "I cannot believe any of the patronesses, not even Lady Sefton, would invite a common bruiser into our gentle fold," he was saying to Sir Rupert Whitebeard. "But there he is, and it looks as though he's brought a half-dozen seconds."

Her father caught notice of her then and grabbed her arm. He moved his mouth to her ear and whispered, "Isobel, stand by my side; do not even turn your head toward the door. Your name cannot survive additional scandal."

Isobel did not argue. He was entirely right, but she had to look, had to see whose reputation instilled such loathing in her father.

And so she straightened her arm and, as a ruse, allowed her reticule to slip to the floor. "Oh dear," she muttered, and then bent to retrieve her bag before her father was able.

As she rose, her gaze flitted toward the doorway, and her eyes met *his*—the mannerless, wicked, impudent brute who'd humiliated her at the club. Behind him was a collection of the tallest, most beautiful beings she had ever seen. The women were the height of most men, their features delicate and perfect. The men were giants, at least a foot taller than any other gentlemen in the assembly room. Like those of the fighter himself, their muscles were pronounced beneath their dark blue coats, protruding like great river stones embedded in a shallow creek.

She sucked a deep breath into her lungs. *My word, where had these huge, beautiful creatures come from?* The tickle that had lodged in her throat moments ago suddenly plummeted into her chest and then expelled itself in a hail of coughs that drew the attention of several members of the ton standing nearby. Unfortunately, it also brought her to *his* notice.

One corner of the fighter's lips lifted in a cocky grin, and he tipped his head toward her. *Lord above, he's recognized me. Perfect. Just what I need this night.*

Isobel straightened her back and cast her eyes to the floor, as though to confirm that nothing had spilled from her reticule.

In the periphery of her vision, she saw that he

and his party of gods and goddesses had been greeted by Lord and Lady Carsden.

"Father, my—my head pains me. May we adjourn for the evening?" Isobel wrapped her hands around her father's arm, hoping to charm him into sharing her thinking, the way she'd been able to do before their lives had changed forever . . . when her parents learned her brother had been killed at Corunna.

Sir Rupert chuckled. "Miss Isobel, if you were to leave, how will I ever convince my Christiana to stay?"

"Christiana?" Isobel's gaze swept the assembly room until she saw her dear friend leaving the dance floor, and a handsome young buck in her wake.

"Ah, here she comes now." Sir Rupert nodded his head toward her. "Are you sure, Miss Isobel, I can't persuade you to stay a moment longer?"

Isobel didn't know what to say. The brute could approach at any moment. "I—I . . ."

Her father cleared his throat. "I think she is quite right in wishing to leave. The company tonight is not what it once was."

Sir Rupert shook his head. "Carington, that is where you and I disagree. For you see, the fighter, that young man, will be a duke."

"A d-duke?" Her father could not seem to form

additional words. His lips moved and his cheeks bounced, but he said nothing.

"The bruiser, as you put it, is Sterling Sinclair, Marquess of Blackburn. Can you not see the enormous diamond on his ring?"

"I can, what of it?" Carington asked sourly.

"It is the Sinclair diamond. Come now, have you truly not heard tale of it? It is presented by the duke to his heir apparent on the day he reaches his majority." Sir Rupert chuckled. "You do spend too many hours in the House of Commons, don't you, Carington? Ought to reward yourself with a few more social gatherings, like your Isobel."

Isobel smiled politely. She had heard of the Sinclair diamond, but never in her wildest imaginings had she guessed *he* was the heir everyone gossiped about of late.

Miss Christiana Whitebeard skipped the last few steps that stood between her and Isobel. "There you are. Where have you been hiding? On the dance floor, making some poor soul fall in love with you? Oh, do tell me it is so . . . for once."

Isobel's cheeks heated. "No, nothing so grand, I fear. Father and I were about to leave."

"No, no, you can't. The Sinclairs are here!" Christiana caught Isobel's arm and without a thought, pulled her away from her father. "Haven't you heard?"

"I have no interest in these . . . Sinclairs." Without meaning to, Isobel frowned at Christiana.

"Not interested in the Sinclairs? Why, you must be mad. Just *look* at them!"

Isobel let her gaze flit to the doorway once more. He was still looking at her. Heat surged through her body. She tore her gaze away. "What about them?"

"Have you ever seen such an amazingly handsome family?" Christiana gave an exaggerated sigh. "I haven't."

Isobel extricated her arms from Christiana's. "They may be beautiful, but I know for certain that Sterling Sinclair, the Marquess of Blackburn, is the most ill-mannered man in all of England."

"I heard about your encounter with him at the Pugilistic Club." Christiana covered her mouth with her gloved hand and laughed. "Why, pray, would you ever decide that entering a gentlemen's establishment, a sparring studio where men are often half naked, would be a prudent thing to do?"

Isobel shrugged. "It was impulsive. I do not need to be reminded of my folly. I saw gentlemen of Society crowding into the Pugilistic Club—and I knew that while so many widows' and orphans' stomachs were empty, these men were heading into a club to throw away money as though it meant nothing! The thought even angers me now."

"Well, what did you receive in exchange for your daring?" Christiana raised her eyebrows as though to wait for a reply, except she didn't bother herself with the waiting part. "Nothing," she said abruptly.

"Not true." Isobel smirked. "The Widows of Corunna Charitable Foundation received a tidy donation the very next day. Someone in the club heard me. Someone with heart—even if he hadn't the sense not to frequent the Pugilistic Club."

"Well, your father must have forgiven you." Christiana leaned close to Isobel and lowered her tone so that no one nearby would hear her next words. "I suppose requiring you to attend this ball was your father's punishment."

"He has yet to learn of that particular indiscretion." Isobel glanced at the doorway again, then back at Christiana. "I do wish the Sinclairs would move farther into the assembly room, so my father and I may pass through the doors without their notice!"

Christiana redirected her gaze toward the door. "Hmm. The fighter is watching you."

"I know." She fought the urge to look up at him. "Which is why I must leave, directly."

"Oh, Issy, what I wouldn't trade to be you tonight." Christiana clasped her hands over her heart. "He is so beautiful . . . but so broken. It's every woman's dream, to heal a man with her love."

Isobel wrinkled her nose at Christiana's nonsensical fantasy. "What are you prattling on about? Is it not evident that I despise that man?"

"How can you when you've heard about the Sinclair family?" Christiana's lips turned downward, and she clasped her free hand over her heart dramatically. "It's really quite tragic."

Isobel shook her head. "I do not know what you mean."

Christiana's eyes went as wide as the mouth of a goblet, and she pulled Isobel with her into the nearest corner of the assembly room. "Truly, you have not heard?"

"I vow, I have not." Isobel tried to pull away, but Christiana tugged her back.

"I must tell you then. Why, it may change everything." Christiana turned her head and nodded toward the Sinclairs. "They are known as the Seven Deadly Sins." It appeared to Isobel that her friend was trying very hard not to show her glee in being able to share a juicy bit of gossip with her.

"What do you mean?" Isobel could not help but mentally count the number of Sinclairs standing near the doorway. *Seven.*

"It's true. Word over scandal broth is that the Duchess of Sinclair died birthing the twins, Lord

Killian and Lady Priscilla. It is said that their father mourned deeply, finally retreating to the comfort of drink, and for years allowed the seven children to run wild, do whatever they pleased."

Isobel lowered her head. She well understood losing a mother and the devastating effect death can have on what is left of a family. Heat needled the backs of her eyes. Unbidden, her mind recalled the night her mother had slipped irretrievably into grief—and, by her own hand, had put an end to her pain and sense of loss, forever.

"Before long, all of Edinburgh Society referred to the ill-behaved Sinclair children as the Seven Deadly Sins."

"That's horrible. They'd lost their mother . . . and their father to drink." Isobel glanced at the fighter again, this time with a little compassion and understanding.

Christiana squeezed Isobel's arm, forcing her attention back to the story she was telling. "There is more. As the Sinclair children grew older, they seemed to embrace the sins Society had labeled them with. Sterling, the Marquess of Blackburn, is cursed with greed." Christiana turned her eyes toward the fighter, and Isobel followed her gaze. "Lady Siusan epitomizes sloth, and Lady Ivy, the copper-haired beauty, envy."

"This is nonsense."

"Is it?" Christiana continued. "Lord Lachlan is a wicked rake. No wonder his weakness is lust. Lord Grant, the one with the lace cuffs, is said to have a taste for luxury and indulgence. His sin is gluttony. The twins are said to be the worst of all." She feigned a shudder.

"Why do you say that?" Isobel pinned her friend with her gaze. "What are their supposed sins?"

Christiana raised her nose toward the Sinclair with a sheath of hair so dark that it almost appeared a deep blue. "Lord Killian's sin is wrath. Whispers suggest that he is the true fighter in the family, but his anger is too quick and fierce. Why, there is even one rumor that claims that he actually killed a man who merely looked at his twin sister! That's her, there. Lady Priscilla. Just look at her with her haughty chin turned toward the chandelier—here, in a room full of nobility! Her sin is, quite clearly, pride."

"Nonsense! I do not believe it," Isobel countered. "I do not believe any of the story. The tale is naught but idle gossip."

"I believe it." Christiana set her one hand on her hip and waved the other in the air as she spoke. "Why else would they have come to London, if not to leave their sinful reputations behind in Scotland?"

"I am sure I do not know." Isobel saw Christiana's jaw drop, and then felt the presence of someone behind her.

"Perhaps I have come to London to ask you to dance with me, lassie." His rich Scottish brogue resonated in her ears, making her vibrate with his every word.

Isobel whirled around and stared up into the grinning face of none other than the marquess.

"I apologize, I would address you by name, but alas, I don't know what it is. Only that you are easily the most beautiful woman in this assembly room." Before she could blink, he reached a bare hand toward her, startling her. He saw her staring at it and was compelled to explain. "I beg your pardon." He moved his hands away, but held his right fist before her as though he meant it as proof of his coming assertion. "My hands are too swollen and injured to fit into gloves. The patronesses understand my lack of gloves has nothing to do with lack of respect." He chuckled softly. "And there are some advantages to forgoing gloves." Within an instant, he raised his knuckles, stitched with black threads, and brushed the backs of his fingers across her cheek—just as he'd done at the club. He sucked in a surprised breath. "English lasses don't stir me the way you do. You must be a wee bit Scottish."

Isobel gasped, drew back her own hand, and

gave his cheek a stinging slap. "My lord, you overstep!"

"I only wished to ask you to dance."

"*Dance?* To dance? You caressed my cheek. You humiliated me, made light of my charity and my attempts to help widows and orphans of war. Why would I ever agree to dance with an ill-mannered rogue like you?"

"Because I asked, and I saw the way you were looking at me when I entered the assembly rooms." He lifted an eyebrow teasingly, bringing to the surface a rage Isobel could not rein in. She slapped his face again with such force that his head wrenched to the left.

He raised his hand to his cheek. "Not bad. Have you thought about pugilism as a profession?" He grinned at her again.

Isobel stepped around Sterling Sinclair, the beast of Blackburn, and started for her father. But the minister was only two steps away. Staring at her, aghast. She reached out for her father's arm, but he stepped back, out of her reach.

She glanced to her left and then her right. Everyone was staring. Everyone.

Isobel covered her face with her trembling hands and shoved her way through the crowd of amused onlookers. She dashed out the door and down the steps to the liveried footman who opened the outer door to the street for her.

She ran outside and rested her hands on her knees as she gasped for breath. Her father would surely send her away for embarrassing him this night.

No matter what punishment he chose for her, Isobel was certain he would never allow her to show her face in Town again.

And Lord Blackburn, the wicked Marquess of Blackburn, was wholly to blame.

Chapter 3

Much of our activity these days is nothing more than a cheap anesthetic to deaden the pain of an empty life.

Unknown

Four of the clock in the morning
The Sinclair residence
Grosvenor Square

A shadow fell over Sterling as someone stepped between him and the light of the single candle that lit the fore-parlor where he and Grant had gathered to share a late brandy. He squinted his eyes and tried to discern from the shape of the silhouette which of his sisters had come down from her bed to chide him.

"Does your cheek require my embroidery skills, dear brother?"

Siusan. He should have guessed from the rigid fold of her arms over her chest.

"You left so quickly after that miss humiliated you before the *ton.*" Her tone was as stiff as her stance. "I didn't have a chance to see if you were injured from such hearty slaps."

Sterling glanced at Grant, who leaned as far back as possible in his chair, as if it would make him less noticeable to his angry sister. "There wasn't anything for a Scot to drink at Almack's, so we left."

Siusan strode toward him and set her hands on her hips. "There was lemonade."

Sterling chuckled and raised his crystal of brandy. "Allow me to rephrase. There wasn't anything for a *real* man to drink."

Siusan snatched his glass and tipped a bit of the amber liquid into her mouth before handing it back again. "Nay, you had the right of it the first time." She sat down on a gilt-rimmed settee beside Grant. "So, will you tell me where you went?" Her tone was much softer now, after a taste of brandy, something Grant did not miss, and he quickly filled a crystal from the decanter for her.

Siusan accepted it, without comment. Her attention still lay with Sterling. "Everyone we met wanted to know you, Sterling. Wanted to hear all about you—and our family. It was almost like being in Edinburgh for the Season again . . . well, except for the very different way people treated us tonight. Och, it was wonderful . . . like we were special, our company a gift to all of Society."

Grant shifted his golden-green eyes to Sterling. "Mayhap we should have stayed a bit longer, eh?"

Sterling shook his head. "What is more important, paving our way into Society . . . or *this*?" He reached into his waistcoat and withdrew a weighty leather bag and tossed it, the contents clanking loudly as it landed on Siusan's lap.

His sister looked up at him. Her pupils grew until her eyes looked black, ringed with a thin band of silver. "What is this?"

Sterling leaned back and grinned. "Seeds to plant and watch grow into a fortune."

Confusion etched a fine line between Siusan's eyebrows. "We used all the winnings from the fight to purchase the requisite finery to enter Society. Where did you get this?"

"I'm not daft, Su. I held out what we'd need to run the household for another month or two." Sterling leaned forward and snatched the bag back. "These coins are residual winnings from the bout at the Pugilistic Club. One of London's best needed a little time to pay, is all. Actually, I was damned right astounded when he admitted he was a bit shallow in the pocket. Comes from an old, respected family. Curious, eh?"

"I am sure if the ton knew of our true circumstances, they'd be scratching their pates too," Siusan said. " 'Curious,' they'd say. 'Would have reckoned the Sinclairs were in want of nothing.' But it isn't true, is it? Our da saw to that."

Grant shifted uneasily upon the settee. "We all have it in our power to change our circumstances."

"Aye, we do," Siusan agreed, "but Sterling isn't making it easy for any of us with his wicked ways."

Sterling raised his brow most innocently. "I only asked the lass to dance."

Grant snickered. "Well, you must have done something more to earn two open-palmed slaps from her." He glanced forlornly at the last few drops of brandy in his glass, and then looked at the nearly empty decanter with a sigh.

"Too bad too," Siusan interjected. "Judging by the way all the misses and their mamas were clamoring over the likes of you, Sterling, all you likely needed to do was be a gentleman, and Miss Carington would have swooned."

Grant nodded. "You've got the right of it, Su.

Word is that she is the daughter of one of the most prominent and noted members of the House of Commons. Who knows, Sterling, had you simply charmed the lass, you might have been betrothed to a woman from a respected family by the end of the Season—and been halfway to earning back the Sinclair honor Father demands of us. I have no doubt he would have approved of such a match."

"But instead you created a spectacle, and every member of the *ton* was witness to it," Siusan huffed. "Who knows what your very public blunder has cost us all!"

Grant leaned forward in his chair, palming the empty glass and thrumming his fingers against its side. "Sterling, you could have at least told me what you planned to do before the ball. Why, I might have been able to stir up a wager for the book at White's." Grant set his glass on the table, then raised a hand and moved it before him as though he was reading from the betting book. "A miss of good breeding will slap a duke at Almack's—twice." He laughed, obviously quite amused with himself. "I'm sure someone would have taken the bet. Could have made us a few bob, don't you think?"

A jolt cut through Sterling at Grant's words. He sat upright, suddenly wide awake despite the early hour and the brandy flowing through his body.

Siusan seemed to ignore Grant's comment. She grabbed the bag from Sterling, plucked out a shiny coin, then tossed the bag back to him. "Pin money." She flicked her long sable hair over her shoulder as she rose and, without another word, quit the fore-parlor for the passage.

Sterling cocked his head and listened to her ascend the stairs until her footfall faded from his hearing. He whipped his head back around to face Grant.

His brother set his hands on his knees and leaned forward. "What is it?" he asked quietly. "What has so aroused your brandied mind that you could hardly wait for Siusan to leave—a bet of some sort?"

Sterling stared blankly at his brother for some moments as he followed the logic of his idea through. *Could it be possible? Could this be the answer?*

Unbidden, his head began to nod, slowly at first, then faster as he began to believe he had stumbled upon a perfect way to earn the money they now lacked. Sterling reached out and grabbed Grant's arm. "What do you know about this Miss Carington?"

Grant blinked. "I dunno. I heard a bit at the club

when she showed up waving about a fan of pamphlets and spouting off about her charity."

A slow smile eased over Sterling's lips. "Tell me everything you know."

Two days later

"I did not ask him if I may leave to shop, I just did," Isobel told Christiana as they walked along Pall Mall in the direction of St. James's.

"Y-you just left?" Christiana sputtered. "Why, if my father was only half as angry with me as yours was with you after embarrassing him at Almack's, I wouldn't dare set foot outside the house without his express permission—in writing. You are certainly braver than I!"

Isobel gave a short laugh. "I am not brave at all. Parliament is in session and therefore he is not at home. Ah, here we are." Isobel hooked her arm around Christiana's and turned her into Harding, Howell & Company.

Christiana stopped a few feet inside the door. "What if you are found out?"

Isobel walked to a counter and lifted a painted silk fan in her hands. "Why should I be? He always returns home late in the evening from the House of Commons. I simply need to arrive at home before him. Honestly, Christiana, I could not endure another day restricted to the house without dying of boredom. La, it has been a full week." She set the fan back down. "Dresses and millinery are in the fourth department. Come on, I haven't got much time, you know." She giggled and caught up Christiana's hand and pulled her toward the back of the store.

They were passing the glazed partition that marked the beginning of the haberdashery, when a wiry-haired gentleman suddenly looked up and stared at Isobel, dropping the reticule he had been holding for the woman beside him while she examined a swath of blush-rose silk. "Gorblimey, it's her, Dorthea."

"Who, dear?" the woman replied in a decidedly uninterested tone.

"Miss Carington," he replied in a hushed voice. "You know, *her*."

The woman whirled around. "Oh my goodness!"

Isobel felt their gazes upon her and her cheeks warmed, but she kept moving, tugging Christiana along with her. How could it be that days later people were still buzzing about her slapping Blackburn at Almack's? Honestly, it should have faded from memory by now. She was simply not that interesting. Her father had told her as much time and time again.

"Excuse us, Miss Carington." Each of the woman's words grew louder, and it occurred to Isobel that she was being pursued through the store. "Please, might we have a word or two with you?"

The gentleman's voice trailed after them. " We just wondered if you would share your intentions."

Lud, would they not just let her be? Isobel walked faster to put as much distance between her and her pursuers as possible.

"Isobel, they are speaking to you. Please stop." Christiana stopped walking mid-stride. She held firm to Isobel's hand, preventing any further movement.

Isobel looked down at her slippers and sighed. She heard the couple move behind her instantly, and so she took a steadying breath and turned around, a forced smile upon her lips. "Were you speaking to me? I hadn't realized, I do apologize. I do not believe I've had the pleasure of meeting you both."

Then, finally realizing he had forgotten his manners, the gentleman smiled and introduced himself. "Do forgive me. I am Lord Triplemont, and this is my wife, Lady Triplemont." Lord Triplemont bowed, and Lady Triplemont tipped her head toward them.

"I am Miss Isobel Carington, and this is Miss Christiana Whitebeard." Isobel bobbed a quick curtsy, trying not to tip over in her confusion. "I apologize again, but I do not know what *intentions* you desire to glean from me."

Lady Triplemont laughed. "Why, if you will marry Sterling Sinclair, the Marquess of Blackburn, before Season's end."

Isobel tore her head around and stared at Christiana, hoping she might make some sense of this, but her friend's expression was as blank as her own must have been.

"I beg your pardon, Lady Triplemont, but I have not the faintest notion what you are about." Isobel crinkled her brow. "Why do you ask such a thing? I am sure I am the last miss in London he would wish to marry, and he most certainly is the last man I would ever consider after his rudeness at Almack's."

Lord Triplemont handed his wife's reticule back to her. "You see, Dorthea. The wager is naught but madness. I told you as much when I first heard of it."

His wife shook her head. "No, no. There is something to it. Ten thousand pounds that Miss Carington will marry Sterling Sinclair, the Marquess of Blackburn, before the end of the Season.

There is something afoot between her and the Marquess of Blackburn. She just is not admitting to it."

"I beg your pardon, but did you say—a *ten-thousand-pound* wager?" Isobel cocked her head. "I am quite certain that I did not hear you correctly. You could not have said—"

Christiana was nodding her head as she blurted, "Ten thousand pounds that you will marry the fighter before Season's end." She giggled and clapped her hand over her mouth for an instant. "Preposterous! But oh, how exciting, don't you agree, Issy?"

"No, I do not!" Isobel's heart started pounding and she suddenly felt very light in the head. "Lord Triplemont, please, tell me you jest and there is no wager."

"The wager was recorded in the betting book at White's last eve," he told her.

Suddenly Isobel could not seem to catch her breath. It simply could not be true. Such an enormous wager was certain to create a stir among the *ton*, and then her father would be bound to hear of it. *Unless* . . . unless she could appeal to the gentleman who had logged the bet and convince him to withdraw it immediately. "Lord Triplemont, pray, wh-who placed the bet? I must know the truth of all of this. I am but a miss whose reputation is in great danger. I must stop this nonsense. I am sure you can understand. Won't you help me?"

"I wish my husband could tell you the gentleman's identity." Lady Triplemont placed her hand comfortingly on Isobel's arm. "The bet was placed anonymously directly through White's. A sizable portion of the ten thousand pounds is being held in escrow at the club to preserve the bettor's true identity. It is my understanding that the anonymous nature of the wager is part of what makes it so enticing."

Isobel shook her head, and a nervous laugh slipped through her lips. "Surely no one would accept such a wager. I am just a plain miss, not titled, not a rich woman. I am likely fretting for naught." She looked to Lord and Lady Triplemont, waiting for them to confirm this idea.

"Well, begging your pardon, Miss Carington, but you did request the truth from me, so I will give it to you. The betting book is already filled with gentlemen accepting the wager."

"The book is f-filled?" Isobel stammered. "Why would anyone care if we marry or not? I do not understand."

"Because the wager is a sure bet. You publicly spurned the marquess. It is clear to most everyone, except my wife, it seems, that you will never marry Blackburn."

Lady Triplemont studied Isobel for several moments. "I disagree, dear. I saw the fire between them at the ball." She turned to face her husband. "I want you to place a wager at White's for me. I believe Miss Carington will marry Lord Blackburn."

"Dorthea . . . be reasonable. I can't," Lord Triplemont said with no little amount of embarrassment.

"You can." Lady Triplemont tipped her head at Isobel and Christiana. "Good day, ladies." She began to turn around to leave when something occurred to her. "There is a lovely pale blue silk in the fourth department that would make a splendid gown for your wedding. You should take a look." With that parting comment, Lady Triplemont took her husband's arm and they strolled toward the front of the store.

Isobel stood, mouth fully agape, as the couple passed through the front door and out onto Pall Mall. "This is most distressing, Christiana. We should leave before we encounter another member of White's."

Christiana turned, and instead of making to leave, she started for the rear of the store.

Isobel jerked around and stared at her. "Where are you going?"

"I assumed you would wish to have a look at

the blue silk Lady Triplemont suggested before we leave." She started to walk again when she realized Isobel wasn't joining her. "Aren't you coming?" She pointed toward the fourth department. "I believe I can see the silk she meant from here, and it is lovely."

Isobel became aware just then that several ladies were listening to everything she and Christiana were saying. So, to make her feelings perfectly plain, she replied in a tone more appropriate for an orange seller than the daughter of a minister from the House of Commons. "I have no intention of looking at silk for a wedding gown. I have no intention of marrying anyone—especially the Scottish marquess Blackburn."

"Really?" Christiana grinned. "Hmm."

Isobel tipped her head toward the door to the street, and Christiana turned around to follow her out of the store. "Yes. It is the truth. I have not the least bit of interest in him. Not one bit."

"Oh, Issy, methinks thou doth protest too much," Christiana muttered beneath her breath.

Isobel whirled around and peered warily at Christiana, who was running her hand along a case of fans and gloves as she walked. "Did you say something?"

"What?" Christiana glanced up innocently. "Oh, only that . . . um . . ." Color charged into her cheeks. She stilled her step, and her gaze flitted around the first department. Then she turned her attention back to Isobel. "I did not mean to say so aloud, but Issy, I think the fan you admired earlier costs too much."

Isobel's eyes momentarily narrowed with suspicion that it was not the fan Christiana had commented upon. "Yes, I agree. Too dear." She hurried back to Christiana and grabbed her hand. "So let us not tarry any longer. I wish to return home." She pulled Christiana close and lowered the tone of her voice. "Please, let us leave now. I do not wish to encounter any other members of White's, and the longer we remain near St. James's Street, the more likely we are to tempt ill fate."

Chapter 4

Materialism is the only form of distraction from true bliss.

Horton

Sterling's throat tried to close in upon itself to prevent the vile soup from making its way into his body. He sat very still at the formal dining table, praying for his stomach to accept the potage.

"It was my mother's favorite recipe." Mrs. Wimpole stood behind Sterling with her hands on her wide hips, expectantly awaiting his reaction to her meal. "I couldn't quite recall all the ingredients, so I made do and added a little this and that to the soup."

Sterling nodded his head and forced back every instinct to the contrary to swallow. Though the soup looked appetizing, it reeked like a blend of rotting flounder and whore's breath in a chamber pot.

She tugged anxiously at her blond lace fichu. "Well, my lord, what do you think? Delicious, no?"

Sterling turned his head just a bit and sealed his lips as he smiled, lest his gullet chase the swill back up again.

When he was sure he could open his mouth, he grabbed a goblet of watered ale and drained it before setting it to the table again.

Mrs. Wimpole was wringing her hands and chewing on her lower lip. "Is the soup too . . . hot?"

Sterling seized on her suggestion. "Aye, but just a wee bit." He warily eyed the yeasty-smelling roll on his plate. "And . . . you made the bread as well?"

Mrs. Wimpole laughed. "Oh, goodness no. Those are from the baker. Baked yesterday, but right tasty when you warm them up."

Safe enough, Sterling supposed. He grabbed it up and pulled off a large bite. "Where are the others? I am only a few minutes late for our noonday meal."

"Oh, they came down, but not a one took more than a sip of soup before your brother Killian remembered that they all had an engagement at the tea garden . . . The Garden of Eden, that was the one."

Sterling felt his eyes widen, and he immediately came to his feet. "Aye, the Garden of Eden! How could I have forgotten? Well, I must away at once."

Mrs. Wimpole's fluffy little white eyebrows inched toward her nose. "Oh dear, please do not say you must leave as well. Please. My lord, I cannot waste the soup. Poplin charged me with the responsibility to stretch our market coins as far as I am able."

Reaching down, Sterling grabbed up the roll and took it with him as he hurried toward the passage. "Do not fret, Mrs. Wimpole. I am sure you and Poplin will see that the potage isna wasted. Please, enjoy it yourselves. Good day, Mrs. Wimpole."

His long legs took the stairs three at a time until he reached his garret. Three measured strides took him into the center of his bedchamber, where he bent to pry up a short floorboard and withdrew a leather coin pouch. He plucked out two shillings from it, then tied it off and tossed it into the breach in the flooring. He started to rise, but paused momentarily. "Damn it all."

Why didn't they choose a cheaper dodge? 'Tisna like we have money to give away.

He exhaled a hard breath of resignation, then reached back between the boards to the pouch, and his fingers closed around a single gleaming guinea. *Damn, damn, damn.* Wasting money on tea and cakes when he could be using it to rebuild their fortune.

The Garden of Eden
Marylebone

Priscilla hoisted the falsest of smiles the moment her eyes met the sight of Sterling entering the tea garden. "Look there, our greedy brother approaches. Stayed for Mrs. Wimpole's soup, did you, Sterling?"

Sterling sighed inwardly. Grant must have confessed everything. He cast a disapproving glance at his closest brother. "Which of you paid her to poison me, eh?" His gaze circled the small tea table his brothers and sisters had gathered around.

Priscilla grinned.

The sweet scent of the yellow-centered climbing roses skirting a hawthorn fence around the tea garden was as cloying as his sister's smile. "So you've heard." He pinned Grant with his gaze. "My thanks, brother, for sparing me the difficult task of confessing my use of our allowance." He focused on each of them for the briefest of moments, gauging as best he could their individual judgments of him.

"Sterling—" Grant raised his finger and fluttered it before his lips, but his meaning was taken too late.

Siusan came to her feet. "Our allowance?" She slapped her palm upon the table, making the dishes of tea rattle on their saucers. "Y-you wagered our allowance?"

The color from Ivy's rosy cheeks drained away. "Sterling, do tell us it isna true!"

He turned his gaze to Grant, who winced sympathetically. "Sterling, I did not tell them anything. But you're in it now."

Sterling clamped his mouth closed. *Bluidy hell.*

Killian shot to his feet, but Priscilla caught his sleeve and drew him back into his chair. Killian leaned forward over his tea and ground out his words. "Did you think we would not hear of this wager? All of bleeding London is chattering about it. Everyone of breeding wants a piece of your wager. Everyone."

Hearing that, Sterling felt oddly proud. It was a good bet. It would seem a sure thing. Only he knew better. "The bet was placed—" He quieted for a moment and glanced around them to remind them all that they were not in a place to discuss the secret wager. "I *heard* the bet was placed anonymously." He dropped his voice to the slightest of whispers. "That a *percentage* of the stake was required for White's to allow such a large wager by an unknown bettor."

Killian's teeth were clenched. "London Society may not have an inkling who would have placed such an audacious wager, but you are our brother. Though this is leagues beyond what we would have believed you capable of, Sterling, the moment we learned of the wager we knew its source."

"Only we didn't know you posted what little portion our father provided us to live." Priscilla patted Killian's arm, the way she always did to calm him when ire was about to consume him.

Sterling scanned those at the table. Lachlan alone was smiling. "Och," his brother said. "Why are you all pretending to be surprised? Leave a shilling on the table and Sterling will have it in his pocket just long enough for it rub another the right way and multiply." He clasped his hands behind his head, his elbows jutting outward as he rocked backward until he balanced his entire weight on his chair's two rear legs. "But he always makes a coin, one way or another. Have faith in our greedy brother here. He will make us all rich—from the fight at Fives Court, or through his wager to convince Miss Carington to marry him."

Killian's flame-blue eyes lit into Sterling once again. "I don't doubt you will double our allowance, brother. But I take you to task over wagering what little coin we have without discussing it with us first."

A steward bustled between several other crowded tables, carrying a dainty gilt chair. He gestured politely for Sterling to be seated while he hurried off to collect another porcelain tea setting.

This momentary distraction garnered Sterling the time he needed to align his thoughts. He'd hoped he'd have at least one full day before the others learned of his wager. It was anonymous, after all. "It is a solid bet. But had I asked each of you to support it, you would have denied me the opportunity." He waved his hand at his sisters. "Just as the three of you grimaced over the wager on my battle with the Irishman."

Siusan crossed her arms over her chest and raised her chin as she exchanged pointed glances with her sisters. Behind her was a most puzzling sight. A lamb walked across the green with a rainbow-hued parrot perched upon its woolly back. Sterling rubbed his eyes and focused over his sister's shoulder again—but what he comprehended grew stranger still. In the center of the garden was an apple tree draped with a huge yellow snake. Sterling surveyed the tea garden more closely, and realized that the Garden of Eden was populated not only by London's finest citizens taking tea, pipes, and glasses, but by an amazing menagerie of God's creatures.

Londoners were completely mad. That was all there was to it.

He had no choice at all. He had to win Miss Carington's hand and be allowed to return to Scotland. There was no way in hell he could spend his life in such a frothy town.

"Sterling, you might have lost the battle and with it our money," Siusan admonished.

Sterling focused again on Siusan. "You hated that I wagered our money, you chided me for my greed, and yet none of you had any difficulty spending the wages of my sin."

Priscilla cleared her throat in a thinly veiled attempt to calm Sterling by drawing his attention to her. "Sterling, we appreciate what you have done to help us. I believe our foremost concern is . . . do we have any money *left*? Though you may not be aware of this, your upcoming battle and the interest the anonymous wager has produced is drawing the favorable attention of the *ton*, something we need as greatly as coin to redeem ourselves."

"Aye, we have a bit," Sterling admitted. "Enough to house and feed us for the Season."

A strangled whimper slipped through Ivy's lips, and for an instant, Sterling was not sure she even breathed. "But what about clothing and baubles?"

Siusan glanced at the tables of matrons on either side of their own. She leaned nearer to Ivy and spoke without moving her mouth at all. "Dear, calm yourself. We are in public." She lifted Ivy's cup and moved it to her mouth. "Aye, the cake is a mite dry. Wash it down with some tea. Here you go." She tipped the dish and forced Ivy to drink to stifle her panic.

Ivy gulped loudly then, glaring at Siusan as she pushed the dish of tea away. This time her voice remained in the realm of a whisper. "How can we move through Society, making the connections we need to earn the respectability our father requires of us, without the necessary accoutrements? I tell you, it is impossible. It cannot be done!"

Lachlan shook his head. "Lassie, it can. We just need to be as cunning as our brother here."

Sterling's fist clenched at the backhanded jibe, but he carefully straightened his fingers. Reaching out, he took a cake from a plate on the table, then spread sweet cream atop the confection. This too was a diversion, for had they not been surrounded by London's fine set, he might have kicked Lachlan's chair just enough to send him tipping backward into the pea gravel. Instead he simply munched on the cake, aware that his brothers and sisters all most patiently waited for his reply.

He swallowed, taking his time, making them suffer ever so slightly for doubting him. When he did look up again, Sterling gazed first upon his ungrateful sisters. "If you can manage to survive only a few more weeks wearing clothing from last year, wearing paste jewels instead of treasures"—he redirected his gaze to his three brothers—"dressing yourselves and condescending to having your neck cloths starched and sloppily ironed by Mrs. Wimpole—my wagers on the Fives Court battle will reverse our financial position dramatically . . . for a time."

Damn it. Didn't they understand? He was doing this for *them.* He should not have to explain himself. He was the eldest, after all, and had always looked out for them.

Sterling's ire peaked. He pushed up from the tiny chair so forcefully that had he not reached out and just caught its back, it would have been knocked into the elderly patron sitting behind him.

He steadied the chair, then flipped a single guinea down, sending it spinning across the tea table, knocking into Ivy's dish of tea before settling beneath the rim of Priscilla's cake plate.

His voice remained low, but firm. "But if you can trust me, and assist me in winning Miss Carington's hand by the end of the Season, I promise you all, whether Father forgives us or not, we will be rich."

He touched his waistcoat pocket, needing to feel the two shillings inside before abandoning the guinea on the table. When he felt them, heard them clink together, he smiled confidently, and turned to leave.

Oh, that he only felt as confident in his Fives Court wager as he pretended to be.

"Wait," Siusan called out. He heard a chair crunch and roll across the pea gravel paving. "Sterling, please."

Looking back over his shoulder, he saw sincerity in his sister's eyes and slowly turned his body around to face her.

"Sterling, you must know that you will always have our support," she said quietly. She waved her hand to the others and pinned each with her steely gaze until one by one they nodded. "We will do what needs to be done to help you win the wager. *Whatever* it takes."

"You have my gratitude," Sterling managed. But his thanks felt as empty as their promise to him.

He started walking for the street, his chest aching, for he knew, in truth, he did have their support. They backed him now, not because they trusted him, as they should, for he'd never let them down. Not because he'd always taken the blows, physical or verbal, for them when he could. Not because they loved him. Not even because they trusted his skill as a gamester.

It was only because he'd left them no other choice.

Chapter 5

Nothing makes us more vulnerable than loneliness, except greed.

Thomas Harris

The Carington residence
No. 9 Leicester Square

Isobel untied the ribbon of her poke bonnet as she slinked through the front door. She sighed with exasperation at the thought of the dratted wager that, through no fault of her own, was going to plunge her headfirst into boiling water the moment her father learned of it.

She stalked toward the course of brass cloak

hooks in the nook just off the entry hall and pulled off her bonnet.

It was then that she came to a startling realization.

While the wide brim of a poke bonnet was a most stylish way to protect a lady's face from sun and weather, making it the absolute hat of choice for a modest yet fashionable miss, Isobel belatedly learned it prevented a young lady from noticing the approach of her father from the side.

He set his knuckles on his hips and rocked onto his toes before slamming down loudly on his heels, in the event, she supposed, that she hadn't already realized his foul disposition.

"Good afternoon, Father," she said meekly. "I did not expect you at home so soon."

She decided to smile and say nothing more. Though she could not yet see it on his face, she was sure that his irritation with her over her latest *disappointment* was bubbling up inside and would spill over at any minute like a pot of milk left too long over the cooking fire.

The seam of her father's mouth stretched thin, and had he had any visible lips, she would have said that he was actually smiling. But this was not possible. He never smiled.

Could it be that he hasn't yet heard of the wager?

"Isobel." The nod of his head was spirited, not

at all resembling the perfunctory manner he usually reserved for addressing her.

She was certain now. He had *not* heard.

If she didn't know better, she would say he was almost . . . jubilant. A hard-won victory in the House of Commons, that was all that could explain his cheer this day. *Yes, that must be it.*

She drew a deep breath in relief as she set her bonnet and mantle to their hooks, then edged past her oddly cheerful father and absently tossed the packet of ribbon she'd purchased during her outing on the small beech wood table in the passage.

Her father raised his hawkish gray eyebrows. "I see you have been shopping."

Isobel's fingers scrabbled for the packet. "It is nothing, really. Just a bit of ribbon for my bonnet, nothing extravagant. Only cost a penny or two . . . truly."

Her father focused on the packet and then grimaced. He raised his eyes to hers. "I'll not have my daughter scrimping on clothing or adornments. Tell me what you need and I will see to it that you have it."

Is he actually telling me to spend more money? Who is this man, and where, pray, is my true father?

A sense of unease coursed through her body. He must be delirious with fever. Nothing else

could explain his behavior just now. "Father"—
hesitantly she reached out and touched his lapel—
"are you . . . feeling completely well?"

He took her hand and, drawing it from his coat,
gave it a quick, insincere squeeze. He cleared his
throat, then rubbed his nose as though it itched
fiercely. "Why would you ask such a thing, Isobel?
Is it so impossible to believe that a father would
wish to see his young daughter dressed in a way
that accentuates her beauty?" He pulled her into his
library, then let go of her hand and hurried around
to his desk drawer. "Tell me, Isobel, how much
would a new gown cost me? Something grand . . .
silk or satin, perhaps?" He looked up at her as if
the answer would be poised on her tongue.

But how was she to know? Since her mother
died, she had made do by altering and remaking
her mother's frocks, splurging on a run of lace or
ribbon from time to time to fashion a more stylish
look. The rest of the small portion her father provided her went to the charity she had founded for
the widows of Corunna.

She shrugged her shoulders sheepishly.

His mouth puckered and his brow furrowed,
carving four deep creases across his forehead.
"Well then"—he snatched up one his cards and
handed it to her—"have the dressmaker send the

request for payment to me. Probably for the best anyway. Can't have you giving your clothing allowance away this time, can I?" He shook the card toward her.

When, in her shock, she did not reach for it, he circled back around the desk and pressed it into her hand.

Isobel eyed him speculatively. He'd never acted this way. Never even pretended to be so generous.

"Oh, dear." He gave a decidedly ingenuous smile again. "Be sure to expedite the creation of the gown, won't you? You will need it in two days." He walked around his desk and sat down in a high-backed leather chair. Easing his spectacles to his eyes, he opened a book and began to read.

"In t-two days?" Isobel sputtered. "Whatever for?"

He looked up and, seeming perturbed, plucked off his spectacles and set them on his desk. "We will be attending Lord and Lady Partridge's spring ball."

"But . . . I had planned to wear my blue gown. I always wear it to balls and routs, and you have never discouraged my doing so."

"It is time you wear something new."

"I tell you, Father, no dressmaker can create a gown so quickly when the whole of the *ton* will be demanding attention." She shook his card at him. "I am but a simple miss—the daughter of a politician, not a grand lady of note more deserving of a gown!"

He pushed up from his chair and slammed his hands to the center of his desk, then leaned over it. "You *are* of note, Isobel, and everyone in Society is well aware of it. Did you assume because I frequent the House of Commons that I would not hear of the goings-on at White's when it concerns my own daughter?"

Isobel double-stepped backward. "I—I had nothing to do with the wager, Father. I swear."

"Bah! You did. You slapped a marquess, *twice*, at Almack's. You made a grand spectacle of yourself and drew the notice of all, and started tongues wagging. People began asking questions, guessing that for a miss to overstep so greatly in public, she and the marquess must be closer than anyone knows."

Isobel gasped at that. "It is not true. I despise him!"

"Do you deny the rumor that you had actually met Sterling Sinclair, the Marquess of Blackburn, before?" He tilted his head, and the edge of mouth twitched.

So he had heard about the incident at the Pugilistic Club. "We were not introduced."

"You met him. Admit it."

Isobel lowered the card and her gaze as she nervously fumbled with it. "I encountered him, yes. It is evident to me that you know this already." She tucked the card beneath her sleeve and hesitantly raised her eyes. "What is that you want from me, Father?"

"To marry him—if he will have you. He asked you to dance, commented on your beauty; therefore I must conclude that he has some interest in you."

Isobel choked on her reply. How mad this was that her father could be charging her with such a demand! "Sterling Sinclair . . . *that fighter* has no true interest—other than to toy with me, rile me. Believe me, he does not wish to marry me—and I would rather . . . rather move to Yorkshire and raise pigs with Great-aunt Gertrude than to marry a beast like him."

Her father leaned back from the desk and sat down again. Slowly he reset his spectacles on his nose. "If that is your wish, Isobel."

"Wh-what do you mean by that?" she asked, though she feared hearing the very explanation she requested. Her eyes began to sting.

He did not look up. "I am weary of your unladylike public displays, and will not tolerate it any longer. If you are not married by the end of the Season, I will write to your mother's aunt to make arrangements for your relocation. At least in Yorkshire, you will have far less opportunity to embarrass me with your behavior." He turned his head upward at last and peered over the top of his spectacles at her. "I am finished with your antics, Isobel."

A dread as cold as an icicle plunged into her. "You cannot be serious. You would cast me out if I do not marry by the end of summer?"

"I assure you, Isobel, I do not jest. In fact, your idea is growing on me." He looked down at his thick book again. "The choice is yours. You haven't much time, dear. Were I you, I would be headed to Bond Street to have a gown fitted . . . but if you'd rather, a stop at the perfumers might be in order. Judging from the scent of your great-aunt, the stench of swine does not wash off easily."

The heat in her eyes threatened to spill onto her cheeks, and she spun and hurried to retrieve her bonnet and mantle. She had no intention of marrying Sinclair. She had no intention of marrying anyone!

She had dedicated herself to aiding the widows of Corunna in memory of her brother . . . and the family he once had. If her father truly meant to toss her into a pigsty at the end of the Season, then she would simply take up lodging with one of the widows she assisted through her charity.

Grabbing at the ribbons of her poke bonnet, she tugged too hard, and instead of it slipping off the hook, the headband snagged on it and ripped.

A tear that had balanced inside her lashes splashed hotly upon her cheek and ran down her face. Not worrying over the torn band, she mashed the bonnet down upon her head and whirled her mantle around her shoulders.

Her father's card slipped from her sleeve and fluttered to the entry hall floor. She bent and picked it up. She had no desire to seek out a mantua maker for a gown to attract the attention of that wicked Sinclair, but neither could she remain in the house with her father just now. And so she stashed the card inside her sleeve once more, and jerked open the front door.

A hackney, whose passenger she could not see, abruptly pulled away from the pavers before her house. Its sudden and unexpected movement startled her to such an extent that she did not at once notice the small bag beside her foot.

She crouched and opened it. Two guineas and one shilling were inside, along with a folded card.

She released the card from its creases and read: *So noble a lady. So noble a cause.*

It was written in a gentleman's heavy hand, this she could tell, but there was no signature.

She rushed to straighten and stand, to call out and stop the hackney so she might thank the occupant for supporting the widows. But the hackney had already turned from Leicester Square for Green Street.

She peered down at the card again, and gulped down the residual sob poised in her throat. Hers was a noble cause, a worthy one. The stranger, her secret benefactor, was right about that.

She threw back her shoulders. No, she should not cower from this unimaginable chain of events that made her the center of interest for all of London Society. It would not last long, the *ton*'s appetite for scandal was fickle, and her humiliation would soon be exchanged for some other poor soul's misfortune.

No, suddenly she knew just what to do.

A smile lifted the downturned edges of her lips. She raised her skirts from the ground and skipped down the steps for the street. She would hire a hackney to take her to Bond Street, where she would make use of her notoriety to quickly have a gown fashioned for her.

Then, while it was still hers to trade, she would use her fleeting fame at the upcoming ball to garner the *ton*'s support for her charity.

And if smiling prettily at a certain brute of a marquess, or rebuking him for his rudeness, brought her additional attention and extended her influence a little longer, she would do it—to generate as much money as she could for the widows of Corunna.

For her noble cause.

St. James's Street

The hackney passed White's four times before Sterling finally spotted Grant's tall form heading up the slope of St. James's Street for Piccadilly Street. "Turn right, here," Sterling bade the driver, "then stop just around the corner."

Grant hurried past two shops, then boarded the hackney. "Good news."

While his brother struggled to catch his breath, Sterling waved the driver onward and back to Grosvenor Square. "How favorable is our position?"

"Very." Grant was grinning now. "The wager has been accepted."

"I know that. How much is in the book?"

"You don't understand, Sterling. The wager has been met—all ten thousand pounds." He chuckled. "A few other members are starting to duplicate your anonymous bet, since yours has already been accepted."

Sterling covered his mouth with his hand and thought about what Grant had said. It had been only two days since the bet was made, and the full amount had been met by an astounding number of White's members. "We cannot allow that. Not when the potential of this wager is great. We've got to put up more."

Grant turned to face Sterling. "But we haven't got more. Due to your wish to remain anonymous, White's required us to hold the entire amount of the bet in escrow."

"We have a bit more."

"Living expenses, that is all. We need our mutton . . . and whisky." Grant narrowed his gaze. "Och, I see that glint in your eyes. We cannot do it. Our sisters will use our heads for stew meat if we wager our last few bob."

"Now, hear me out, Grant. The wager is extraordinarily popular . . . both sides of the coin, it seems. Everyone is talking about it, and about White's."

Grant nodded. "There wasna an empty seat at

the club. Barely any room to stand. Even more extraordinary are the number of contrary wagers showing up in the book—bets that you will *not* marry Miss Carington by Season's end."

"So what if we petition White's, through our proxy, to double the anonymous bettor's exposure without requiring an additional ten thousand pounds to be held in escrow?"

The day was fine and the windows of the coach were open as the hackney rolled slowly up Piccadilly Street. Ladies and gentlemen, taking advantage of the sunny day to stroll and shop the length of the street, stopped to stare when the Sinclairs' cab passed them by.

Grant slumped back against the cracked leather squabs, trying to move out of sight. "Gads, they're pointing."

Sterling smiled out the window and nodded his head in greeting at anyone who noticed him.

"Och, cease at once, Sterling." Embarrassed, Grant covered his eyes with his hand. "Who do you think you are, the bluidy Prince Regent?"

"Just trying to stir up a little more interest in the wager."

Grant dropped his hand from his eyes and grabbed Sterling's shoulder, crumpling the clean slope of his coat. "We cannot ask to double the wager. What if we lose? What if you can't win Miss Carington's favor? Have you thought of that?"

"Nay. Because I will not fail. I saw the way Miss Carington looked at me. She may pretend to despise me, but in truth, I think she fancies me." Sterling wickedly blew a kiss to two young misses walking behind their chaperone, sending them into a fit of blushes and giggles. "And I ask you, Grant, what miss, especially one slightly older than what is considered in London to be in her marriageable prime, would refuse the troth of a handsome man who will one day become Duke of Sinclair?"

"Maybe one who is daft enough to step between two massive pugilists in the middle of a battle." Grant raised his dark eyebrows at Sterling. And he wasn't jesting.

"She is passionate about her charity, and I always have been attracted to women with great *passion*." He flicked his left eyebrow to clarify his double meaning.

"Aye, but remember that this woman's passion is giving away money." Grant lowered one eyebrow, but left the other high and questioning. "If you lose this wager, you and she will have a lot in common, eh?"

Sterling glanced out the window again. His

smile dissolved. "I will not let that happen, Grant. Ivy told me this morn that Miss Carington will be in attendance at the Partridge ball. I plan to be there as well . . . ready to do whatever I must to win."

"Well then." Grant sighed amusedly. "I would not miss this particular ball for all the whisky in Scotland."

Chapter 6

Most of the luxuries and many of the so-called comforts of life are not only not indispensable, but positive hindrances to the elevation of mankind.

Thoreau

Partridge House
Hanover Square

At the exact moment the Whitebeard carriage turned onto George Street, Hanover Square still some distance ahead, Isobel realized that the Partridge spring ball was not the annual intimate affair it had always been in the past.

Gleaming carriages jammed Hanover Square, packing it as tightly as a pricked sausage casing, extruding their gaily dressed passengers through narrow gaps where they might, between horse teams and vehicles, allowing them to flow onto the pavers and into Partridge House.

Sir Rupert Whitebeard, who didn't give a tail flick for appearances, instructed his footman to dispatch their party where they were on George Street, and he, Christiana, Isobel, and her father would hoof their way to Partridge House rather than spending the entire evening waiting inside a carriage that was not going anywhere.

Though the night was chilly for spring, Isobel saw that every window in Partridge House had been thrown wide. Three young misses were leaning out one of the upper windows, laughing loudly, and gleefully using their splayed fans to draw cool air into the crowded room.

Isobel tightened her hold around Christiana's arm. "I do not have a good feeling about this. The house has never been this crowded."

"I am sure the dressmaker simply told a few patrons that yours was the most glorious gown she'd ever stitched, and everyone must come to see it for themselves. No debutante could wear that color . . . or that daring neckline." Christiana laughed, but Isobel would have none of her levity this evening.

She knew better. She knew why the house swelled with the upper ranks of Society. They were there to see her. And him. The common miss and the Scottish marquess, whose possible romance had become the most discussed topic in all of London—at least so wrote the *Times*. The idea was ludicrous. The country was at war, for heaven's sake. Men were dying! Isobel stopped abruptly and stared at Partridge House. A shudder shook her.

Oh God. Why had she ever believed she could do this? She fought the urge to spin around and run back to the carriage.

Then, inside her head, she heard the answer oh-so-quietly.

For your brother.

For the lost husbands, lovers, and sons.

She sucked down a deep breath of cool air, and listened with her heart.

For the widows of our soldiers.

For their children.

Yes. She could do it. She could. She must. Whom else could they turn to when they were in need? Only her.

Isobel pulled Christiana close so that their two fathers, who walked solemnly and slowly behind them, would not overhear her plan to coax a few guineas from every prosperous family inside the house. "I will need your assistance this night, Christiana."

"With what, avoiding that handsome Scottish marquess of yours?" Christiana whispered back.

"Not at all. I fully intend to engage Lord Blackburn, while drawing as much attention from the *ton* as I might." Though she tried to restrain any outward reaction that might call her father's notice, the right side of her mouth twitched and lifted upward.

Christiana's eyes grew as round and bright as the full moon above. She stopped walking. "Whatever do you mean?"

Startled her father might see Christiana's delay, Isobel tugged her along. "The moon does seem to be shining directly upon Partridge House, Christiana. Look at that," she exclaimed, before lowering her voice to a confidential tone again. "You mayn't believe it, but I wish for as many people tonight to become interested in the wager as possible."

"Do you take me for a fool? I do not believe it for one instant. No one would ever wish such a thing upon herself." Christiana was still staring at Isobel as they walked.

"You have to stop peering at me that way. My father will get the notion that I am meaning to cause mischief—and I am not. What I am about to do this night is for the widows and orphans."

"Lud, Issy, what is it that you are going to do?"

Christiana pressed her hand to her side. "Your teasing is making my breath come so hard that my corset is creaking. Please, do tell me now and end my suspense."

Isobel shot a hunted glance over her shoulder to check the distance between the two of them and their fathers. "Very well. I am going to dance with Lord Blackburn, if he asks me. I am going to give him the cut direct if he is rude to me. I am going to flutter my lashes like a young miss in love. I am going to ignore him horribly, and I am going to remain breathlessly poised on his every utterance."

"You are being nonsensical, Issy." She frowned at Isobel. "Did you, perhaps, sip some of your father's brandy before leaving the house?"

As they merged with a crowd thinning to pass through the front door, Christiana stopped again and waited as if to force Isobel's answer.

"I am not being nonsensical. I vow that I mean to do all of those things . . . and more. If not tonight, then at some other gala. I mean to keep the *ton* interested in the two of us—and the wager." Isobel put her mouth to Christiana's ear. "And while I have the *ton*'s interest, I will use it to voice the plight of war widows and their children. My mission is to collect as much as I can from those who have so much money that they eagerly relish the chance to throw it away on such a meaningless wager."

Christiana responded with a gasp just as they entered Partridge House. She said nothing as they surrendered their wraps, her face impassive as she seemed to consider Isobel's request for assistance. But when their fathers belatedly crossed the threshold, ensconced in a crush of humanity, Christiana turned her wide eyes to Isobel's and nodded. "I will do it. You know I will do anything for you. But Lord help you if your father learns what you are about this night."

"No, *I* will be helping the Lord, for if my father learns of my strategy, I will surely be dispatched to my great-aunt's pig farm in Yorkshire."

"What? Your great-aunt Gertrude—the one whose lingering swine scent of pig makes your eyes water?"

"*Yes.*"

"Well, Issy, you will pardon me, won't you, if I do not come to visit you in Yorkshire?" Christiana asked. "You know I detest pork."

Isobel scowled. "So, Christiana, now you understand why I simply cannot fail. If I am forced to leave London, the widows will have no one to assist them, to help find rooms and employment. To give them money when they have none to feed their children."

"Yes, but *especially* because you do not wish to perpetually smell like pigs," Christiana added, quite seriously.

"R-right. That too." Isobel swallowed deeply, girding herself for the evening. As their fathers rejoined Isobel and Christiana, their party moved together up the staircase to the ballroom.

Sterling stood beside his brother Grant at the perimeter of the opulent Partridge ballroom. Or rather, where the perimeter would have been if the grand room had not been filled from the center to each of the four walls with far too many overcurious guests.

He glanced across the room at Killian and Lachlan, who were easily visible over the waves of shorter Englishmen, and saw that they were already making their escape from the crush.

Sterling groaned inwardly. He supposed he couldn't fault them for leaving; after all, he would do the same had he not been here for the sole purpose of encountering Miss Isobel Carington— without humiliating her or earning a slap this time.

He had the wager . . . and his family's financial future to consider.

His sisters were each swathed in a vibrant hue: indigo, saffron, and emerald. They stood out from the misses dressed in "purity" white, and the matrons in dull shades of metal, each seeming to repel attention more efficiently than the last.

Then a wave of silence rippled through the swarming ballroom. Sterling turned his head, his eyes just catching a flash of crimson in the doorway before everyone in the room seemed to move at once.

Suddenly the crowd opened like a loose seam until he alone stood at its apex, and in the doorway stood Miss Carington.

Her crimson gown shimmered in the flickering light of the chandeliers. The color of the gown seemed to heighten the porcelain smoothness of her skin, yet at the same time enhancing the fullness of her exquisite mouth, and heighten the beguiling flush atop her high cheekbones. Her hair, glistening like spun gold, was drawn elegantly atop her head and pinned into place with sparkling ruby brilliants.

She did not move, but all eyes were drawn to her.

Sterling didn't move either. He couldn't. He was too dazzled by her beauty and wholly stunned by her passive but entirely visceral command of him.

Grant clapped a hand to Sterling's back and pressed him forward, just as the crowd closed behind Miss Carington and, like a wave-surge, washed her straight toward him.

Her eyes were wild and wide as revelers rushed her across the dance floor so quickly that she did not even have the forethought to raise her hands to brace herself for the inevitable collision with him.

Sterling opened his arms, and within an instant, she was thrust hard against his chest. He felt her start to fall backward, and instinctively wrapped his arms around her and held her fast.

Her hair smelled faintly of flowers, bringing to his mind the welcoming scent of pink heather on the moors. Without thinking, he closed his eyes for a moment and reveled in the earthy sweetness that so reminded him of Scotland.

The smallest sigh fell from her lips in that momentary silence of the ballroom, and she turned her brown eyes up to meet his gaze.

"Are you well?" he asked her softly and sincerely.

She nodded slowly at first, then faster as she found her feet and sense enough to raise her palms and push away, breaking his embrace.

It was too fast, it seemed, for she staggered backward, and he reached out and caught her hand to steady her.

Slowly she lifted her eyes to his again, and to his astonishment, she lifted her lips as well, and smiled warmly at him. Then, without releasing his hand, she graced him with a most unexpected curtsy. "Thank you, Lord Blackburn," she said quietly.

By instinct alone, for thought seemed well beyond his grasp just then, he bent and bowed deeply, nodding his head to her. "Miss Carington, I am grateful I could assist you."

The crowd roared and clapped, jolting Sterling and making his eardrums vibrate as the sound reverberated off the walls, consuming his senses.

As the applause melted, the musicians began to play, and the attention that was wholly theirs only a moment before dispersed and scattered throughout the ballroom in the form of conversation, dancing, and merriment.

Miss Carington, oddly enough, did not seem unnerved by the cheers of the assembly seconds before.

She peered up at him with her expressive eyes, then she arched the fine slash of her right eyebrow as though waiting for something.

He realized then that he was about to blunder socially again if he did not honor her in some way. "Miss Carington, it seems we are being given a third chance to meet properly"—he raised his lips and flashed a gallant smile—"which is only right, since I have recently learned that we are to be married." Inwardly he winced, belatedly regretting his reference to the wager.

Miss Carington did not falter. She lowered her head slightly, tilting it to the side as she looked up at him through her thick lashes. "I have heard the same, Lord Blackburn. Interesting, is it not?" She rose up on her toes just a bit, then whispered in hardly a quiet tone at all, "It is my belief that the reports of our upcoming wedding are only rumors . . . though I could be mistaken." She did not smile.

Though the room was close and still, the hair upon Sterling's head seemed to spring on end as surely as if a cool breeze had whisked through. What could he offer in reply? He did not know exactly how to take her comment. Was she toying with him, as he had with her the last two times they encountered each other?

He studied her more closely, gazed at her eyes and her mouth for clues of her true meaning. But there were none. Could it be that she was delicately communicating her interest in a possible match? She was but a miss, after all, and he a Scottish marquess. It was possible she finally saw the logic in such a strategic match.

Then too, it was also conceivable that . . . she felt some level of fondness for him.

He glanced desperately around to see if Grant

still lingered nearby. His brother always seemed to understand the secret motivations that caused women to confound men.

Sterling spied Grant with their sisters standing near a long table stocked with dozens of glasses, bowls of punch and lemonade. Bewigged and liveried footmen ladled their glasses full, and as the four Sinclairs turned in his direction, Sterling caught Grant's notice and frantically summoned his brother to him.

He turned to prompt Miss Carington that his brother and sisters approached, but a young copper-haired miss had taken her arm and was hustling her away.

Miss Carington glanced up apologetically, but allowed herself to be drawn from him and into the chattering fold of several elderly ladies and gentlemen.

Damn it all. He had her attention for but a clutch of minutes before losing her again.

"So, what did you say to send her running away, Sterling?" Grant asked in a low tone, just loud enough for Sterling and his sisters to hear his kidding.

"I didn't do a thing—or say anything. I didn't have a chance." Sterling rose up to his full height and watched her conversing in the distance. He whirled on Grant. "I ought to flatten that straight nose of yours for shoving me into her like you did."

Ivy giggled. "Och, don't blame Grant. You could have remained still as a marble statue and the crowd would have seen you together regardless. You don't realize how entertained London Society is by your wager."

Sterling shook his head. "It is difficult to believe a bet, solid though it is"—he sought the gazes of his siblings to ensure they heard the addition of those few words—"would interest so many in the possible match of two people—especially a couple with nothing in suit but that they both hail from the outskirts of proper Society."

Priscilla gave Siusan a covert nudge with her elbow as if prompting her to speak.

Siusan nodded and shook open her painted silk fan and spoke from behind it. "Sterling, how thick you are being. The wager has nothing to do with the money—though a grand sum it is."

"What do you mean, Su?" Sterling angled himself so he could see behind her fan. "Most certainly it has *everything* to do with want of coin."

"Nay," she replied. "It has to do with *romance and love*."

Sterling looked quizzically at her, then at his brother. "Tell her, Grant. Tell her she is the one being thick if that is what she believes."

"Well, she is right by half," Grant admitted. "I will give her that."

"Have you lost your senses as well, brother?" Sterling raised his brow in surprise.

"Now, now, let me finish." Gesturing for them all to draw closer, Grant lowered his tone. "The gentlemen from the club are interested in the coin, and certainly the sport of wagering."

"There, I told you." Sterling nodded firmly.

Grant raised a hand. "The ladies, their wives and daughters, from what I have heard over brandy at White's, are the true sources of the counterwager. They, according to the members' complaints, are solely concerned with the prospect of a love match between a handsome Scottish marquess and an ordinary miss from Leicester Square."

Priscilla wrinkled her nose. "D-did you say Leicester Square? That's not such a smart address in Town. Are you certain she is from a good family, Sterling?"

"She is, and you should not be so swollen with pride, Priscilla," Ivy said through clenched teeth. "You no longer have license. Though we reside in a most fashionable square, I am sure *Miss Carington's* home is at the very least . . . furnished."

"Sterling . . ." Grant centered his gaze on his glass of punch and swirled the liquid around inside. "Don't look up abruptly, but you should know that Miss Carington's lovely brown eyes are upon you."

Sterling raised his gaze and saw that it was true. His chest swelled, knowing she had sought him out. Perhaps this hand was still in play. "So they are."

"Another dance set is about to begin," Siusan advised. "As popular as Miss Carington seems to be this eve, if you wish to further your position, you will wish to approach her now."

"I will request a dance . . . soon enough."

"Nay, Sterling, *now*." Priscilla tipped her head at a tall, auburn-haired young man, only three strides away from the Sinclairs, who was unabashedly studying Isobel. "For if you don't lead her to the dance floor now, *that* gentleman surely will."

Sterling knew the look in the Englishman's eyes all too well. The man was not merely considering a dance with Miss Carington. He was appraising her, admiring her . . . and more.

Sterling did not wait another instant, but bolted for Miss Carington, heedless of the startled ladies and gentlemen forced to leap from his path.

He held Miss Carington firmly in his sight, but from the periphery of his vision, he caught a glimpse of the Englishman racing for her as well.

Sterling jerked his head to gauge his competition's progress. Two other older gentlemen in tails seemed to be clearing a path for the Englishman, who smirked back at Sterling and hastened his strides toward Miss Carington.

The Englishman was going to reach her first.

Devil take him.

Suddenly a large, round-faced woman, in a lurid cerulean turban, seemed to purposely step directly in front of the Englishman, blocking his path. She sucked in an audible breath and squeezed her eyes tightly as though girding herself for impact.

Sterling pinned Miss Carington with his gaze. He heard a shriek, and guessed what might have happened, but his focus remained only on the doe-eyed beauty before him.

He would have this dance.

And no other.

Chapter 7

An object in possession seldom retains the same charm it had in pursuit.

Pliny the Younger

Isobel feigned an amused laugh in response to Lady Marigold's story, and was about to beg off from the dreary conversation to fetch a glass of punch, when she glanced up to see two gentlemen racing toward her—or rather one gentleman and a Sinclair.

Grown ladies leaped out of the way of the rogue bulls' charge, giggling like misses just out, while men, seeming unaware, turned their shoulders into the way of Lord Blackburn.

"Lud, Issy, they are headed straight for you!" Christiana exclaimed. She grasped Isobel's arm in her surprise, which only prevented either of them from fleeing. The matrons who had been standing with the two younger women, chirped their delight with the unexpected race and hurriedly chasséd behind them.

Isobel struggled against Christiana's grip until she noticed that all eyes were upon her. She stilled, and in the few seconds she had remaining before the gentlemen would arrive before her, she schooled her features and donned a mask of absolute amusement.

La, she only hoped Lord Blackburn would not reach her first, but rather the other man whose features were more delicate. His appearance gave Isobel the impression that he was gentle and cultured, unlike the Sinclair brute. But her hope was not to be.

Sterling was not the least breathless, as she assumed he would certainly be after running the *ton*'s gauntlet. His pride in his victory was clear in his pale eyes, gleaming down at her like fine polished silver.

The other gentleman was at his back within an instant, still trying to make his way to her, but the ladies of the *ton* would not have it. They closed the circle around Isobel and Lord Blackburn, standing hip to silk-covered hip to prevent anyone from approaching.

Lord Blackburn raised his arm to Isobel. "Dear Miss Carington, would you do me the very great honor of dancing with me?"

Isobel gulped, and suddenly she felt as though she might begin to weep. It was ridiculous to feel this way, but, la, in all the years she had been coming to the Partridge ball, no gentleman under fifty years of age had ever asked her to dance. Ever.

She was the miss who had almost reached the altar—before her beau was sent to battle, never to return. The very young miss who, some matrons surmised wrongly, had likely made it into the handsome lieutenant's bed, as so many misses had recklessly done before their soldiers headed off to war.

But when the months passed, and Isobel showed no sign of ripening with child, the gossip finally ended—but the damage had been done. In her father's heart, and in the minds of the gentlemen of the *ton*, Isobel's reputation was irreparably tarnished.

There was a certain freedom to being the miss no one would truly consider. There was no pressure to impress, and her days were full with her charitable concerns.

Still, she never stopped yearning for love. She just reconciled herself to the fact that the love of a man was something she would never have.

Isobel peered up at the Scottish lord through rapidly tearing eyes. She had imagined this, her first true dance with a suitor, many times over the years. Dreamed of this exact moment. And now, when a devastatingly handsome man actually offered his arm to take her onto the dance floor, it was the one man she abhorred—Sterling Sinclair, Marquess of Blackburn.

She glanced at Christiana, who gave her head an almost imperceptible nod, before she finally gave him her answer. "I—I would be most honored, Lord Blackburn"—Isobel gave him an embarrassed smile—"but, my lord, I fear there is no music."

Lord Blackburn turned toward the musicians and shook an open palm to them as if in command. It was a gesture they understood, for the violinist plucked a string thrice and the musicians raised their instruments.

The Scot turned to the crowd behind him and raised his other palm as well. Ladies grabbed their husbands' arms and dragged them forward, and within a blink of time, the floor teemed with dancers.

Lord Blackburn returned his gaze to hers and

bowed. "Miss Carington, I believe you were mistaken. The next set is about to commence."

A flush rose up from Isobel's middle and flooded her cheeks with heat. She did not know why his command of the ballroom filled her with a sense of pride, but it did. And so she took his arm and allowed him to guide her, past her astonished father and a dozen other equally surprised gentlemen, to the very center of the dance floor.

Lord Blackburn took his place beside her without a word, but his eyes said more than a comment ever could. For the first time in her life, Isobel felt what she believed it must be like to be desired.

As the music began, his hand, warm and larger than she would have imagined a hand could be, closed over hers protectively, and they began to move across the floor.

She could not help but marvel at the grace a man as enormous as Lord Blackburn could possess. And yet he danced with a skill and ease she had rarely seen in London.

Worriedly, Isobel tore her attention from him and focused on her own dancing, not wishing to stumble or misstep when it seemed clear she was partnered with a master.

As they turned around each other, he gazed deeply into her eyes, and suddenly she could not hear the music. No longer was she aware of others dancing beside them or great numbers of ladies and gentlemen gazing upon them.

The dance floor seemed to fade and disappear as surely as if a fog off the Thames had descended, obscuring everything from her eyes . . . except for *him*.

It was hard for Sterling to concentrate on the dance, with Miss Carington looking at him that way. Could the wager actually be the reason? It seemed impossible to him.

Why, though his heart had oft raced at the heft of a full coin bag, no amount of money had ever made him gaze at a lass the way she looked at him.

Not that it bothered him. It merely confused him. Truth to tell, the thought of what notions might be behind that intoxicating gaze of hers was beginning to stir him to no little extent. Enough that as the last notes of the music played out, Sterling was already plotting how to leave the brightly illuminated ballroom—where very soon every member of the *ton* would know the extent of his physical attraction to Miss Carington.

"Miss Carington," he began as the musicians lowered their instruments, "since we are to be married, shouldn't we at least know each other's names?"

She looked down at his hand, still holding hers,

but he did not release it. He wouldn't until he was sure she would not leave his side for the Englishman who flitted about nearby like a bothersome moth.

"Sterling Sinclair, Marquess of Blackburn. I believe I am correct, so . . . Sterling would be your first name, no?" The haze in her eyes had lifted, and the tone of her voice—which surprisingly did not offend his ears like those of the gaggle of English matrons and misses clamoring throughout the ballroom—was decidedly sarcastic.

"Aye, it is." Why did she make him feel like a lad wanting to press his lips to a lass for the very first time? "Though I don't know yours . . ."

"Do you not?" She raised both eyebrows in doubt. "I somehow doubt that, my lord. But if by some set of circumstances you have not heard my name bandied about in connection with the wager at White's, I will tell you. My name is Isobel . . . Miss Isobel Carington."

"*Isobel*," he muttered unintentionally beneath his breath. When he heard her name on his lips, he straightened and took rein over his words. "It suits you well. Much better than Miss Carington."

"Is that so, my lord?"

"Aye, 'tis."

"Though knowing my name does not give you leave to use it—even though you clearly feel at ease enough with me to hold my hand well after the dance has ended." She dropped her gaze to their clasped hands once more.

It was then that he realized his thumb was caressing the top of her hand. Still, he was not about to release it.

"A house this grand must have a garden or a terrace, aye?"

Her face lost all expression. "Y-yes, it does." She raised her free hand a few inches from her side and gestured to the doorway to the staircase. "But . . . I do not think—"

"I don't think it wise to remain in this sweltering ballroom either. Some cool air will be most reviving." Sterling gave her a playful tug toward the doorway.

The idea of leaving with him seemed to startle her, and she did not move from her spot on the parquet dance floor.

"Och, come now." Sterling gave her an easy, comforting smile. "Joining me in the garden, where I am sure dozens of other guests are taking the air, is much less apt to cause talk than the two of us holding hands in the center of the ballroom—which we'll do until you agree to come to the garden with me."

The twitch of her chin was hardly a nod of assent, but Sterling took it as such anyway. He released her gloved hand and offered his arm, which, to his relief, she took, and allowed herself to be led from the ballroom.

Isobel understood her father's mingled expression of pleasure and worry as she left the ballroom with Lord Blackburn. She was feeling the same unsettling rush of feelings.

It was a godsend that she had managed to snare Christiana's attention just before she and the Scot had disappeared through the doorway to descend the sweeping staircase for the garden. At least she was sure they would not be alone for long.

It was less apprehension than excitement she felt as they walked through the open French windows and out into the garden.

The night air was crisp and bracing, in complete contrast to the ballroom, which had left her skin damp and her chemise clinging to her. She had been so warm, and entirely distracted by Lord Blackburn, that she didn't register that the footmen at the foot of the staircase had been positioned there to bring wraps for those who might wish to stroll through the moonlit garden.

He escorted her directly to an oyster-shell pathway ringing a lush garden of early white moss roses.

As they strolled the shell-paved walk, the crunch

beneath their feet sounded abnormally loud, but the sound matched their pacing exactly.

She stopped, causing Lord Blackburn to do the same. The crunching of shells stopped. When they started again, the sound did too, only this time a chorus of giggles rent the night. She whirled around and saw a herd of women running through the open doors and into the house.

The larger of the two footmen, at the direction of Lady Partridge herself, closed the French windows. A metallic click reverberated through the walled garden.

"No!" Isobel pulled away from Lord Blackburn and raced to the door. She tugged on the brass knobs, but the windows were locked. Peering through the glass, she rapped hard, calling out to the ladies, but they and the two footmen had retreated down the passageway and were already disappearing from her sight.

"They've locked us in the garden!" Isobel cried out to Lord Blackburn, who hastened to a narrow window at the edge of house. But that too slammed closed before it could be reached.

"Och, you don't really wish to go back inside the ballroom so soon, do you now?" Sterling turned from the house and slowly walked in the direction of an iron bench in the farthest corner of the garden. "Come this way. We will sit and enjoy the cool air while the rest sweat through their finery."

She tried jiggling the lock again.

"Lassie, they will not open the French windows any sooner if you stand there."

Isobel sighed, then as she crunched toward him, an unsettling thought sailed into her mind. She peered warily at her lone companion in the garden. "You did not have anything to do with this, did you, Lord Blackburn?"

He chuckled at that and slapped his knees. "What sort of Scotsman would contrive to trap an English beauty in a garden, only to be observed by half the women in London?" He gestured to four open windows high above, filled three-deep with ladies of the *ton*.

Isobel groaned. She rolled off her gloves and pinned them against her side with her arm as she rubbed her temples with her fingers. "Why would they do this?"

"Why, they are playing Cupid. Surely you realize this." He patted the bench. "Come, they cannot hear us so far from the windows, and the roses screen their view . . . if we only lean back a wee bit."

He was right, and more than anything Isobel needed a respite, no matter how brief, from the prying, probing eyes of Society. Isobel closed the short distance to the bench, then stepped out from the fan of rose bushes, just enough to be sure she was completely visible, then gave a pronounced curtsy to the gallery above before sitting down beside the Scotsman.

Isobel could not help but be amused at the absurdity of all of this. Lud, the entire wager, and that she was at the center of it, was completely mad.

Lord Blackburn chuckled along with her, making her laugh even harder.

She looked at him. Could it be that he wasn't really as wicked as she first believed? In truth, he was as much of an unwitting victim in this blasted wager as she herself.

"Lord Blackburn, perchance have you seen White's betting book? Who placed this wager?" she asked. "No one seems to know."

He sucked his lips into his mouth as he seemed to consider his answer. "I have not seen the book or the entry myself, though my brother has."

Isobel felt a jolt rush through her. "Who is it? Please tell me. Who is this bettor with so much to risk on such a worthless wager as whether we will marry?"

"Lord Anonymous." He shrugged. "I wish I could tell you more, but the wager was placed anonymously."

"But why would the bettor wish to keep his

name a secret? I would think all the gentlemen of White's would be congratulating him on his ability to inspire the whole of the *ton* to participate."

Lord Blackburn rubbed his hand across his mouth, drawing her gaze momentarily to the glittering ring on his finger. "I would say he did it to increase interest in the wager—and it seems to have worked brilliantly." He peered hard at her. "Do you really believe the wager was . . . *inspirational*?"

"No, *I* do not!" Isobel drew a deep breath through her nostrils to calm herself. "I believe the wager exemplifies the greed . . . the completely selfish nature of men—and women, evidently." She glared up at the crowd-filled windows.

He seemed to flinch at her impassioned response.

"I apologize for being so blunt, but it is sometimes hard to restrain my true feelings when so many people are in such great need of money, while others waste no opportunity to cast it willy-nilly to the four winds." Without realizing it, she set her hand on his atop his arm. "When we first met, I had been walking by the Pugilist Club on the way to pass along a few shillings I had managed to save for a war widow and her children. I had walked from Leicester Square instead of hiring a hackney, so I could give her as much as I might."

Lord Blackburn exhaled and stared down at the broken oyster shells beneath his feet. He raised his toes and absently ground a few shells with the heel of his shoe.

Isobel realized he was uncomfortable hearing her recount the night at the Pugilist Club— the night he treated her so abominably, but she couldn't seem to stop herself from continuing. "When I saw so many gentlemen of breeding and wealth entering the club, drawing pouches of money from their waistcoats, I was incensed."

"And so you took the opportunity to ask for money . . . for your charity," he said flatly.

"You know of my work? That I am trying to raise funds to purchase Wenton Inn to provide a permanent place of lodging for them—at least until they find their own bearings in this town?" she asked, somehow feeling very surprised.

He scratched his neck. "Och, I know. You showed up during my battle waving pamphlets in my face, if you don't recall."

She widened her eyes. "But you ridiculed me and what I was trying to do."

"I didn't know what you were trying to do, except get your nose broken by stepping between two fighters." He looked down at her hand upon his arm.

She pulled it away.

"That doesn't mean I did not hear you, and admire you."

Isobel was filled with warmth and, admittedly, no little amount of confusion.

How could she have misjudged this man so entirely?

He saw her staring at him, assessing him as though for the first time. Heat surged through her cheeks, and she waved her gloves before her like a fan. What a cake she was making of herself. The night was cool. Only he was making her feel very warm. "D-do you think someone will come for us soon?" she stammered.

"Don't fash, Isobel," he told her. "The gentlemen of White's will hear what the women have done soon enough. They will not want to lose their position in the wager and will free us from the sweet fragrance of the moss roses."

His eyes, as bright as quicksilver, held her gaze as surely as his arms had held her in the ballroom, so strong and unyielding. Making her want to lean closer, to fold into him and savor the moment of rapture again.

"Soon enough, they'll come and . . . shade the shimmer of the moonlight," he whispered so softly that she was compelled to turn her head up to his to be sure she heard him, "and they'll save us from the blessed silence of the garden . . . any moment now." He moved his lips so near that his breath warmed her cheeks with every tantalizing word he uttered. "So don't fret, dear Isobel."

His moist lips hovered just above hers, inviting her. The roses were tall, a lush, perfumed fan. No one would see. She closed her eyes, knowing that she needed only to tilt her chin upward, an almost imperceptible shift, and their mouths would touch . . . in a gentle kiss.

And then the unimaginable happened.

Before she realized it, her lips brushed his warm mouth. For the briefest instant, their breath mingled, the pressure of lips increased as the thrum of her heart trebled with desire.

She sighed at the sensation of it, her mind reeling . . . before settling into the present again.

"Oh, oh blast." Her eyes flew open. Lud, she had given in to a moment of missish musing. "I didn't mean to . . ." Her fingers hurried to her mouth, and then awkwardly to his, before she realized she was touching his mouth—again. "I do apologize, my lord. I do not know what came over me . . . Please forgive me, won't you?"

She felt her eyelashes fluttering.

His brow rose, and he looked confused. "I don't know what you mean, Isobel. You did nothing wrong. The heat made you swoon a wee bit, 'tis all."

She stared up at him. Was it possible that he truly thought her kiss was naught but faintness? No, she could not be so blessed with luck.

But as she gazed at him, his expression gave suggestion he thought otherwise. Could it be?

"Issy!" came a female shout.

Isobel leaped from the bench and saw Christiana standing in the open French windows. "Oh, thank heaven!"

Christiana beckoned. "Hurry, come inside before the footmen return. They've been instructed to keep you locked in the garden."

Isobel started to rush for the open doors, but stopped when she realized Lord Blackburn was not following her. "We must hurry. You heard Christiana, did you not?"

Lord Blackburn leaned forward on the bench until he could see the upper windows. "Just as I thought." He pointed to the upper levels of the house.

Isobel yanked her head upright. Dark-coated gentlemen were drawing the women away from the windows, amid a flurry of protests.

"I think they've had their entertainment for this evening," he said, grinning. "More than enough excitement for tonight, eh?"

Isobel swallowed hard. No, tonight could not be at an end!

She'd managed to extract promises from the guests for only a few pounds to support her charity. And, from what the other ladies had witnessed, they likely believed they were halfway to winning the wager.

She couldn't have that. She needed their attention. She needed their fascination with her and Lord Blackburn for as long as possible.

She needed money for the widows. A whimper slipped from her mouth. "I shall see you inside, Lord Blackburn. Mayhap the musicians will play a Scotch Reel." She offered what she hoped was a beguiling smile, but her nerves were strung tighter than violin strings.

She bobbed a quick curtsy, then turned on the ball of her slipper and left him in the garden.

Surely he would return to the ballroom, if only to bid her good night. She had until then to come up with a way to shift any too-firm perceptions.

Mayhap there had not been enough excitement this night. Not for her purposes anyway.

No, not by a league.

Chapter 8

He is no fool who gives what he cannot keep to gain what he cannot lose.

Elliott

Sterling had not yet reached the top of the staircase when Grant trotted down to meet him. His brother hooked his arm around his shoulder and urged him hurriedly toward the ballroom. "Where the hell have you been?"

"In the garden." Sterling clasped his brother's middle finger like a filthy rag and pried Grant's arm from his shoulder. "You could have guarded the French windows and given me a wee bit more time with the lass."

Grant's eyebrows nearly met at the bridge of his nose. "I don't know what you are blaming me for now, but if it has to do with Miss Carington, you have to listen. You cannot be makin' it look too easy. Especially now."

"Make exactly what look too easy?" Sterling paused before entering the ballroom and lowered his voice. "Winning her?"

"Aye." Grant glanced around before speaking to ensure they wouldn't be overheard. "Killian and Lachlan have returned—with news. Wait until you hear what has transpired. The *anonymous* bettor has doubled his bet . . . without having to escrow his additional stake." He waggled his eyebrows meaningfully.

Killian charged through the door to the ballroom with Lachlan at his heels. "Did you inform him, Grant?"

"I would have never believed it, but I know you must have a plan for this contingency, Sterling." Lachlan tipped a glass to his lips and drained it of arrack punch.

Sterling looked quizzically at Grant. "There's more you want to tell me, isn't there?"

"Word hasn't yet reached the ballroom, but it will, and we need to know our position before it does." Grant urged Sterling away from the door.

"I am not sure what we ought to do now. White's has taken an unprecedented measure and has opened this wager only, and its book, to the public as a whole."

"The hell, you say." Sterling scratched at the stubble beginning to breach the skin of his chin and began to pace.

This was an event he had not considered. He glanced up at each of his brothers, but he could see they all looked to him for direction. "Why do you stare at me so? The field has changed but the wager has not. It is of no consequence."

He turned and started for the ballroom once more. None of his brothers followed. Doubt and, aye, a bit of worry too, was plain in their eyes. "Our exposure is no greater than we planned. This development, if anything at all, bolsters our chances of winning. More bettors to accept the wager."

Through the open door of the ballroom, Sterling glimpsed Isobel standing before her father, head downcast. As if she felt his attention, she looked up at him, and a wisp of a smile appeared briefly upon her lips before she returned her gaze to her father.

Grant moved beside Sterling. "Aye, more potential bettors enhances our chances of winning—but only if you do not make your successful courtship of Miss Carington seem like a given. The irresistible lure of the wager was that she spurned you publicly." He exhaled in disappointment. "Now look at the two of you. You are both smitten."

Sterling stiffened at the accusation. "Nonsense." For that was all it was, wasn't it—utter nonsense?

Lachlan drew alongside Grant, and Killian came up shoulder to shoulder with Sterling. "Bah, he's not smitten in the least, Grant. I believe our brother has a new strategy to encourage others to accept the wager."

Killian leaned forward past Sterling and exchanged a concerned glance with Grant. "I hope you've got the right of it, Lachlan. I really do."

Sterling started again to enter the glittering ballroom, but stopped short of the doors, thinking better of it.

He knew he could not battle the urge that pounded within him to rejoin Isobel. To take her into his arms on the dance floor . . . or wherever else she might consent to join him this night.

But his brothers were right. No one would take a bet he was sure to lose. He needed to separate himself from Miss Carington for a time. He couldn't make it appear too easy to woo her.

Her huge brown eyes peered at him as he stood

motionless in the doorway. His body reacted, forcing him to whirl around. He started for the staircase.

"Where are you going?" Grant called out.

Sterling maintained his course down the stairs and did not look back. "Please advise our sisters that we are leaving now."

"But Sterling, they will not wish to go so soon," Lachlan called back down to him.

"I don't care in the least. Tell them."

The next morning
The Carington residence
Leicester Square

Isobel stood silently before her father's desk, waiting for him to finish reading the morning paper. When at last he looked up, he bade her to sit down in the chair nearest his.

He removed his spectacles from his nose, and laid them atop the newspaper, before thinking better of it and sliding them to the side. "Well, Isobel, what have you to say for yourself?"

Isobel didn't know quite what he wanted to hear. The *on dit* column detailed so many events from the night before, she wondered how they managed to have it printed so soon. Her right eye started to wink of its own accord, as it always did when her father was about to chastise her for something she had done or *might* have done. "I am sorry, Father, but I am at a loss."

He tapped on the newspaper. "Have you read this?"

Isobel nodded. "Only partly. I did not finish because I saw no need—because it is not true."

"Which part? That you entwined your fingers with the Scotsman after the dance had well concluded? No, no, it cannot be that, because I saw you with my own eyes." He thrummed his fingers on his lips. "Mayhap it was the paragraph that mentioned how the daughter of Minister Carington ventured alone into the garden with Lord Blackburn."

"That bit is only partly true." Isobel cupped her hands on her knees and leaned forward to argue. "When we entered the garden, we were not alone. There were at least a dozen ladies there as well . . . for a time anyway."

"But you did remain with Lord Blackburn, alone, even after the others departed, did you not?"

Lud, he was arguing the merits of the column as though he were in the House of Commons!

"I did remain with him after they left"—Isobel shot to her feet—"but only because they closed the French windows and locked us out of Partridge House!"

He stared down his nose at her, until she quieted and reseated herself. "And why would ladies of Society lock you in the garden with Lord Blackburn, hmm?"

Isobel felt her eyes begin to narrow. She was not to blame for this! "Because *you* forced me to attend the ball."

"I admit, I did request you attend because I can no longer tolerate your antics in public, and if Lord Blackburn is willing to have you, I shall happily grant him your hand and pack you off to Scotland myself."

Isobel gasped at that.

"Oh, do not pretend to be stunned at the thought."

"I do not pretend to be surprised that you *had* the thought, Father." She rose from her chair and made to leave the room. "I am only distressed that you said such a cold thing to your own daughter. When Mother and Clive were alive—"

"Sit down, Isobel."

"I will not!" She folded her arms over her chest. "You practically ordered me to seduce Lord Blackburn, against my wishes, and then you admonish *me* when others join in your quest to see me married to him. I tell you, Father, I danced with Lord Blackburn because it would have been most rude of me not to accept his invitation. I left to take air with him because the ballroom was sweltering from the heat of so many gazes upon us. But *I* did nothing wrong."

"Evidently you did." He flicked the newspaper from its folds and began to read aloud. ' "What had seemed to guests at the Partridge ball to be the budding of a true romance between the Scottish marquess and Miss C. ended abruptly with His Lordship turning his back on the commoner.' " He folded the paper neatly and returned it to his desk.

Isobel shrugged her shoulders nonchalantly. "Did he? I do not recall seeing him after Christiana freed us from the garden." But she did remember. A pang of hurt had pricked at her when, after looking at her across the ballroom with such passion in his eyes, he turned away and departed only minutes later.

"Well, the column claims he did." He picked up the newspaper and tossed it to her, sending it skittering across his desk to the carpet.

She did not move from the sunburst medallion where she stood on the carpet. If she bent, she worried that in her state of anger and humiliation, a tear might form and slip from her lashes unbidden.

"So, Isobel, what did you do to douse his interest in you? Certainly you did something. A mannered gentleman does not focus his attention so wholly on a young woman and then leave without so much as a good evening."

"He is not a mannered gentleman," she sniped. "He is a Scotsman."

"And one day that Scotsman will become a duke. So I urge you to dissect your actions last night and identify where you erred."

"I am telling you the truth, Father, when I say to you that I did not err."

He flicked his fingers toward the passage, dismissing her. "I will make some inquiries and determine when the next opportunity will be to right your wrong with Lord Blackburn. Now, go on. Away with you."

Isobel spun around and stalked into the passage.

"Might you be wanting some tea, Miss Isobel?" the maid-of-all work, Bluebell, asked. "If you don't mind my saying, you look a bit pale in the face. I could fetch you some if you like."

"No, Bluebell, but I do thank you for offering the tea." Isobel slowly started up the staircase for her chamber. The maid followed her.

"Maybe I can help you figure where you got it wrong, with His Lordship, I mean," Bluebell told her. "After all, how could a miss like yourself *know*?"

Isobel had just reached the landing above. She grasped the rail and turned. "What do you mean?"

"I don't mean nothing, really, only that you haven't had any suitors, none that truly count anyway. So how could your father expect you to know what you got wrong?"

Isobel stepped down a tread and grabbed Bluebell's arm and marched the maid up the stairs and into her bedchamber. "You listened to my conversation with my father?" Isobel crossed the room to her dressing table.

"I didn't mean to. I was replacing a taper in the passage and I sort of . . . overheard." Bluebell rushed toward Isobel. "But I can help you with His Lordship. I have . . . *experience*." She bounced her eyebrows up and down. "You know what I mean."

"Oh, good Lord!" Isobel did know what the maid meant.

"Miss Isobel, I don't expect nothing in return." Bluebell looked sheepishly up at her. "Except maybe a little whisper if you would marry him . . . if he asked you."

Isobel raised her brow. "Why would that information be of any possible interest to you, Bluebell?"

"Well, because I have a few shillings put away, and since the wager is open to everyone now—"

"What?" Isobel grasped the maid's upper arms. "What do you mean by the wager being 'open to everyone' now?"

Bluebell scrunched up her nose. "You didn't hear? Why, it has been the talk of the houses and the streets since last night."

"Bluebell, *please*, tell me what you mean!" Isobel felt like shaking her.

"White's opened the betting book to the whole of London. Anyone can place a bet. You don't got to be a member of the gentlemen's club either, but it's only for one wager and you can't go inside the club. You have to place your bet with White's master of the house at the corner of Piccadilly and St. James's at noon and six in the eve."

Isobel's head began to spin. She released her hold on Bluebell and then walked to her bed and plopped down upon it. "And that one wager is—"

"The only one anybody who is something in this world cares about. Whether you and Lord Blackburn will marry by the end of the Season."

Isobel clapped a hand over her eyes and dropped back against the coverlet. "Well, certainly. What other wager would it possibly be?"

Chapter 9

Purposeless activity may be a phase of death.
Pearl Buck

Only minutes after Isobel and Christiana stepped down from the hackney cab, the low, dark clouds, which had threatened rain all morning, finally burst, sending sweeping curtains of gray down upon Piccadilly Street.

Huddling together beneath a wide umbrella, Isobel hooked her arm in Christiana's and hastened her down the pavers toward the corner where Piccadilly met St. James's Street. Rain splashed up from the puddles collecting in the gaps between the pavers, but Isobel was not about to slow her pace. It was nearly noon.

"We have passed three shops I would have dearly liked to have entered—at least until the rain stops," Christiana complained, glancing back over her shoulder at Fortnum and Mason growing more distant as they headed toward St. James's Street. "Your invitation was for shopping and tea—not skipping through muddy puddles!"

Isobel slowed and tilted the brim of their dripping umbrella back just far enough that she could see the crowd collecting on the corner before them.

"Do you think there has been an accident of some sort, Issy?" Christiana asked, cupping her hand to her brow to see through the rain.

"No accident," Isobel replied, then tugged at Christiana's arm to propel her into a forward gait. "I think the reason for the gathering is quite deliberate."

Christiana looked quizzically at Isobel. "What, other than some sort of accident, could bring such an odd collection of people together?" She raised a finger beyond the protection of the umbrella until a large, cold raindrop plopped atop it and disappeared far beneath her sleeve, causing her to wiggle and shake for an instant. "A chimneysweep, a shopkeeper, a general, I think . . . two maids, and, my word, my father's physician!"

"Oh, they all have reason to be standing on the

corner in the rain," Isobel confided. "They are here to place a bet—on me, well, and Lord Blackburn as well." She suddenly stopped and pulled Christiana back against a building. "We cannot go any closer, for I do not wish to be observed."

"Do you mean all of these people, from all parts of London, are here to enter in the wager at White's?" Christiana shook her head. "Impossible. Look at that gathering. I do not see one possible member of White's."

"As of last evening, apparently, membership is no longer a requirement to place a bet on this one particular wager." Isobel tilted the umbrella back again, sending a sheet of water over Christiana's backside.

"Oh! Issy, watch what you are doing!" Christiana reached behind herself and grasped a handful of her calico skirt to squeeze the water from it. "Why are we here if you already knew of this?"

"Because I wanted to see for myself," Isobel muttered. "Somehow I had nearly convinced myself that it was not true. That our maid had been mistaken."

Isobel peered at the two gentlemen standing in the center of the crowd. A bear of a liveried footman stood exposed to rain while holding an ivory-handled wide umbrella over a squat man writing in a heavy book.

By happenstance, at that very moment, the shorter gentleman turned his head just enough that Isobel was able to discern his distinctive profile. It was Mr. Raggett, the master of the house at White's. She had attended a dinner party at which she clearly recalled being introduced to him. He was brusque and not the sort someone would easily forget. Isobel brought her hand to her mouth. If the man on the corner was Mr. Raggett, then the book he held could not be anything other than White's infamous betting book.

She watched Mr. Raggett work for several moments. He listened briefly to each person, one by one, jotted something in the book, and then turned the book to the bettor for a signature or mark if that was all the bettor could provide.

Suddenly a hackney cab turned the corner, but instead of continuing onto Piccadilly Street, it stopped abruptly as the driver reined in the horses toward the pavers.

"Someone does not want to miss out on the chance to enter this wager," Christiana said. "Lud, if we'd been standing nearer the street, we might have been run down."

No one disembarked; however, Isobel heard her name being called through the partially opened window. "Miss Carington. Good day! Miss Carington."

Isobel glanced confusedly at Christiana, and warily the two young women walked over to where the hackney had stopped.

The window snapped down farther, and though Isobel tried to see who was inside, it was too dark. "You should get in" came a young woman's voice from the interior—a voice marked by a distinctive Scottish burr. *Oh God.* The woman was certainly a Sinclair.

"Miss Carington, you and Miss Whitebeard are getting wet," the woman called out to them.

"We have an umbrella," Isobel replied softly. "It will suffice."

"Och, just get in and hear me out. If you still wish to squish your way home to Leicester Square in soggy boots, you may do so. At least show me the courtesy of listening to what I have to say." A face appeared on the other side of the foggy window. Isobel could see that gloved fingers struggled with the latches, but the window would not be opened any farther. "Gads," the voice ground out, before swinging the door to the cab open.

Inside sat a tall, beautiful woman with silky red hair.

Christiana leaned her mouth to Isobel's ear. "It is Lady Ivy—one of the *Sinclairs*." A muted squeal of excitement slipped through her lips.

Isobel swallowed nervously, all too aware that

her surreptitious arrival was likely no coincidence at all. Had Lady Ivy followed them from Leicester Square? "Good day, Lady Ivy. May I ask what you wish to discuss?"

"Nay, you cannot. Just get in." She beckoned and slid across the leather bench.

My, Isobel thought, aside from their commanding height, the trait every Sinclair she'd chanced to meet shared was extreme confidence.

Christiana wasted not an instant boarding the carriage. "It is dry in here, Issy. Stop being a stubborn goose. Get in."

Isobel collapsed her umbrella, then with a parting look at the crowd beyond, she stepped up into the hackney.

"You really were being a goose," Lady Ivy said bluntly.

"I beg your pardon?" Why did it surprise Isobel that a female Sinclair would be no more mannered than Lord Blackburn? Lady Ivy, like her brother, seemed to have no reluctance to say exactly what entered her mind at the very moment.

Lady Ivy swapped her place for the rear facing seat and rapped with her knuckles upon the cab wall. The hackney driver snapped a whip, and the cab lurched forward. "You *were* being so daft! What were you thinking?" Lady Ivy shook her head at the two of them and gave them a most disappointed look. "I was merely passing by, and I saw the two of you lurking near the bookmaker's. You both make very poor spies, I tell you that. Why, another moment and someone else might have recognized you as well—an *on dit* columnist perhaps. How would that have been, eh? Or do you enjoy seeing your exploits reported in the newspaper?"

Judging by the sheepish expression on her face, Christiana seemed almost embarrassed for Isobel. "She is correct, Issy. It might have looked like *you* were wishing to place a bet on the corner."

"But I wasn't!" She turned her head to face Lady Ivy next to her. "Lady Ivy, I tell you, I wasn't. I only wanted to see for myself that it was true—that the wager has been opened to all of London."

Lady Ivy smirked. "Och, it is true. The wager is open to the world. My brothers heard about it last night at the ball. Sterling was so angered by it that he ordered all of us to leave the ball at once before the *ton* learned of it—who knows what games they might have played with you both had we not quit the ball."

Isobel's mouth fell open and remained that way until Christiana reached across their laps and, with the tips of her fingers, forced it closed again.

Isobel blinked. "So I didn't do anything to offend your brother—to cause him to leave Partridge House."

Lady Ivy chuckled. "Why would you have thought that?"

"Well," Christiana offered, "the newspaper column said so."

Lady Ivy clapped her hand over her mouth to stifle an uproarious laugh. "Och, you are very innocent, aren't you both? We Sinclairs never pay any heed to what the *on dit* columns print about us. The columnists are much more interested in entertaining than reporting anything remotely approaching the truth. The sooner you learn this, the better."

Isobel and Christiana traded shocked stares, unable to respond.

The hackney jerked to a halt. "Ah, here we are, Grosvenor Square," Lady Ivy announced.

The door of the hackney opened, and a gray-haired manservant hurried from the house and offered Isobel a hand.

Isobel flashed her eyes at Lady Ivy. "Wh-where are we?"

Lady Ivy rose from the seat and moved past Isobel to take the old man's hand to step down. "My home. Won't you come inside and dry off?

We can take our tea in the fore-parlor by the fire. Come now."

Christiana grinned. "Well, I'm going with her. You can sit here and wait if you like, Issy, but a fire and tea sounds delightful to me just now." Christiana leaped up and stepped from the hackney.

A little squeak of a voice in Isobel's head told her to walk to Leicester Square if she must, but as she often seemed to do, she ignored the warning.

She too climbed down the steps to the carriage and followed Lady Ivy into No. 1 Grosvenor Square.

It never even once occurred to her that a long-nosed columnist might have been standing beneath an umbrella on the corner.

Nor that he might have observed her entering the home of the man half of Society thought she would marry—Lord Blackburn.

Chapter 10

Thousands upon thousands are yearly brought into a state of real poverty by their great anxiety not to be thought of as poor.

Mallett

Sterling had just reached the landing of the first floor when dulcet female voices, drifting like perfume up the staircase, met his ears. His pulse quickened, and he paused to listen. These were not the familiar Scottish tones of his sisters. Nor did the soft words belong to Mrs. Wimpole.

He crept as quietly as he could down to the ground floor, but the old stair treads groaned under his feet just the same. The voices stopped before he reached the passage. Resting his back against the wall, he remained still and listened.

"I should greatly enjoy meeting such a . . . well, I will say it, such an infamous gentleman as Lord Elgin," said a voice that was not unknown to Sterling, but he could not dress it with a name. "Certainly I have heard about the Parthenon marbles, but have not had the opportunity to actually view them for myself. It would be most diverting to have the opportunity to discuss their acquisition with Lord Elgin."

"Well, it is settled then." He recognized the lilting voice as Ivy's. Sterling smiled, withholding the urge to chuckle. His clever sister had actually convinced someone it was safe enough to call upon the Sinclairs.

He straightened his waistcoat and moved to the doorway to greet her guests as any hospitable head of the household should. "And you will join us as well, Miss Carington?" Ivy added.

At the mention of her name, Sterling's lungs seized. His throat felt as though it was closing upon itself, and he started to choke. He coiled his fingers and brought his hand to his mouth, but a hail of coughs assailed him, making his presence instantly known to the ladies.

Before he could form a word, Isobel's huge doe eyes turned upon him, and her pink lips parted, moving as though she too grasped for words.

The memory of her soft kiss, the one she'd so wished to pretend had not happened in the garden, fixed in his mind. Unbidden, his gaze went to her lips.

Ivy smiled delightedly. "Och, ladies, look there, it is my dear brother Sterling." She settled her teacup on the small table before the flickering fire, then rose and approached him. "Sterling, I did not know that you had returned from Gentleman Jackson's saloon. I thought you were sparring until this evening to prepare for the battle at Fives Court."

She glanced at Isobel and the other young woman, as if to be sure that they understood that she did not expect him to be at home.

But Sterling had never planned to spar this day, and Ivy had no reason to expect that he would. As his coughing subsided, he lifted an eyebrow at Ivy, to let her, if not the others in the room, know that she was not half so clever as she thought herself to be in bringing Miss Carington and him together once again.

The ladies hurried to their feet. Sterling stepped into the doorway of the fore-parlor and bowed, his eyes never once leaving Isobel's own. "Miss Carington." An urge to go to her charged unexpectedly through his body, but his mind's counsel won his favor. He remained standing in the doorway.

Isobel tipped her head and honored him with a graceful curtsy.

He turned to the other young lady. "I do apologize for my lack of formality, but other than knowing that Miss Carington calls you Christiana, I do not know how to address you properly."

Ivy stepped quickly into the breach. "Sterling, may I present to you Miss Christiana Whitebeard?"

The young woman's lashes fluttered as she nervously pushed a lock of reddish-gold hair over her ear. "My lord." She stepped away from her gilt chair, bowed her head, and curtsied.

"It is so kind of you to call upon my sister," he managed to utter before his gaze drifted to Isobel once more.

The tenseness in the small fore-parlor was palpable to all, but only Ivy had the audacity and pluck to seek to disperse it. "Actually, Sterling, I found our dear friends here drowning in the rain on the corner of St. James's and Piccadilly. It was my duty to rescue them and bring them here for tea and a fire to set their skirts to dry." She grinned meaningfully at him.

"The corner of St. James's and Piccadilly, you

say?" *Christ*. Isobel obviously had heard that the wager had been thrown wide to the public. Why, though, would she have gone to the betting corner? "The lure of shopping must have been great to draw the two of you out on such a miserable, wet day at this one."

"Oh, look at us all standing about like palace guards when there is hyson tea to be had. Please, let us all sit down . . . so our necks will not get crooks from having to look all the way up at my tall brother." Lady Ivy gestured for everyone to be seated again. She patted madly on a fourth chair, but Sterling did not sit down.

Christiana folded her hands atop her lap. "Actually, my lord, we did not venture into a single shop—if you can believe it."

Isobel's eyes went impossibly wide, and hot color suffused her cheeks.

Sterling did not miss Isobel's heightened reaction, and furrowed his brow. He was about to press Miss Whitebeard into explaining herself when Isobel leaped into the awkward breach in conversation.

"N-no, we didn't manage to shop at all. The rain ended our day of shopping before it even began, I fear." Her eyes darted between Sterling and the cup of steaming tea she held in her hands. "Thankfully, Lady Ivy spied us from a hackney.

Else we might have been washed all the way to the Thames." The weak smile she managed to foist to her mouth quivered, and she bit into her lower lip as if to fix it into place.

He could not bring himself to look away from Isobel, though he was firmly aware that his mere presence in the house completely unnerved her. His gaze was distracted by a droplet of water clinging to the ringlet of her golden hair. As she seemed to become more aware of his attention, her breathing quickened again, making the bulb of water quiver and roll until it dangled from a single hair.

She snatched her gaze away from him, tilting her head down as she reached to the table for her dish of tea. The rain droplet lost its grip as she moved, and splashed down upon her swan-like pale throat, before trickling slowly down her décolletage, where it disappeared from his sight beneath her gown.

Ivy cleared her throat. "Why, I hope the chill, damp air doesn't set a cold upon my chest." She fashioned a smile for Isobel and Christiana, then turned a cold warning glare upon Sterling. Her eyes' rebuke transformed into a placating hostess's smile, and she slapped the squab of the chair beside her, harder this time.

When he saw that the other women were now

focused on Ivy's hand gesture, Sterling edged past Ivy's long legs and seated himself at last.

It was damned awkward and uncomfortable, sitting there, about to take tea with his sister and another miss, while willing his body not to reveal that his mind's eye had followed the rain droplet beneath Isobel's chemise, between her full breasts, and over the smooth skin of her belly until it finally nestled into the tight curls between her legs. He rushed a teacup to his lips and drank deeply.

Ivy reached out and gently urged the cup from his hands. "My cup, dear." She laughed softly, glancing up at the misses across from them both, causing them to echo her. "Allow me to pour a fresh cup for you."

Sterling struggled to right his thoughts. He lifted his gaze to Miss Whitebeard, but noticed a clear droplet peeping in and out of her nose with every breath.

He snapped his head around to Ivy and saw that she was balancing a dish of tea before him in her hands. He reached out and accepted it with a gracious nod. "Forgive me, for I did not intend to eavesdrop, but as I came down the stairs I thought I heard you mention an invitation to our guests."

"Aye, you did indeed." Ivy pressed her fingertips together in a steeple. "Lord Elgin, whose wife's family is kin to our own, sent a card this very day."

"Did he now?" Sterling studied his sister, wondering what she was on about. He had been at home all day and not a single card had arrived.

"Aye." Ivy's voice trembled. "So I thought, wouldn't it be splendid to draw together friends, such as Miss Carington and Miss Whitebeard, with our family for an evening here to meet the esteemed Lord Elgin?"

"You thought that, did you?" Sterling raised a single eyebrow. "And has he agreed to attend your soirée?"

Ivy masked a scowl. "Nay, not yet, because I have not asked him. His card arrived only today . . . but since his wife is kin, I am sure he would greatly desire the opportunity to spend an evening with us and our diverting guests."

"And when did you *think* this evening might transpire—I would need to consult my sparring schedule to be sure there is no conflict." Sterling turned up his lips most innocently.

Ivy did not falter. "Thursday evening." She looked at Isobel and Miss Whitebeard. "You do not have another *engagement*, do you?" She raised her ruddy eyebrows and stared pointedly at Isobel.

"No, no, I do not believe so," Isobel replied softly.

"I do not care if I do," Christiana chirped excitedly. "La, such an event sounds utterly diverting. I would not miss your evening for any reason, Lady Ivy."

"Well, then." Ivy clapped her hands together, settling the matter. "Thursday it is . . . assuming Lord Elgin can attend, but since we are practically family, I do not see why he would not do the same as Miss Whitebeard here and make the time to attend my soirée."

Within a few minutes, Isobel had found a way to extricate herself and Christiana from Ivy's tea party, and they were safely seated inside a hackney that was now turning from Grosvenor Square.

Sterling stood at the front window of the fore-parlor and watched Ivy wave until the carriage could no longer be seen.

He shook his head. Just what the hell was his sister trying to do? And why was she so certain a man both as lauded and as ridiculed by the *ton* as Lord Elgin would wish to come to dinner?

The Sinclair family was not known to Lord Elgin—and they most certainly were not kin . . . in any way or form. Why, Elgin and the controversy over the Parthenon marbles was in the newspapers nearly every day of late. He had become quite famous. Why would such a man condescend to call upon their family?

Something was afoot, and Ivy was at the center of it.

"La, Isobel! It is as certain as the coming morn that the marquess truly wishes you to be his bride. It is no game to him," Christiana told Isobel as the hackney wheeled its way back to Leicester Square. "His eyes could not leave you even when the conversation had, and his focus should have, out of politeness, been on the person speaking."

Isobel laughed. "Do I detect a smidge of jealousy in your statement, Christiana?"

"No, you do not." She turned her head abruptly and gazed out the carriage window. "But I am not wrong about his feelings. Or yours for him . . ." She turned her head slightly and peered surreptitiously at Isobel.

Isobel folded her arms over her chest and leaned back against the squabs. "I cannot deny that Sterling . . . Lord Blackburn is quite handsome and entertaining, but he is certainly not the man for me."

"Really? Handsome, rich, and diverting." Christiana huffed a sarcastic laugh. "Yes, I can see how those qualities warrant crossing his name off your *lengthy* list of gentlemen wishing to marry you."

"No need to be cruel. You know as well as I that I would have been married by now had—" Isobel waited for the tears to bud in her eyes, but none came. She waited a few seconds more, for the tears always poured into her eyes whenever she thought of Lieutenant Harbinger, the man who had promised to marry her when he returned from the war. Only, like her brother, he never did. The Battle of Corunna had taken them both from her in a single night.

Christiana slid across the bench to be close to Isobel. She wrapped an arm around her, waiting too for Isobel's tears to come. "It is only by the grace of God that my Mr. Stanley's service has kept him safe from battle thus far."

Isobel looked up at Christiana and gave her a weak smile. She knew how quickly one's life could change. One moment she and her mother were planning ball gowns with their modiste, and the next she was standing with her father at her mother's graveside, after having just attended a memorial service for her brother and the gentleman she would have married. "I had the perfect man, once."

Christiana sighed. "You were so young. I daresay you did not know what a perfect man was. And, la, if you do not see perfection in the Scottish marquess, I fear you are blind."

Isobel pulled away from Christiana and stared at her in surprise. "I do know! The gentleman I nearly married, and the man I would marry if he would only present himself, is generous, kind, loving, and responsible. Sterling Sinclair, grr . . . Lord Blackburn is a fighter who bloodies others for money. Truth to tell, I believe my perfect man and Lord Blackburn could not be more different!"

"Are you so sure of that?" Christiana asked. "What I see is a man who loves you. If you cannot see that, might there be other qualities that would recommend him that also remain unknown to you?"

Isobel leaned her shoulder against the cab door and stared out the window in silence. She had met the one perfect man in her life, and now he was gone. Why should she waste her days believing another existed, when she could use her life helping women and children who'd also lost the men they loved in Corunna?

No, Christiana was completely wrong.

The Carington residence
Leicester Square

"Lord Elgin will also be attending," Isobel told her father.

"Are you certain you heard correctly, Isobel?"

He sprang up from his desk to his feet. "Are you quite sure? *Lord Elgin*."

Isobel huffed a breath from her lungs. "Yes, Lord Elgin, who absconded with the Parthenon marbles. Lady Ivy claimed some sort of familial connection with his wife . . . what, I do not know precisely. But I do know that Lord Elgin left a card at the Sinclair residence just this day and that Lady Ivy had no doubt he would attend her soirée on Thursday night. I should like to confirm that you and I will both attend, Father."

Minister Cornelius Carington absently twisted several long gray hairs protruding from his eyebrows. At first, owing to the growing controversy about Lord Elgin's procurement of the Greek antiquities, Isobel thought he was about to refuse attendance, and moreover, was about to disallow her attendance at the soirée as well. Not that she would have argued, had this been his intent, but it was not.

"The timing could not be more perfect." He released the twist of eyebrows, and flicked a loosened hair from his index finger onto the Turkey carpet. His mind topping with thought, he sank back down into his chair and set his elbows on the desktop. Rubbing his palms together, he looked to Isobel to be almost gleeful.

"So, how shall I respond?" Isobel crossed her

arms over her chest, growing more curious, yet increasingly impatient with his reaction.

He lifted his chin and peered at her almost as if he only now realized she was standing before him addressing him. "Why, we shall accept. Yes, yes, we shall." A deep chuckle welled up from inside his chest, making Isobel more than a little nervous. "Lord Elgin will not yet know that a committee has been formed to consider his request that Parliament purchase his collection—and even if he had assumed a committee would be convened, he certainly would not know that I have been appointed to it."

"What do you mean, Father?" Isobel slowly undraped her arms and settled them to her sides. "You are not thinking to quiz Lord Elgin about the marbles with him unaware that you are part of the committee making recommendations to Parliament? Why, that is entirely unethical."

"What he did was unethical. Why, he acquired—some say stole—the marbles while acting as our ambassador to Constantinople. He may have used his own fortune to have the marbles chipped away from the Parthenon, the most beautiful building on earth, but he used British warships to transport them back to London."

Isobel was taken aback by his accusations, but was even more surprised by the color of his face.

His cheeks took on a throbbing blend of color—
red, pink, white, and purple—and they began to
puff out with each breath like an angry dog. "And
only now that he has squandered his wealth on
his ridiculous notion to bring the marbles to his
estate in Scotland, he asks the government to buy
the marbles from him—for the cultural education
and advancement of our people!"

Isobel stiffened. She rarely, if ever, agreed with
her father, but in this instance, it was possible
they might think alike on this matter. For if what
her father said was true, Lord Elgin's greed made
those involved with the wedding wager pale in
comparison.

Chapter 11

Let us treasure up in our soul some of those things which are permanent. . . , not those which will forsake us and be destroyed, and which only tickle our senses for a little while.

Gregory of Nazianzus

The Sinclair residence
Grosvenor Square

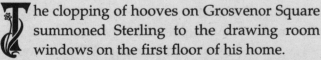he clopping of hooves on Grosvenor Square summoned Sterling to the drawing room windows on the first floor of his home.

As he peered down, Sterling tried to ascertain which of his sister's guests was so eager to attend the festivities that they'd have the audacity to arrive a quarter of an hour before the appointed time.

Sterling did not, at first, recognize the man standing in the lamplight on the pavers below, but curiosity obliged him to place his palms upon the windowsill and lean forward for a better look.

The smartly dressed gentlemen momentarily removed his hat and primped his hair with a quick pass of his fingers through his graying locks.

It was then Sterling noticed something over the man's nose. It appeared to be a bit of plaster or a lint bandage.

A fighter perhaps? Sterling squinted his eyes and peered harder still. Nay, too small and delicate in frame.

As if he felt Sterling's attention upon him, his gaze was drawn up to the window. Sterling started to step behind the curtains, but realizing he'd been seen, tipped his head in greeting.

The gentleman lifted his hand good-naturedly, then, giving the plaster over his nose a checking over with the pads of his index fingers, headed for the doorway.

Sterling realized the early guest's identity at that moment and expelled a long sigh.

Ivy hurried up behind Sterling. "Who has come? Nay, let me make a game of it. It is . . . Miss Whitebeard and her father. She was ever so excited to attend. Am I correct?"

Sterling turned around and caught his sister by

her shoulders. "Didn't you tell me you did *not* extend an invitation to Lord Elgin?"

"I didn't, truly. I only *said* I did. I might even have told several guests who condescended to join us this eve that I did. But, in truth, I never so much as inquired after the direction of his house."

Sterling's gaze bore deeply into her eyes. Ivy often toyed with the truth of things, and now might be one of those times. He squeezed her shoulders slightly. "*Ivy.*"

"I swear to you, Sterling," she replied, her eyes beginning to burn with the indignant questioning of her word. "I did not invite him to the soirée."

Sterling smoothed his hands over the shoulders of his sister's saffron-shaded gown. "Well, do not be too surprised when he is announced within the next moment. For Lord Elgin has indeed arrived." He stood tall and affixed a welcoming smile to his lips.

Ivy, suddenly appearing shaken, did the same. "Are you certain he is here?"

"Aye, I am."

It seemed all the Sinclair brothers and sisters had heard their manservant Poplin announce Thomas Bruce, seventh Earl of Elgin, and had hurriedly entered the drawing room to make themselves known to him.

It did not matter to any of them that he was both greatly esteemed and loathed at once, depending upon whom in Society was asked. The matter of position on Elgin's marbles was as cleanly divided as Society's position on the wager.

Nor did it seem to matter to any of them that Lord Elgin had not actually been invited—for Ivy had earned the privilege of uncovering the mystery of why he had attended anyway.

Priscilla could not wrench her gaze from Lord Elgin's plastered nose, or what would have been a nose. The usual protrusion was all but gone, and no amount of plaster could hide that. "Sterling." She dragged him aside and stood near the rear festooned window so Lord Elgin would not overhear her. "What happened to his nose? I dare not ask, but I cannot stop observing him until I know his affliction. Was it an accident? Nay, he was attacked in Athens, wasn't he, while trying to take the marbles?"

Sterling fashioned a scowl for her. "It is not polite to inquire about one's infirmities or sensational past."

Priscilla sank her elbow discreetly into his side. "*Sterling.*"

He grinned at her. "I will trade the information you seek for some bit of knowledge I require."

"Very well. I have no secrets."

"Nay?" Sterling glanced across the room at Ivy. "But our sister does."

Priscilla groaned softly. "You wish to know where she obtained the money to fund the soirée."

"Aye. She said she will not divulge her source until every guest had departed." He waited, rocking slowly back and forth on his feet.

"You could throttle it out of her. I know I should like to," Priscilla said. "Do you see that she is wearing my burgundy ribbon? She didn't even think to ask me first."

"I could, but that wouldn't be gentlemanly . . . or I could simply ask you." He was getting impatient.

"I might as well say. It is not as if I am to blame—at all." Priscilla opened her mouth and smiled brightly at Ivy, while she spoke through her teeth. "From beneath your floorboards."

Sterling sucked in his breath. "You had best be playing at something, Priscilla, for if you are not, I am liable to off your sister this very night."

"No folly. She did it." She shook her head. "Och, don't be so surprised. We all knew the money was there. Every time you pry up the board the entire house creaks."

"But I would have noticed." Sterling's gaze

scanned the finely appointed drawing room, until he spied her standing between Killian and a blue damask–lined wall.

"Ivy dropped a few metal skirt weights into the bag to match the weight of the coins we took—so you wouldn't know the money was missing until she'd already spent it."

Ivy turned her head and became snared by his gaze. Sterling narrowed his eyes. Her own golden-green eyes widened as she realized she'd been found out, and with a silent gasp, she scurried to stand beside Lord Elgin.

Priscilla skewered Sterling's side with her thumb. "Your turn. You can deal with Ivy later."

Sterling led Priscilla to a marble refreshment table. "I have this on good authority, but like anything else, it mayn't be the complete truth."

"Go *on*." Priscilla glanced nervously over her shoulder. "We havena much time."

"After the marbles were crated and set upon the warships bound for England, Lord Elgin decided to take advantage of a fleeting peace between England and France and travel overland rather than by sea. It was a mistake that would cost him his nose . . . and his wife."

"What do you mean?" Priscilla asked. "The French hacked his nose off?"

Sterling shook his head. "He was captured and held as hostage for years. When he was finally released, he returned to England to find his wife had left him for another, he had lost his seat in the House of Lords, and his finances were in as much a state of ruin as his diplomatic career."

Ivy's gaze flitted to Lord Elgin. "But his *face*. Why, he resembles those marble statues missing their noses."

Sterling rolled his eyes. "Word is that while he was in Constantinople, he contracted a severe skin disease beginning on his nose, which later became inflamed and ulcerated while he was imprisoned. Ultimately the sore caused his nose to rot and to fall off."

Priscilla turned and stared at Lord Elgin in horror. "How does he remain so jovial? I should have wanted to leap from a bridge if my life had disintegrated so horribly."

"I expect his spirits are raised because Parliament may approve the purchase of Elgin's Parthenon marbles for the people of England."

Priscilla shuddered. "But his *nose* . . . how terrible. How does he endure it?"

Sterling gave her a parting look of disappointment, then turned to find Ivy and his stolen coins.

Just then, Poplin's raspy voice called into the drawing room. ". . . and Miss Isobel Carington."

Sterling's body tightened and his heart quickened as he turned to see Isobel and her father enter the drawing room.

Isobel stood alongside her father, who was unrepentantly scanning the large drawing room for Lord Elgin. She spied the man before her father did. He seemed to be involved in a lively conversation. He gestured animatedly and his eyes were bright with the excitement of the tale he seemed to be recounting for Lady Ivy and two of the others, who clearly were Sinclairs, judging by their height and muscular forms.

Lady Ivy, seeing them arrive, excused herself and greeted Isobel and her father at the doorway. She ushered them into the room, and when Minister Carington excitedly requested an introduction to Lord Elgin, she promptly led him away to do just that.

Sterling strode purposefully over to Isobel, lifted her gloved hand, and pressed a gentlemanly kiss atop it. Even through the kidskin, she could feel the warmth of his mouth on her hand, making her wish with all her being that he would move his lips to her mouth.

And kiss her . . . not the way it had been in the

Partridge House garden . . . by accident. But purposely.

Her eyes suddenly felt lazy, her body as though she'd taken a wine, but she had not. The elixir that had drugged her was simply the presence of Lord Blackburn.

He released her hand then, and smiled, almost embarrassedly. Could he be feeling what she felt?

"I see you are able to wear your gloves again. I trust your hands have healed?" Isobel cringed inwardly at her pale conversation. But her mind had been wiped of all thoughts the moment he kissed her hand.

He chuckled at her comment. "A fighter's hands are never completely healed, but the swelling is gone, and so, aye, I can wear my gloves again."

Isobel stared up into his eyes, and her heart quickened. She comprehended only a few of the words he spoke, but from those she gathered that, like her inane comment about his gloves, his reply was unimportant. His gaze was locked with hers, and what they were communicating to each other, most unintentionally, had nothing to do with gloves.

"Ah, there we are!" Lord Grant appeared beside them and set a palm on Isobel's right shoulder and Sterling's left. "So, how is London's favorite couple this night? Set a date for the wedding yet?" He chuckled, volleying his glance between both of them as if they might suddenly join in his laughter.

Sterling groaned at Grant's quips. "Miss Isobel, if you have yet to make the acquaintance of the poorest jester in all of England, this is he, my brother Lord Grant."

Isobel gave a hardly serviceable curtsy to Lord Grant and greeted him. Her mind was too distracted by Sterling, who stood a little too close, looked a little too magnificent in his dark blue cutaway coat and close-fitting breeches.

Giving his brother a quick glance, Sterling took Isobel's hand, without requesting leave to do so, and then set it upon his arm, littering the air between them with some words to the effect that he wished to make her known to their esteemed guest Lord Elgin.

As he took command of her and led her across the room, for the first time in her life, Isobel felt the impulsive, clumsy miss who could do nothing right suddenly disappear—and in her place walked a strong, confident, and passionate woman.

Her eyes began to blink back the heat rising into them. This queer feeling—of transformation, for the all-consuming sensation could be nothing less—shook her to her very center.

It unnerved her like nothing she had ever

known, and for an instant, Isobel wondered if she would recognize her own reflection if she looked in the gilt-framed mirror as they passed it by.

Why, suddenly, did she feel this way; so full, so complete?

Strangely, it was as if the simple act of being near Sterling somehow awakened a strength that had always lay hidden deep inside her, buried and protected from spiteful words, ridicule, and the judgment of others.

It was as if he somehow shared his own courage, his great confidence, with her.

She wondered then what gave Sterling the strength to care so little about what others thought. Such freedom that gave him! He seemed to do what he wished and followed his heart rather than the rules. He was fearless.

She cocked her head and through her lashes peered up at him, admiring him. The hint of a smile appeared on his lips, and he tightened his grip, drawing her closer against him.

Isobel smiled too, even as Sterling interrupted her own father to introduce her to Lord Elgin. For as long as Sterling was beside her, his strength and courage infusing her, she knew for certain that she was at last becoming the woman she was meant to be.

* * *

An hour later, the guests had assembled around the dining table and a liveried footman, hired from a neighbor, began to serve the soup.

This event worried Sterling, who recalled all too vividly Mrs. Wimpole's fish potage—and the need for every member of the Sinclair family to quit the house to avoid being poisoned by the cook's mother's favorite receipt.

His stomach turned as he watched Isobel lift her spoon and dip it into the green soup. The world seemed to slow, and he knew he had to stop her from tasting it, even though preventing her from being poisoned would horrify his sister Ivy.

Coils of steam curled up, reaching for his nose. He held his breath. He could not allow Isobel to do it. He couldn't. He shot his hand out and grabbed hers, steadying it over her soup dish. "Wait—"

Isobel turned her confused eyes up at him, and she carefully lowered the spoon until he released her.

Everyone at the table sat silently staring at him. He opened his mouth to explain himself, when a tendril of pea-flavored steam slipped into his mouth.

"Pea soup," he said under his breath, wholly surprised. Damned if it didn't look exactly like Mrs. Wimpole's potage. The consistency was identical, but . . . "It's pea soup."

"Aye." Ivy blinked slowly. She sucked her lips into her mouth, then relaxed them into a slow smile. "Delicious." She pinned Sterling in her sight. "Don't fash, Sterling. The steam rising off the soup is deceiving, I know, but I promise you, it isn't too hot for our guests." Once she finished speaking and the dinner guests transferred their attentions to Sterling for his reply, Ivy pinned him with a barely veiled glare.

Siusan, who sat opposite Isobel, scooped some soup into her spoon, and hastened it to her mouth. She swallowed, then addressed Isobel. "The soup is perfect, just right. My sister hired a cook for this event who, until her mother fell ill, had been engaged for years by the Duchess of Devonshire." She looked pointedly at Sterling, then gave him a prodding nod to try his soup.

Sterling exhaled and tasted his pea soup. Priscilla brought her serviette to her mouth to cover her silent laughter.

"Lord Elgin"—Mr. Carington thankfully drew the attention of the guests to the other end of the table—"we are all so fortunate that Lady Ivy thought to bring us together this night."

Isobel, who had started to lift her spoon, replaced it in her dish, and looked wholly startled. "Yes, Lady Ivy, I agree." Her demeanor changed abruptly, and she flashed her hostess a bright smile.

"Though you could not have known this, since the appointment was quite recent, my father—"

Mr. Carington's eyes widened, and he raised a hand to interrupt Isobel. "Oh, allow me, my dear. *Please.*" He turned his attention to Lord Elgin once more. "I was recently appointed by the trustees of the British Museum to form a committee to consider the purchase of the Parthenon marbles. So, as you can imagine, Lord Elgin, that you and I were both invited to Lady Ivy's debut soirée is quite a coincidence indeed!" He forced a delighted chuckle.

Lord Elgin lifted his dark eyebrows. "But Minister," he said, addressing Isobel's father, "I—I was not invited to the soirée this night."

Ivy gasped, and her pallor closely replicated the green hue of the pea soup. "Och, Lord Elgin, you *were.* In fact, you are our guest of honor." She looked helplessly at Siusan, then at Sterling as well.

"Certainly you received my sister's invitation. Our runner confirmed its delivery to"—Siusan looked back at Ivy, waiting for her to insert the direction of Lord Elgin's house, but Ivy widened her eyes for an instant, making clear to Siusan she could not assist—"your home."

Lord Elgin lifted his linen and dabbed the edges of his lips in embarrassment, "I did not see the invitation, though you may be assured I would have come."

Sterling leaned inward over the table. "But . . . you did come to the soirée, Elgin."

Lord Elgin glanced around the table and saw that every eye was centered on him. He laughed. "Oh, dear me, I can see how I have confused everyone." He spoke directly to Sterling. "I confess, this is all rather embarrassing to me, but it is not as though the newspapers have not reported my circumstance."

"Lord Elgin, you needn't concern yourself with appearances in this house," Grant interjected. "We are Scots, like you, *brothers*."

Lord Elgin lowered his head, and when he raised it again, his eyes welled. "I came to this house this night not to be celebrated, but to ask for your help, Lord Blackburn, to see the marbles to Scotland, which had from the start been my intention."

"What?" Mr. Carington began coughing into his serviette. "But what of the British Museum? I know for certain that you requested that Parliament consider buying the marbles—"

Sterling leaped to his feet and crossed to Lord Elgin. "Dear man, please come with me and we will discuss this privately."

Lord Elgin's eyes were full of emotion. "I do not wish to disrupt—"

Ivy came to her feet. "Och, you aren't disrupting anything. Please, *go* and talk. There is plenty of food to be had." She smiled almost coquettishly. "In fact, my lord, we shall be dining for hours. There are twenty-three dishes to be served."

Siusan cleared her throat. "Thirteen, dear sister."

"*Thirteen* dishes!" She smiled, doing her utmost to appear to have the uncomfortable situation in hand.

Lord Elgin bowed to her. "Thank you, Lady Ivy."

"Do excuse us, please." Sterling leveled a hard gaze upon Mr. Carington before extending his hand and guiding Lord Elgin from the dining room.

His parting glance was at Isobel, and he hoped she took his meaning when he silently asked her to stay.

Chapter 12

What a miserable thing life is: you're living in clo-
ver, only the clover isn't good enough.

Brecht

Burlington House
The shed

This street is Piccadilly, not Leicester Square.
Lord Blackburn, you promised you would
see me home." Isobel looked up at the im-
posing structure visible through the window.
Why were they here at all?

After Lord Elgin's confession, the evening de-
clined quickly. Isobel's father became sick with

worry that the committee he'd been charged by
Parliament to form, to assess the viability of acquiring the Elgin marbles for the British Museum,
was doomed to fail. His coloring became as green
as the pea soup, and he left the Sinclair home early
with nothing more than a request that someone
escort Isobel home to Leicester Square.

Of course, after emerging from his long discussion with Lord Elgin, Lord Blackburn volunteered
for the honor.

"Why are we here . . . Sterling?" A wand of
moonlight illuminated naught but his pale eyes.

When the carriage came to a wobbling halt at
the farthest edge of Burlington House, Sterling
opened the door and leaped out before the hackney driver had even called their destination.

He stood in the bright moonlight and raised
his hand to her. "I want to show you something.
Something amazing."

Warily, Isobel slid to the edge of the seat, then
grasped his hand and stepped down from the
hackney.

Sterling looked up at the hackney driver. "I bid
you to stay here, sirrah, even if we do not emerge
until daybreak."

Daybreak? Just what was he intending? Isobel
looked at the huge, dark castle of a house. "Is
anyone at home?" she asked hesitantly.

"Nay. The house has been sold." He took her hand and walked to the tall gate in the fence surrounding the property. From his waistcoat pocket he withdrew a key and set it into the iron lock that securely barred entry into the gardens at the rear of the house.

"Then why are we here? What do you wish to show me?" Isobel felt her body tense. Not from fear, but from the knowledge that she was alone with him, a wicked fantasy that had pestered her mind and caused sleepless nights since the very first day they had crossed each other's paths at the Pugilistic Club.

The gate was nearly twice his height, but a doorway set into the left gate made it possible for Sterling to gain their entry. He swung the door wide and ducked through, then ushered Isobel forward, closing it behind them.

The yard was bright given the illumination of the near full moon, and it took but a moment for her eyes to adjust and see the amazing scene before them.

Marble pediment sculptures, column bases, and figures fenced a huge coal shed in a wall of luminous silvery blue.

It took Isobel several moments to realize what she was truly seeing. "These are not . . . Elgin's Parthenon marbles?"

She knew the answer already, and she shivered in amazement.

"They are." Sterling neared her, hesitantly at first. "You're cold, lass."

She shook her head, but moved into his embrace regardless. "Elgin has left the marbles here, out of doors, in the dampness of London?"

He shook his head. "Not all. Come. Elgin lent me the keys." Sterling separated from her and took her hand and led her to the doorway of the wooden shed.

It was no ordinary coal shed. Even in the moon-touched darkness, she could see that the structure was at the very least as large as her home on Leicester Square.

Sterling withdrew a very small key from his waistcoat pocket and inserted it through the rusted escutcheon and into a lock. He looked at her, and she nodded expectantly, then he turned the key and pushed the door open.

They stood together in the open doorway for several moments, waiting for their eyes to adjust to the dimness. Though two great windows on the large gables of the shed's roof admitted rectangles of moonlight, it was still very dark inside.

"It is too dim to appreciate the marbles." Sterling looked at Isobel. "I apologize. I truly wished to show you something extraordinary."

"You've seen them then?" Isobel asked.

"Nay." Sterling reached out his hand and ran it along the sculpted neck of a marble horse. He smiled. "Tonight Lord Elgin asked me to purchase the marbles. It is why he came to the house this eve."

"What?" Isobel was astounded at this. "A-and did you agree?"

Sterling laughed, but it was a soft, sad sound. "I wish that I could. There is no other collection like it in the world, but I do not have that sort of coin . . . yet."

Isobel scrunched her brow. "What do you mean?"

Sterling left her side and began to feel his way through the marbles inside the dark coal shed. "Lord Elgin is not the greedy collector so many suppose him to be."

"There are some who may argue that position," Isobel countered. She listened for his reply, and when he spoke, let her hearing guide her.

"Until tonight, I might have been one of that number. But no longer." He passed beneath a wedge of moonlight. "Elgin's original thought was only to make plaster casts of some of the greatest marble sculptures known to mankind before they were destroyed."

"What changed his mission?"

"The Acropolis was being used as a Turkish fortress, and already pieces of the marble were being used for hovels or crushed, then burned, to make lime to whitewash other buildings. Elgin's artisans worked quickly to make the casts, but because the governor of the fortress would not allow them to erect scaffolds, after one year only a few pediments had been cast."

"But . . . these are not casts." Isobel touched the marble folds of a woman's garment, marveling at the realism and artistry of the sculpture. "These are works of art."

Sterling was nearby, his voice told her so, but she could not see him unless he passed beneath one of the bright windows above. "A chaplain of the British Embassy, who was passionate for antiquities, petitioned Constantinople for permission for Elgin to remove any sculptures that did not interfere with the walls of the citadel. The timing was perfect, Nelson had just won the Battle of the Nile, and the British were on the rise in the Mediterranean. Permission was granted."

Isobel considered the story. "And so Elgin's belief is that by removing the marbles, he saved them from being destroyed."

"Aye. The collection is a gift to mankind that must be protected."

Isobel did not wish to be alone in the darkness.

She raised her hands and felt her way toward Sterling's voice. "Then why does Lord Elgin seek to sell the marbles?"

When Sterling spoke, she felt the heat of his breath, and honed in on him.

"Because he cannot afford to keep them," Sterling replied. "And his reason for acquiring them in the first place no longer exists."

"But at dinner, he mentioned bringing the marbles to Scotland," Isobel reminded him. She stilled and listened for his voice.

"Aye, it was his grand hope, but he assumed my means are much greater than they truly are. I cannot help him, though I wish that I could."

She was near now, her heart pounding with anticipation of finding him in the darkness. "But why Scotland? I understand that it is his homeland, but he resides here now, in London."

Sterling sighed, and she hurried toward the sound of his breath. "Elgin was taken captive by the French when he returned to England overland, while the marbles were being transported to England by sea. His wife, to whom he'd promised to bring the grace of Greece to Scotland, left him for the man who supposedly worked to obtain his freedom from France. You see, illness had rotted and took his face, and sadness over losing his beloved wife stole his heart."

Isobel knew Sterling was close. She stepped into the light from the window in the gable above and raised her hands in the air to him. "But my father, he and Parliament will save the marbles. Place them somewhere safe and protect them from the elements here."

"Or will Parliament follow the ideas of others who claim Elgin robbed Greece of her culture?" He exhaled. "I don't know. And neither does Lord Elgin. To hear him, the government sides with popular opinion. He believes Parliament would rather let them disintegrate here than to buy them for only what he paid for his workmen and for the marbles' transport to London."

"My father will not allow that," Isobel claimed, but in her heart she did not know for certain that her words were true.

Seeking Sterling's heat, she moved forward until she felt his chest against her. She inclined her head and rested it upon his shoulder, and felt the welcoming warmth of his arms encircling her.

They held each other for some time, for no reason other than want of each other. But at length, Sterling broke their embrace. "Even though we cannot see the true beauty and art of these sculptures, we cannot lay waste to this opportunity. We may never have it again."

Isobel looked up, to where his face would be, only darkness obscured. "What do you mean?"

She felt his hand on hers, moving it through the air until it met with the cool stone of a marble sculpture.

"We will feel the mastery with our hands," he told her. "We will learn through touch."

Isobel slid her hand down the marble sculpture, his hand atop hers, moving it, slowly.

"Magnificent, is it not?" Sterling stood behind her, his mouth just above her ear. She closed her eyes and let her fingertips see the smooth, cool muscle and sinew of a man's leg, and imagined, so wickedly, that it was not marble she touched, but Sterling. That instead of guiding her hand, he was running his hand over her body.

And in the next moment, to her great surprise . . . he was.

He'd moved directly behind her; his free hand slid around her waist, his thumb gently tracing the slope of a rib.

A profound silence filled the musty air of the shed. She felt his hardness pressed against the Y where her back met her buttocks. For some seconds neither of them moved, as though each of them waited for the other to break away from the carnal threat building steadily in the stillness.

Isobel wrapped her fingers around the hand poised on her ribs. She drew in a shaky breath as she ran his hand up to her breast and cupped her hand around his until he held her there.

"Isobel?" The sound of her name riding his breath was deep and raspy, and it sent a vibration through her, making her quiver against him. His tone did not question what she was doing; she knew this. He was asking her if she wanted to tread farther.

And she did. What happened beyond this night was of no consequence. She was destined to remain unmarried, her father told her that oft enough, and she knew he was right.

This wager was but a game that brought two mismatched people together, but she knew their time was fixed. By the end of the Season, their paths would veer and part forever. She would die a miss, but not a maid.

She wanted him, wanted to know what it was like to merge her body with his. To feel desire and experience it fully. She wanted a night to remember for the rest of her lonely life. One night, with this beautiful Greek sculpture of a man.

And so she let the courage he infused her with fill her, and she turned slowly around, until she was standing pinned between the reclining male pediment sculpture and Sterling, who felt as hard and unyielding as the marble.

She raised her lips and he kissed deeply, stealing her breath away. Dizziness stole her balance, and her hands came down behind her. The open knees of the statue bumped her shoulders from behind, imprisoning her on either side. Sterling stepped into the breach, not allowing her to right herself. And so she hoisted herself back along the statue's torso until she rested on his chest.

In the dimness she had the impression that Sterling was smiling, but she did not know for certain. She leaned up and caught the lapel of his coat and began to drag him over her, but he resisted.

She had been too bold, too brazen. A flush of humiliation rushed up from her chest and filled her cheeks. Lying back down atop the statue's ancient stone torso, she covered her eyes and willed back any tears.

One night, it was all she wanted. She had used all the courage she had, and he had rejected her.

Suddenly a weight covered her for an instant. Sterling's warm lips were kissing hers. His lips opening her mouth to his, his tongue probing the flesh inside.

She raised her hands and felt that the stone-hard muscles of his chest were bare. She slipped her hands down over his chest, feeling a crisp mat of hair between the great mounds of muscle. A sigh slipped softly from her mouth.

His kisses grew harder. He threaded the pins from her locks, then, casting them aside, slid his fingers through her hair, as he plundered her mouth with intimate kisses, so passionate that they both stunned and made her need more. Much more.

His hands raced over her body as he fed on her mouth. His breath came in pants, so shallow that she almost didn't hear him. "Are you sure of this, Isobel?"

She caught his cheeks with her palms and pulled him back just far enough that he could see her in the blue dimness. "Yes, I want you."

"But, lass, you are—"

She laid a single finger across his lips. "—a woman who finally realizes that she has been living a half-life. But no more. I want you. I don't care about tomorrow. I want you more than you'll ever know."

In a slash of moonlight, she saw his silver eyes peering down at her. She knew what she was asking of him this night probably made no sense to him, but she was more certain that she wanted him to make love to her than she had ever been about anything in her life. She peered back up at him, then smiled.

He closed his eyes, then tilted his head up and muttered something in Gaelic, something she could not understand. And then he kissed her, long and deep.

He'd never felt such a passion throb within him, not like this. Never before had he felt such an insane drive to feel a woman beneath him. But then Isobel was not any other woman. She was the only woman he wanted. The only one he somehow . . . needed.

Pushing up on one hand, he dipped his tongue into her mouth, then ran it gently over her upper lip. She writhed beneath him, brushing her thighs against his hardness straining against his breeches.

Her hand slid down his side, raising goose bumps on his skin; then she moved her hand between them and ran her fingers lightly over his breeches and along his penis, making it throb and twitch.

God, how he wanted her.

Didn't she know what her touch did to him?

He could not restrain himself any longer, and pulled at the thin slip of ribbon that cinched the neckline of her gown. The ribbon slid back through its satin casing, and the gown opened to him.

Cool air rushed over her skin, and as he lowered the bit of silk chemise that concealed her from him, her nipples hardened. He lifted her breasts up from the confines of her corset and, in the soft haze of moonlight, gazed at the full roundness of her. He leaned up and kissed her again, urging a little sigh from her lips, and then he slid down her and took a nipple into his mouth.

He swirled his wet tongue over the rose tip of her taut nipple, then sucked it along with a cool breath into his mouth. As he stroked her with his tongue, he cupped her other breast in his hand, kneading the soft flesh, heating the pebbled nipple until it began to soften under his touch.

Isobel slapped her palms down on his shoulders and gasped at the sensation, arching her body against him. Pressing the most intimate part of her against his erection. This was his undoing.

Sterling leaned up and caught Isobel under her arms and moved her higher against the huge statue. She looked down at him, confusion bright in her eyes.

Sterling peered at the tangle of marble and female legs, and frowned for a moment until he realized what he needed to do.

Grasping Isobel's ankles, he lifted them in the air, parting them, and placing one on either side of statue's outer legs, opening her to him.

Isobel began to pant and tried to sit up. "Sterling—"

He reached out a hand and pressed it against her middle, guided her back against the marble chest as he lowered his head between her legs.

Gently he spread her feminine folds, exposing the pink pearl to his mouth. He flicked that most sensitive part of her with his darting tongue before drawing it into his mouth and sucking it, sending Isobel's body into tiny spasms.

"Sterling, *please*," she whimpered. Her fingertips dug into his shoulders.

As he swirled his tongue around the tiny bud, he eased one finger, and then another, into her wet heat, gliding them in and out of her until her thighs quivered and bore down upon his fingers with each thrust.

"Sterling," Isobel moaned, reaching down and cupping the back of his head until he looked up at her. "Please come to me." He nodded and turned his head, kissing her silky inner thighs before moving higher, over her bunched skirts. He suckled at one of her breasts, and then along her throat until he reached her full lips.

He leaned to one side for an instant to lower his

front fall, and then positioned his penis between her hot, wet cleft. She bucked against him, but if she was indeed a maid, he must restrain himself. He pressed just his plum-shaped tip inside her at first, but she tightened around him, making him squeeze his eyes in concentration. "Isobel, slowly."

Isobel shook her head frantically from side to side. "No. *Now*. I want you, Sterling. Now."

He leveled his head with hers and looked deep into her eyes. "Isobel, I—"

She slid her bottom down then, moving him into her, past the veil of her maidenhead. She gasped at that moment, and clung to him for several seconds. At last he felt her body relax, and he began to move inside her.

He thrust into her, long, slow strokes at first, building a rhythm between them, before plunging deeper and harder into her.

Isobel never stopped looking into his eyes. Her mouth chased his with every thrust. Her muscles gripped him tightly and began to pump his penis faster and faster, making his body slam harder into her depths.

Sterling felt the beginnings of rush and broke his gaze with her. He had to stop. But at that instant, Isobel lifted her right leg from behind the marble knee and wrapped it around Sterling's back. She bucked wildly against him, and at the moment she cried out in her ecstasy, her body clenched around him so tightly that he could not stop himself. "Oh God, Isobel."

A flash of heat swept over him, and he caught her gasping mouth with his lips and kissed her hard as his essence pumped into her.

I love you.

Chapter 13

The be-all and end-all of life should not be to get rich, but to enrich the world.

Forbes

The Sinclair residence
Grosvenor Square

The sun imbued the sky with graduated shades of violet and pink. Sterling stood at the door admiring the sunrise, and trying earnestly to remove the giddy smile from his mouth before entering the house.

He had just begun to turn, his fingers already on the door latch, when a gleaming carriage drawn by four matching bays entered the square.

Och, he didn't need any more gossip in the newspaper, and so he hurried inside and closed the door before he could be observed.

He had only just removed his coat and set it upon a hook in the passage when the front door opened again and Poplin stepped inside.

Poplin seemed every bit as surprised to see Sterling, as Sterling was to see the manservant. "Oh, good morning, my lord. My, you have certainly risen early." His gaze swept Sterling's rumpled evening attire. "I—I mean, I trust you had a good evening, my lord." The old man's usual chalky pallor flushed as pink as the sunrise.

"Excellent, actually." Sterling passed Poplin and opened the door in time to see the posh carriage passing the house. He closed the door and studied Poplin. "I know that part of your arrangement, and Mrs. Wimpole's as well, is that you are not required to live in this house."

"That's right, my lord." Poplin gave a quick bow. "But if you will please excuse me, I need to tend to the fires. Good chill in the air this morning. Wouldn't want your family to catch their death while they sleep. It is still several hours before noon. Your brothers and sisters will not be down for their breakfast until then. Might I ask Mrs. Wimpole, when she arrives, to take a morning tray up to you?"

"No need, Poplin. I can wait to eat with the others."

"Very good, my lord." Without waiting for any further requests from Sterling, Poplin turned quickly and tottered off down the passageway.

Sterling opened the door again and peered out. The fancy carriage was gone. He rubbed his hands over his eyes. "Our manservant arriving to work in a carriage? Och, what am I thinking?" Mayhap he should sleep—for his mind was making some illogical leaps—but oddly enough, Sterling did not feel the least bit tired.

He chuckled softly as he closed the front door and then took the stairs to his garret.

"Good afternoon, Sterling. Aren't you the chipper chap this day?" Siusan grinned over the lip of her teacup.

She was alone at the dining table, though the noon hour pinged on the tall case clock in the passage, the signal to all that the breakfast was served.

"Lovely day." He knew he was still smiling. His mouth was sore, causing him to guess that he'd been smiling all night in his sleep as well. He gathered some fruit and toasted bread from the hunt board to break his fast, then sat down at the table with Siusan.

"We were worried something might have happened to you last night. You never came home." Siusan settled her cup on the table and folded her arms to await his reply.

"Well, Su, as you can plainly see, I am sitting right here. So I did come home." He popped a bit of bread smeared with marmalade into his mouth, and could not help but smile as he chewed.

Siusan unfolded her arms and flattened her hands on the table. "Oh, heavens. Just tell me! What are you so insanely happy about?"

Sterling finished chewing his bread, then swallowed and slowly washed it down with a sip of tea. "She is going to marry me."

Siusan leaped to her feet and raced around to kiss his cheek. "How did you ask her? Tell me you said something dripping with romance and passion." When he did not immediately answer, she frowned. "Oh please, Sterling, you did not appeal to her sense of logic, marrying a one-day duke and all that nonsense?"

Sterling shook his head. "I did not ask her to marry me . . . *yet*."

"Well, certainly you didn't. You spoke to her father." Siusan sat down again.

"Nay. I did not ask anyone." He smiled brightly. "I just know. Nay, I am certain she will accept me the moment I offer her my troth."

Siusan propped her elbows on the table and rested her head in her hands. "Sterling, what have you done?" She turned her gaze up at him. "Once word slips out, and it will, for the *on dit* columnists seem to have taken up residence in the bushes on the square, we will be expelled from Society. Everyone will realize that you were not an unwitting victim in this wager, but the driver of it all!"

"It will not matter. I will marry her, and we will win the largest wager in White's history. Don't you understand, Su? Father will approve of my wedding her. She is from a known and respected family. She is not a dancer or actress, like the others."

"Don't *you* understand?" She hissed angrily through her teeth. "This wager is not only about the money. It is about launching all of us into Society, so we can redeem ourselves in Father's eyes as well. Cease thinking only about yourself, Sterling. Everything you do has consequences for us all. You must understand this!"

Siusan stormed out of the dining room, passing Lachlan, who was just entering from the hallway. His brother smiled as he entered the dining room. "Su seems in a good twist this morn. You must have had a *very* good time last night to put her in such a state this early. So what did you do, eh, Sterling?"

Later that afternoon
The Carington residence
Leicester Square

A flash of movement in the passageway beyond her father's library propelled Isobel to her feet. She quickly straightened the newspaper on the desk that she'd been covertly poring over for any mention of her adventure with Lord Blackburn to view Lord Elgin's marbles.

"Beggin' your pardon, Miss Isobel. I didn't wish to disturb you." Bluebell entered the room, not daring to look up, as if she feared seeing something she ought not. "Your father asked if you would come up to his bedchamber. He ain't well enough to come below just now."

Isobel hadn't had time to finish reading the columns, and so she leaned down pretending to smooth the newspaper with her palm. She smiled up at the maid, but it became immediately evident that Bluebell was not leaving.

Blast. She would just have to hope for the best. She probably didn't have anything to fret about anyway. They hadn't left the coal shed until it was nearly dawn. No newspaper reported events so quickly, especially one as trivial as someone viewing statues.

"Absolutely, Bluebell, right away. I was just seeing that . . . everything was straight and tidy for his meeting with his committee this evening." Brushing her hands together briskly, as if to remove some unseen dust, she hurried from the library and then up the staircase to her father's bedchamber.

"Good morning, Father," she announced cheerily as she opened the door. The heavy curtains were still drawn, making the room nearly as dim as the coal shed had been, and it took several moments for her eyes to adjust enough to see the dour expression on her father's face.

He lay propped up by several plump pillows, with a damp cloth draped dramatically over his forehead. "Tell me, Isobel, is Lord Blackburn going to offer?" He brought his hand to his head and groaned.

Isobel felt her eyes bulge in their sockets. Did he know the early hour at which she had arrived home? She was sure he had been asleep and she had been very quiet. "On my honor, Father, I—I do not know what Lord Blackburn's intentions are."

He opened his eyes, yanked the wet cloth away, and sat up. "He has yet to come to an agreement on the price, I am sure that is all that is left of the matter. Not that price should matter a tick. The Sinclair family likely has more gold than the Crown. Have you seen the ring on his finger? That alone must be worth half the metopes."

"The metopes?" Isobel muttered. Oh, thank the heavens, she had misunderstood, and her father was not talking about Lord Blackburn's offer for *her* but rather his intention to assist Elgin!

"The carved spacers between triglyphs on a frieze." When Isobel just peered blankly back at him, his tone grew very loud. "The marbles, Isobel. I am speaking of Elgin's Parthenon marbles! What did you think I meant?"

"Oh," she replied quickly, "the marbles certainly. It is only that I had not heard the term . . . *metope* before."

"I can understand the allure of such a collection, but Elgin must be made an example! One cannot use his position in government to obtain permission to loot antiquities for personal gain. If the cost of this lesson is the loss of the marbles, then so be it."

"No, Father. The marbles are said to be a gift of art to the world. You must not let them waste away to prove a point of honor. Elgin claims he cannot pay for proper storage and preservation. You heard as much at the soirée last eve. *Please*."

Her father seemed suddenly interested in what she had to say to him. He leaned forward, and Isobel had the impression that he was studying her expression as thoroughly as the words she had spoken. "So you do not believe the Sinclair family will pay Elgin's exorbitant price."

"I do not know, Father, but I believe with all my heart that if you have the influence to convince the British Museum to acquire the collection, you should. Else you and your committee will forever be held accountable for the loss of an irreplaceable world treasure."

He father sat silently for nearly the tick of a minute hand, before flicking his fingers to shoo her away. "Send Alton to me. I must send a missive to the committee at once."

Isobel backed from the room and closed the door. She only hoped that her father would do the right thing and save the marbles no matter the cost.

The next day

Isobel had hoped for some correspondence from Sterling. A bent visiting card would have sufficed, but she had not heard anything. She wondered how this could be, because her world had changed so completely since they . . . viewed the marbles.

La, even if the British Museum acquired them, she knew she could never look at one particular statue again without flushing bright scarlet.

Her father and the other trustees tapped to consider the purchase of Elgin's Parthenon marbles had met for hours last night, not adjourning until she had already retired to her bedchamber. Surely this was a favorable sign for Elgin, for had the reigning suggestion been to refuse purchase of the marbles, the meeting would have been much shorter. The marbles were miracles of man's own artistry—and she did not think so just because she'd spent the most amazing night of her life atop one.

"Isobel!" She looked up from the chair beside the window to see her father standing in the doorway, his arms folded tightly across this chest.

"Good afternoon, Father. I did not hear you come into the parlor, I was so taken with the story I was reading." Her eyes focused on the book that lay open in her lap—only to realize it was one of the books she had found among her mother's things—a love story. Her father would not approve of her taking anything of her mother's except the old dresses that still hung in the wardrobe. Her eyes widened in panic, and she hurriedly snapped the cover closed and shoved the book between her skirt and the arm of the chair. She spread her dress over it so her father would not see it. "I did not hear you come upstairs to bed last night. Your meeting with the trustees continued quite late, did it not?"

"It did." He seemed to be studying her, and what he saw did not seem to please him. "Go and put on another dress—a walking gown if you have one."

Isobel blinked in surprise. "But I am not going for a stroll, so I do not understand why I must change when this dress is perfectly suited for sitting at home."

Her father unfolded his arms and set them on his hips. "Isobel, do not argue with me. I do not understand why the gentlemen of Town are suddenly so intrigued with you, but they are."

Isobel's mind swirled with confusion, and she turned her gaze downward to see that she was wringing her hands worriedly. Had Sterling sent her father a letter or a card? Could it be he planned to offer for her? No, surely not. And yet . . .

"Are you listening to me, gel?" came her father's booming orator's voice.

She snapped her head upright. "Yes, Father." She came to her feet, allowing the book to fall like a tree into her seat.

"Mr. Burke Leake, an esteemed protégé of one of the trustees, has requested the honor of meeting you and taking you to Hyde Park for an afternoon ride in his phaeton. You will receive him graciously wearing . . . something else."

"Leake? Father, I do not know Mr. Burke Leake." Nor did she wish to. Now that she had given her heart to Sterling, she did not wish to encourage the affections or attentions of any other.

"I realize you have not been introduced, but I know him, and he seemed quite taken with you when he saw you at the Partridge ball." He pushed out his lower lip and gave a satisfied smile. "Two men vying for my wayward daughter's attention. I am quite sure it was the red gown I bade you to have fashioned." His voice became low then, almost as though he was talking to himself. "Should have thought of that years ago. Had I, someone else might have been worrying over your latest ill-thought-out antic."

A painful sadness rolled through Isobel. She and her father had been so close once. And now, after her brother and mother had died, a time when she and her father should have been closer than ever—there to support each other—he only wished that she was some other man's problem.

"Go on now, gel. You only have an hour to make yourself presentable."

"Yes, Father." Isobel bowed her head, then walked slowly across the parlor, passing her father as she moved into the hallway for the stairs.

"Wait," he said, noticing the book sitting on the chair.

Isobel stopped and turned, barely raising her head to look at him.

He walked to chair and picked up the book and started to hold it out to her when he recognized it, and drew it before him. "Never mind," he amended. "I will do it for you. You need to prepare."

Isobel nodded her head and made her way to staircase. She had taken only three treads when she heard her father sobbing. But that was not possible. He never cried. She crept back down two steps, then crouched down and peered between the rail posts.

Her father was kneeling on one knee, resting his head in one hand and holding the small book against his chest with the other. His shoulders shook, and he cupped his hand over his mouth to mute his sorrowful gasps and cries.

Isobel shot to her feet. She knew too how it felt to miss someone so much. She started down the stairs wanting to comfort him, to remind him that he was not alone. But she stopped short.

He was vulnerable now, a weakness he hated

in others, but especially in himself. If she approached him now, it would only embarrass him and increase the cool gulf that had grown between them since they lost the rest of their family.

She turned, knowing that was what he would want, and climbed the stairs to her bedchamber.

Chapter 14

Three great forces rule the world: stupidity, fear and greed.

Einstein

The Carington residence
Leicester Square

Bluebell opened Isobel's bedchamber door an hour later. "There's another one here for you, Miss Isobel." The maid peered warily over her shoulder and then scooted into the room. "Forgive me for sayin' so, but this Mr. Leake gentleman, he's fine in form and in face, but if you ask me, the Scotsman, he's your man."

As she hooked a string of pearls around her neck, Isobel met the reflection of Bluebell's gaze in her dressing table mirror. "Lord Blackburn is my man . . . for what?"

Bluebell shared a toothy grin. Even in the dim reflection of the silvered glass, Isobel could see color rise into the maid's cheeks. "Well." She paused and turned to make doubly sure that the door was completely closed. "*Everything*."

Isobel shifted her legs and turned around on the stool she sat upon and faced Bluebell. "Everything?"

The maid rolled her eyes and snorted a short chuckle. "Criminy, I have seen him, you know. All the belowstairs women are talking about it. Some have even seen him in a kilt—and prayed to the heavens for a good gust of wind."

"You still haven't told me what you mean by *everything*." Isobel was toying with the long-nosed maid now, but she was not eager to meet this Mr. Leake, and so she fussed over her appearance for a few moments more.

"*In bed*, that's something." Bluebell crept closer. "Those Sinclair men are huge . . . and so are their feet. And you know what they say about men with big feet."

Isobel widened her eyes at Bluebell.

"Big hands too."

"Is that what they say?" Isobel sucked her lips into her mouth to avoid bursting into giggles.

"Well, it is something like that anyway." Bluebell held up her forefinger. "So, there you have one thing: better in between the bedsheets." She lifted another finger. "He is going to be a bleeding duke. Mr. Leake, well, he's just a mister, isn't he?" She raised a third finger. "Have you seen the gleaming stone on His Lordship's finger?"

"Is Mr. Leake wearing a ring?" Isobel asked, trying very hard to appear most serious.

"Only gloves, but, remember, the Scotsman has big hands. Bigger hands, bigger ring, which would cost more so . . . that means he must have money if you think about it." She smiled, seeming pleased with herself. "That adds one more. Big ring. Money." She raised two more fingers. "That's five."

Isobel shook her head. "Only four. You counted the big ring twice."

Bluebell looked confused for a moment, then raised her hand with all fingers straightened again. "Better in bed."

"You already said that. Better in bed was the first thing you mentioned."

Bluebell shook her head in frustration. "That's because it's the most important thing. Miss Isobel, you are so innocent. Don't you know that if you got a man who can make you happy in bed, whether or not he's got a title or money don't matter a lick. If you ask me, if a man makes you happy, you don't need nothing else."

"Thank you for your advice, Bluebell." Isobel sat very still and thought about what Bluebell had said. Her thinking and logic might have been a little convoluted, but her conclusion was sound. If a man makes you happy, what else do you need?

Bluebell bounced a shaky curtsy, then spun around and started for the door. "Oh, don't forget, the *other one* is waiting for you in the parlor, Miss Isobel."

Isobel and Mr. Burke Leake walked out the front door and down the steps to the pavers where the Carington manservant, Alton, stood grimacing. From the put-upon expression on his face, it was plain that he felt that the top-ranking member of the house's meager staff should not have been required to stand in the square holding Leake's matched pair like a common stable boy.

Mr. Leake handed Isobel up to climb into the high perch, then walked around to the other side to board himself. Isobel looked back at the house and saw her father standing in the doorway with a satisfied slip of a smile dressing his lips. Movement above drew her eye to the second floor, where Bluebell stood with Mrs. Bowls, the house cook.

Isobel shielded her eyes from the sun by raising her hand to her brow so that she might better see into the shadow shading the front of the house. She had just focused again on the maid and cook when Mr. Leake cracked his whip and the phaeton lurched forward. Isobel turned around in the seat as they sped away, and would never be quite sure if the servants were all scowling at her and Mr. Leake, or if the shadows were merely playing tricks on her eyes.

"Do tell me if we are whisking along too quickly, won't you, Miss Carington?" Mr. Leake said, a little too proudly to sound sincere. "This particular make of phaeton is said to be one of the fastest in existence."

Isobel flashed a bright smile at him. "Do not worry over me, Mr. Leake. I find the speed exhilarating." *And the sooner we arrive in Hyde Park, the sooner we will return.* It was still possible, after all, that Sterling would call.

"Do you?" Mr. Leake seemed pleased, and he snapped the ribbons, urging the horses into a fast trot.

Isobel's father had been right; she did know Mr. Burke Leake, though they had not been introduced until this afternoon. He had been the handsome auburn-haired gentleman who had raced Sterling through the Partridge ballroom to ask her to dance. He had lost then, and if he truly sought her affections, he had lost again.

Sterling was the victor of her heart.

When they arrived at Hyde Park, Mr. Leake took them immediately to the stables, where a boy took the horses in hand so that their owner and Isobel might partake of a stroll around the Serpentine.

"Miss Carington, since I first saw you at Partridge House, my greatest desire has been to express my interest in courting you." He offered her his arm, and since she could not think of a polite way to refuse his offer, she took it and allowed herself to be escorted down the pathway along the sparkling water.

"Honestly," Isobel said, not wanting to encourage Mr. Leake when she did not share his feelings, "I am surprised that you did call, given that half of London believes Lord Blackburn and I are to be married before the end of the Season."

He laughed. "But the other half believes the two of you will not, and I count myself amongst their strong number."

Isobel smiled and gazed up at him as they walked. His eyes were as blue as the sky this day and his smile just as bright as sun. "What interests you, Mr. Leake? Politics? Art? Travel?"

He glanced down at his feet as they walked, almost bashfully. "Everything you mentioned, distilled into one." Mr. Leake looked up at her, almost, it appeared to Isobel, to be sure she was still listening. "Topographical and antiquarian studies." He waited for her to comment, and now she understood why he monitored her attentiveness. His two elevated interests were not subjects of usual parlor conversation.

"My father told me that you were intimately connected with Elgin's marbles. Was it your knowledge of antiquities that involved you?"

He nodded. "I see you have been well informed. I spent several years in Constantinople for our government, instructing the Turks in marine artillery, and I traveled with them to Egypt to expel the French. During that time I surveyed the valley of the Nile, and grew fascinated with topography. The ship I sailed with was later engaged to transport Elgin's marbles from Athens to England. It foundered off Greece, however, and all my maps were lost, but my interest in antiquities and topography was not."

Isobel studied him. "I wonder," she began, "what a man with such experience in the region and knowledge of antiquities believes should be the fate of Elgin's marbles."

"You do not truly care, certainly," he said.

"In truth, I do," Isobel protested. "My father is one of the trustees deciding whether Parliament purchases the marbles." She could tell that Mr. Leake felt hesitant in providing a reply. "I vow I will not discuss what you say with him. I am only interested in your learned opinion."

He peered into her eyes, and she knew he wondered if he could trust her. A moment later, he proved to her that he did. "I am a member of the Society of Dilettanti, a society of noblemen and gentlemen dedicated to the study of ancient Greek and Roman art. I am the protégé of Sir Richard Payne Knight, who has claimed that the marbles are not Greek at all. Like your father, he is also one of the trustees who will decide the marbles' fate."

Isobel sighed. "So you do not believe Parliament should purchase them."

"On the contrary, I know they are treasures and must be protected."

A smile spread across Isobel's lips, her happiness with his reply so obvious that she covered her mouth.

"Am I to understand that this pleases you, Miss Carington?" He laughed then, and she lowered her hand and did the same.

"Yes, it does please me. You see, I saw the marbles recently, and now feel somehow intimately connected." The image of Sterling making love to her atop one of the statues made her blush fiercely. "I know . . . my passion for them is not easily understood, not even by me."

He turned her to him and took her hands in his. "That is where you are wrong, Miss Carington. I understand your passion for antiquities quite intimately myself." A sweep of heated color flooded his cheeks, and the awkwardness of the moment became evident to both of them.

"Shall we return to the phaeton? I daresay, the warmth of the day is surprising, and a fast ride through the streets of London would be most refreshing, would it not?"

He nodded enthusiastically and led her back to stables. But when they arrived, the stable boy was nearly in tears. "I apologize, sir, but I left your horses to fetch some water, and when I returned, their tack was on the ground and they were gone!"

Mr. Leake was thoroughly flustered. "I am sorry, Miss Carington, but I must look for them. So I will summon a hackney for you, if you do not mind."

Isobel was just opening her mouth to agree when she heard her name on the breeze. "Good day, Miss Carington," said Mrs. Smithly, who waved to her from a nearby carriage. Lady Marigold leaned toward the door from the opposite seat and fluttered her gloved fingers out the open window. "Good afternoon, dear."

Isobel lifted her hand and acknowledged them. She was just turning back to Mr. Leake to suggest she request a ride back to Leicester Square with the matrons, when he took off running toward their carriage. He spoke with them through the open window and then beckoned for Isobel to come.

"They said to tell you to marry the Scot," said the stable boy.

"What?" Isobel spun around to look at the lad. "Who bade you to tell me that?" She furrowed her brow at him.

"Those ladies," he replied confidently, no longer seeming so upset by his failure to tend to Mr. Leake's horses properly. "The ladies who paid me a pounder to let the team loose."

Isobel gasped. The damnable wager.

With a parting scowl at the stable boy, she hurried toward the coconspirators' carriage.

The next evening
Wormesley House
Park Lane

The annual musicale sponsored by the self-appointed arbiters of taste was an event no one who was honored with an invitation would dare miss.

And, owing to the widespread interest in the wager concerning the question of the marriage of

Lord Blackburn and a miss of common birth, but uncommon beauty, the Sinclair family was gifted with just such an honor.

The Sinclair family stood near the window talking among themselves, for, though every devout patron of the arts studied them, no one dared speak to them until Sir Richard Payne Knight had given his approval of the Scots.

Payne Knight rounded the Sinclairs in ever-tightening circles. He was a self-tutored scholar and connoisseur, admired for his theories of picturesque beauty as well as ancient art, especially phallic imagery.

"If he passes me by once more," Priscilla sniped, "I shall walk straight up to him and tell him his musicale is . . . uninspiring."

"He is studying us. Give him a little more time, Priscilla," Ivy whispered. "I have no doubt that such a self-important Englishman is somewhat intimidated by the sight of *real* men."

Sterling chuckled at that, and for some reason it was this break with formality that drew Payne Knight to them.

"I am so pleased that you and your family condescended to attend our musicale, Lord Blackburn." He did not glance sidelong at any of the other Sinclairs.

"There was no condescension involved," Sterling countered. "My family and I were honored to receive an invitation to join you and the Society of Dilettanti this night."

Priscilla could not restrain herself any longer. She moved beside Sterling and dropped a deep curtsy to Payne Knight. "We are all greatly honored by your attentions." She smiled tightly at him. "I wonder, how do you find us?"

From the corner of his eye, Sterling saw Siusan swish open her fan to conceal a grin or look of astonishment, which, he could not tell.

Sir Richard Payne Knight seemed to find Priscilla's comment amusing. "Why, my dear, I find *you* rather forward, but every beautiful rose bears a thorn or two." He walked past them all, then turned and returned to stand before Sterling. "I find you all quite aesthetically pleasing to the eye." He turned his attention back to Sterling. "Even you, Lord Blackburn. Your face is amazingly symmetrical for a fighter whose jaw receives such punishing blows." He paused for a moment and puffed a silent laugh. "You truly are a contradiction, my lord. You enjoy gambling and sport more than most, but then you are also a true devotee of beautiful things as well, aren't you?"

"No more than any other man." Sterling smiled

flatly. The only reason he endured this bore was a whisper that Isobel would also attend the annual musicale.

"Ah, but not every man has developed such a keen interest in Elgin's Parthenon marbles." Payne Knight pursed his lips and waited expectantly for Sterling to respond.

Sterling raised his eyebrows and said nothing.

"Oh, do not be alarmed, my lord. I hear of everything . . . of importance to art, that is."

"I do have interest in the marbles—in *preserving* them."

"Really?" He folded his arms over his chest, then lifted his right index finger to his nearly nonexistent chin. "I have heard that they are not from Athens at all, but rather crude Roman sculptures." Payne Knight pinned Sterling with his watery eyes. "I wonder if you have heard the same."

"I have heard such a rumor, but also that it sprang from your lips, sir." Sterling shook his head. "And surely it was said in jest, because as a connoisseur and scholar of antiquities, one glimpse of the marbles surely convinced you of their authenticity."

Payne Knight paused for a moment before laughing. "I do enjoy your company, Lord Blackburn. You are most diverting."

"As are you, dear sir." Suddenly Sterling saw

Isobel enter the drawing room with her father—and, damn it all, the gentleman who had once raced him across a ballroom to dance with her as well.

Payne Knight's lips curled, and he gestured for the party to join him and the Sinclair family. Greetings were exchanged, until one was left. "Lord Blackburn, are you acquainted with my protégé, Mr. Burke Leake?"

"I have not formally had the pleasure," Sterling said, trying very hard not to look directly at Isobel or search her eyes for any indication of worry. He had not heard a word, or received a message from her . . . and he was sure he would have by now.

Leake bowed his head. "I wonder, do you recall that we were competitors once for a dance with this beautiful and noble lady?" He looked at Isobel, who appeared suddenly stunned. Leake took a step closer to her. "Perhaps we are competitors still, eh?"

Sterling stared mutely at the auburn-haired gentleman before smiling broadly back at him. "Ah, you are partaking in the wager." He looked hard into Leake's eyes, but his smile remained on his lips. "Alas, I don't know the outcome of the bet either." He softened his gaze and let it fall gently upon Isobel, who blushed becomingly, much to the visible consternation of her father.

"So good to know you all," Payne Knight said. He gestured at the musicians who were taking their places upon a small dais. "The musicale is about to commence. Please, won't you all be seated?"

Sterling made to offer his arm to Isobel, but her father stepped between them. He immediately palmed Isobel's shoulder and guided her and Mr. Leake to a trio of chairs on the opposite side of the aisle from where the Sinclair brothers and sisters were just beginning to take their places.

Sterling turned in his too small chair toward Isobel, but her father's hardened gaze intervened and she did not so much as raise her eyes.

He leaned to Siusan, who sat at his right. "I need your assistance."

"What? Now? The musicale is about to commence."

He shook his head slightly and crooked his index finger at her.

She leaned close and flipped open her painted fan and traced the line of a pagoda, prompting Sterling to study the intricate design while he whispered to her. "Something is wrong. I need to speak with Miss Carington. Would you ask her to meet *you* tomorrow noon for tea at the Garden of Eden?"

"What is the matter? I thought you were so sure just yesterday," Su whispered softly.

"I wish I knew, but I don't. Her eyes are worried though. Something has happened. Her father will not even let me near her." Sterling sighed and lowered his eyes to the program distributed by the arbiters of taste, the Society of Self-Puffery. "Will you do it?"

Su touched his arm. "Aye, of course I will. Assuming you still have a few shillings tucked away somewhere for me." She grinned.

He nodded absently at Isobel.

Su turned and glanced at Miss Carington, who stared straight ahead, waiting for the musicians to begin, while Mr. Leake prattled on, gesturing to the ancient vases on either side of the mantel.

Ivy leaned toward him from the other side. "Don't worry so, Sterling. I will assist you as well, by seeing what I can do about distracting our Mr. Leake on the morrow."

Sterling lowered his head, absently crumpled the program in his fist, and waited impatiently for the hellish musicale to end.

As the musicale and the conversation that followed were mercifully drawing to a close, Isobel excused herself from her father and Payne Knight to return to her chair to collect the wrap and reticule she'd left upon its seat. Whisking the silk wrap around her shoulders, Isobel then bent and snatched up the reticule from the chair. She had started to walk back to her father when she felt something heavy in the bottom of the bag. First shaking it once, to be sure of what she felt, she loosened the cord that cinched the silk reticule, then opened it to peer inside.

"What on earth?" A small white calling card and several guineas gleamed softly in the dull light illuminating the purse's interior through the delicate silk. Thrusting her forefinger and thumb inside, she withdrew the card. It was blank except for three hand-inked words: *For the orphans*. The writing was familiar to her, for the note accompanying the donations left on her doorstep recently had been inked by the very same hand. She was sure of it, for she had studied the writing endlessly, hoping it might yield some clue as to the identity of the most generous and thoughtful gentleman.

"Who put this—" She jerked her head up and scanned the room for anyone who might have left the gift. The musicale's attendees still milled around the room, clustered here and there in conversation. She spun around, her eyes shifting wildly as she sought to pick out just who might be the anonymous donor. Just then, from the corner of her eye, she caught a glimpse of a gentleman darting into the darkness through a narrower door, leading not to the passageway and the front door beyond where some guests were going, but, she guessed, into the depths of the house.

Isobel reached out a hand. "Wait," she said softly, knowing already that since the gentleman evidently wished to remain unknown to her, her plea to stop would go unbidden. No sooner had the word left her lips than he disappeared and the door had closed again, so quickly that it left her to wonder if she had even seen anyone at all.

Leake. It might have been he who left the coins. While waiting for the musicale to begin, he had seemed extraordinarily interested when she told him about her charity work, even though he likely had heard of it before. After all, she had been London's parlors' topic of interest since she charged into the Pugilistic Club. She must thank him and tell him how much she appreciated his support of the widows and orphans when so many would waste their coin elsewhere on games of chance.

Isobel turned around and looked for him, but he was nowhere to be seen. This convinced her further that she was correct in her assumption that Leake was her man.

She hastened after him, but her slippers had barely moved two steps before she stopped.

Certainly Sterling would be watching her, as might her father. It wouldn't do for any guest—but

especially not her, the focus of the *ton*'s scrutiny—
to be seen rushing off into the darkness of rooms
obviously not meant to be entered.

More importantly, she desperately wanted to
speak with Sterling before she and her father quit
the musicale, if only for a moment, to be sure he
knew it was her father's invitation, not hers, for
Mr. Leake to join them. And if she had the courage, she wanted to assure Sterling that her fondness for him remained ever steady and strong.

She frantically glanced around the room for
Sterling, but he was nowhere to be seen either.

Never mind, she told herself. *I will return in but a
moment or two.*

Damn it all. He'd walked straight into a library
that was little more than a box broken only by a
single door and a rather small window. There was
no other exit.

He knew his time was short. He hadn't expected Isobel to turn to retrieve her reticule a scant
second after he dropped the coins inside. Instead
of leaving the musicale at that moment, as he'd
hoped, he instead was forced down the row of the
diminutive chairs where the only escape from her
notice was to duck through the narrow door at
the end of the aisle.

Unfortunately, she'd probably seen the door

close behind him, and was already fast on his trail. The only way to avoid her was to heave the window open and dive through it. *Bluidy hell.*

ˋ Sterling hurried to the window and had just started to lift the sash an inch or two when he heard the gentle squeal of hinges as the door opened behind him. He froze where he stood, his face directed at the window. Though he could see that the night's moon was but a sliver of light in a cloudy black sky, Isobel would see him and know the small offerings that had been left for her, all he could manage just now, were from him.

His feet were used to turning about quickly to avoid a combatant's coming blow, but this time he doubted his speed was enough to rescue him. Sterling backed against the bookcase and edged silently toward the corner, where the room was darkest.

"I know you are in here . . . and what you have done," Isobel said, but her voice was thin, as though she was not entirely sure of her words.

Sterling could not see her in the blackness of the library, and knew he would not until she crossed before the muted moonlight breaking through the window. She did not speak further, and her nervous breathing became his only clue.

Silence was his only protection now. He felt like a fool, hiding in the darkness. It eluded him why he so desperately needed to shield his charity from her. He only knew that, for some reason, his meager donations were almost an embarrassment.

In his heart, he wanted to do so much more for her, for what she believed in so passionately, but now, when he wished it most, he did not have it to give. His greed had won out, as it always did, and what coin he owned was held in escrow on a wager that belittled and cheapened Isobel and what he felt for her. He pressed hard into the corner into which he had backed himself.

Isobel's heart pounded against her ribs. He was here, if not Leake, *someone*, a stranger whose heart was larger than his need to be recognized for the good he was doing.

She could smell the polish of the leather book bindings, see the faintest impressions of ceiling-high shelves, but she could not see *him*. The one who believed in her work. Believed in her ability to help others with what coin he could spare. Believed in her.

Walking to the nearest bookcase she could see, Isobel ran her hands along it, hoping that if she only continued around the four corners of the library, she might come upon the man, the good, generous man, she was compelled to thank for believing in her when so many others did not.

Her fingers slid over the humps of book spines, her lead hand feeling the air before her. "*Please*, I know you are here. Answer me. I only wish to thank you for what you are doing for those who would otherwise do without."

A cool stream of air touched the back of her neck and made her shiver. She turned her attention to the soft light slipping through the gap between the window sash and sill, and her spirits plummeted.

"No, please, *no*." Isobel bisected the library to reach the source. Her hands slid down the window until she felt the air pressing into the room from outside. She peered out onto the lawn just outside the window. Very likely he had escaped through the low window and was in the process of reaching up to close it when she entered the library. Her hopes of learning the true identity of the generous stranger were dashed. Her delay in following him had cost her.

Isobel rested her palms on the window sash and sighed forlornly. Pressing her forehead against the cool windowpane, she closed her eyes. "If only you knew what your support meant to me." She exhaled a long breath. "If only you knew."

Unexpectedly, she heard the door latch jiggle, startling her. She tensed, not moving from the glass, and waited for some moments for it to open, but it didn't. She exhaled in relief at not being discovered alone in the library where she clearly did not belong. She blinked and waited for her eyes to adjust to dim moonlight icing the lawn, then peered hard through the window, looking for the stranger.

The heat of large hands was suddenly gripping her shoulders, the warmth of a body pressed close against hers from behind.

"Shhh" came a hot breath against her ear.

"*Sterling.*" She did not need to hear another word. His firm touch was enough to assure her it was he. When she heard the door handle, it was Sterling entering the room. Not some guest or servant testing the door, Sterling. "I was looking for you," she whispered.

"I know, lass." His simple words, his voice alone, made her nipples tighten.

His hands skated over her arms, skimming seductively along the sides of her breasts, then wrapping around her waist and pulling her harder against him.

Her body shivered with excitement as she felt his cock pressing stone-hard against her bottom, but another part of her throbbed madly. She spun around, maintaining contact between their bodies, until his hardness prodded her where she most wanted to feel it.

He started to pull back from her then, knowing as she did, but evidently caring more, that though their bodies craved the succor of the other, this was not the time and definitely not the place to quench their bodily thirsts.

But Isobel's need for him ranked above her worry of discovery, and she wriggled her fingers beneath his breeches, wrapping them around his stiff shaft. Never removing his mouth from hers, he gasped at the surprise of her touch, drawing what little air hovered inside her mouth into his own.

She slid her fingers down to the base of his penis, beckoning his tightening orbs below with a stroke of two fingers, maddening him, hardening him further.

Sterling grabbed a fistful of her silk skirt and drew it up along her thigh, fumbling through layers of fabric until his fingers met the moist heat between her slick folds. He slid his forefinger over her engorged core, circling it until she writhed against him with the want of him inside her.

She twisted until his touch found her entrance, then she pushed down, driving his finger into her depths and making her pulse with pleasure. It wasn't what she wanted, though, not really, and from the way his cock throbbed in her palm, she knew he needed more as well.

"Isobel." His mouth moved against her lips in

a raspy whisper. "Not now." She circled the head of his maleness with her thumb, and felt a droplet of heat emerge. His breath hitched. "Christ, love, I want you more than I know words to express it. But now is not the time. I want you for my own, and though my body craves you, my heart longs for you, sating my need for you this night risks too much."

His finger slid from within her, drawing her dew to the bud of her desire and stroking her there for a moment more.

Isobel whimpered. She thrust her tongue deep inside his mouth in protest, but she knew too that Sterling was right, though she wished he was not.

"Siusan will send a card upon the morrow. Do as she asks, please. For me." Sterling nipped at her full lower lip, then let her silk gown slide back down her leg.

She withdrew her hand from his shaft, but chased his mouth with hers one last time. "I will. I promise."

Chapter 15

*Most men pursue pleasure with such breathless haste
that they hurry past it.*

Kierkegaard

*The next day
The Garden of Eden
Marylebone*

The footman had barely raised his hand to direct Isobel to the table where the two Sinclair ladies waited for her, when she pushed past him and raced to the third chair. "Is everything well? I admit, I am greatly surprised by this invitation to take tea at the garden with you."

"Everything is wonderful," Ivy said louder than

she ought. Clearly she was saying it for the ears of those around them. Then she lowered her voice to a mere whisper. "Are you hungry, dear?" Ivy asked, lifting the reddish slash of her eyebrow.

Isobel nodded. "A bit." She looked down at the plates of biscuits, cakes, and cream, and her stomach growled.

"Good. I have had the Garden cooks prepare a basket to take." Siusan signaled for the waiter and disappeared behind a painted silk screen to emerge with a small hamper of woven willow.

Isobel did not know what to make of this. "Are we leaving?"

Priscilla laughed. "Nay, dear. *You* are." She inclined her head and saw that a hackney had drawn up at the entrance. In the shadow inside, she saw a large man beckoning to her. "It's Sterling. He thought perhaps something was amiss. Your father clearly did not wish for the two of you to be together last evening at the musicale."

"He was right about that." Isobel stared down at the hamper, then let her gaze flit around the crowded tea garden.

"Just go. You know you wish it. As does he." Siusan smiled at her.

"Thank you, Lady Siusan." She curtsied. Turning to the two Sinclair ladies, she blew happy kisses to their cheeks, then turned and walked as slowly as might appear to be normal to the hackney waiting for her.

Her heart hammered inside her as the driver handed her up into the carriage and into Sterling's arms. He settled her beside him on the bench, then tossed the hamper to the seat across from them.

"Beauchamp Grange," Sterling called out to the driver. The cab door closed and latched, and the carriage jolted forward, casting Isobel into Sterling's embrace.

He peered into her eyes, and then he kissed her softly. "It is a long drive to Beauchamp Grange. At least a full hour outside of Town." He kissed her harder, deeper, and she verily melted in his arms.

"Thankfully, you brought sustenance."

Isobel laughed with surprise as Sterling grasped her waist and lifted her high, her skirts billowing up as he spread her knees and sat her down, straddled upon his lap. Her breasts began to ache and her feminine furl throbbed as she became increasingly aware of his hardness straining against his breeches just beneath her core.

The carriage ran through a hole in the road, making the cab, and Isobel as well, bounce hard again and again as the front then back wheels dipped in and out of the gap.

A groaning sound rose up from deep inside Sterling's throat as Isobel clung to his lapels, moving her hips against his, riding him like a horse for balance. Moist heat rushed between her legs, and instinctively she bore down on him, needing so badly to feel him deep inside her, filling her.

"Enough of this," Sterling growled, then cupped his hand behind her head and dragged her mouth to his.

Her lips were warm, sweet, and vaguely salty as he tasted them while his hands skimmed over her walking gown. Closing her eyes, she parted her lips to his kiss, opening herself to his tongue's exploration of her soft flesh. She moaned softly, seeming almost entirely unaware that he pulled at bows, loosened her lacings, and within a few moments, her gown was left bunched around her waist and her soft breasts were bared to him.

He felt her nipples harden to the rush of cool air upon them, and so he cupped the weight of her breasts in his hands, brushing the pebbled pink buds with his thumbs, until they softened pertly from his warm touch.

Isobel wriggled against him with a whimper of frustration, and suddenly became more assertive in making her wants known. She kissed him more urgently then, teasing him, nipping at his lower lip as she unwound his neck cloth. She opened her lids more fully and stared directly into his eyes as she purposively fumbled with his waistcoat, not bothering to remove it, but instead shoving it out of her way. Opening the ties of his lawn shirt, she exposed a deep V of his chest. She released the buttons of his breeches and opened his front fall, easing his throbbing cock into her palm.

A pleased smile stole over her lips. The heat of her hand was searing, and his erection twitched as she ran her curious fingers up and down his shaft before encircling its head with her forefinger and thumb.

She closed her eyes again as she leaned up onto her knees, looped one arm around his neck, leaving her other hand pumping his penis, making him ache for her. She flicked her tongue teasingly over his upper lip as she pressed her breasts against his chest and brushed the tip of the plum-shaped head between her legs, across her heated opening. He leaned into her and kissed her neck, breathing in the scent of her, savoring it.

Christ. She was going to drive him mad. She had to slow down.

Breaking her kiss and then leaning back, Isobel licked her full lips and looked drowsily up at him. Sterling's pupils grew impossibly dark, reducing the pale blue of his eyes to a thin ring of color.

His breath came fast, driving Isobel's heart to

pound with excitement. Suddenly he jerked her arm from his neck and took her hand from his pulsing penis, pinned her hands behind her back in the grasp of one strong hand. "I need you to slow down, Isobel. You aren't playing fairly."

She smiled and nodded, somewhat ashamed of her aggressiveness, and expected that he would release her hands then . . . but he didn't.

Instead he moved his thighs against her knees, opening them wider. She felt his fingers parting the cotton of her pantalettes, and then his forefinger running between her moist plump lips. He dipped it deep inside her, wetting it before slipping his fingertips over the small bud between her folds, and rubbed in slow circles. Isobel gasped and pulled against his hold on her, but he only tightened it and pulled down a bit, tilting her breasts up to him. Her nipples hardened almost painfully and she threw her head back, nearly crying out when he took one into his hot mouth and flicked it with his slippery tongue.

His thumb rubbed her now in ever tightening circles as he plunged two fingers into her depths, pumping her harder and harder, making her head dizzy with sensation.

His mouth moved from one nipple to the other, teasing her breasts. Her thighs began to quiver uncontrollably. "Sterling, oh God." His fingers slid from inside her then, and she felt the thick head of his member parting her lips, warming its tip in her essence. Sterling started moving his thumb against her again, making her hips writhe.

Tension wound tight inside her core. She couldn't endure any more of this sweet torture. She couldn't, she just couldn't!

Sterling freed her hands suddenly, and at once caught her hips and pulled her down hard on top of him. His cock burned inside her, and her muscles closed around it, as his hands slid down and lifted her buttocks, and he slammed into Isobel again and again.

Her mind was spinning, and so she grasped his broad, solid shoulders to balance herself as she began to ride him. She was aflame with sensation, matching his thrusts stroke for stroke. They made love fiercely, feverishly as the carriage bumped through the countryside.

He plunged deeper yet inside her, then lifted her. She felt the bench cushion against her back, and Sterling pounding inside her, kissing her, running his hands over her breasts.

He slipped a hand beneath her, into the small of her back, and pressed upward. Heated bliss slammed through her in time with his thrusts. Spasms so violent that she felt her muscles clench down on him.

Throwing his head back, Sterling stiffened at the moment of her climax, and a sheen of sweat dampened his lawn shirt.

Isobel could feel the pounding of Sterling's heart against her ribs. He leaned up and looked lovingly into her eyes—she thought he might say something, but he didn't—instead he kissed her lips softly.

She smiled and wrapped her arms tighter around him. No, he hadn't said it, but she knew. *He loved her.*

It was a warm day, the first in a full week. Isobel sat on a large stone beside Sterling. She'd peeled her stockings from her legs and was swirling her toes in the cool water of the pond.

Her head rolled around, and she rested her chin on her shoulder as she peered up at him and watched him rolling a pale green reed between his lips. She smiled thoughtfully. "It is so peaceful here. So beautiful. Someday I should like to live in a place like this. No worries about gossip, and appearances. No fears of *on dit* columnists crawling through the hedgerows." She laughed then. "Sterling, what is it like where you come from?"

Sterling cupped her shoulders and moved her so that she rested her back against his chest. "A bit like this. Restful, when there is not work to be done to keep the ancient estate from falling down about our ears."

"Sounds like a bit of heaven."

"Except the work part." When Isobel turned her gaze up to him, he kissed her cheek. "Once we were of age, my brothers and sisters resided in the family house in Edinburgh. We were young and wild, and our ancestral home provided no little opportunity for mischief. We thought it quite boring actually."

Isobel turned in his arms until she almost faced him. "I need to ask you about a story I heard . . . about your family—that you were called the Seven Deadly Sins. You do not need to talk of it if you do not wish it. I shouldn't wish to pry. I only want to know you better. We are complete strangers to each other's pasts."

Sterling flinched at that, but nodded. "It's true enough." He looked out over the water, pausing briefly for a long breath before beginning. "Once our mother died birthing the twins, our father decided that whisky was the best way to deal with his grief."

Isobel ran her hand down his arm to comfort him.

"For years, he gave us leave to do whatever took our fancy. It didn't matter what it was. He did not guide or discipline us. After a time, we wanted his attention so badly that our exploits grew worse, far more extreme . . . some say almost legendary in their wickedness."

Isobel shook her head. "I cannot believe that."

"Och, it's true. I wish I could tell you differently, but I cannot." He bent and reached down beside the boulder to retrieve a flat stone, then drew back his arm and skipped it across the water. "Before long, our neighbors quietly referred to us as the Seven Deadly Sins." His eyes remained on the water, unwavering. "My sisters cried when they heard what we were being called, and my brothers lashed out. Got into fights. Soon the neighbors didn't bother to whisper their taunts anymore."

"That's beastly. You were only children."

"Aye, but we were unruly as they come. We defied any rules, for no reason at all, disobeyed any authority . . . but the names still stung and the tears still came." He looked at her then. "Are you certain you wish to hear more?"

"I do. I want to understand."

Sterling nodded, then sought the visual calm of lapping water again. "Being the eldest, I devised a game to protect us from the pain of others. We each chose one of the seven deadly sins and made it our own whenever we were in public. We became proud of our wickedness and our ability to distress others."

Isobel did not understand this. He could not be talking of himself and his brothers and sisters. "But you are not like that . . . not now—any of you."

"Well, my father may disagree with you on that." He pulled her closer to him. "You see, after a few years, our sins stopped being a game. They became as much a part of us as the color of our eyes or the hair upon our heads. That is, until my father finally put down his bottle and realized the true damage his absence from our lives had caused."

"And this is why he sent you here, to London?" Isobel asked. She ran her fingers through his hair soothingly, coaxing him to continue.

"Aye. He is a rich and powerful man. One day, he had carriages brought to the door and in that instant, cast us out of Scotland. He had his agent acquire a house on Grosvenor Square for us all to share. He gave us a few bob and told us we were not to return until we each had earned back the respect demanded for the name Sinclair."

Isobel stared at him. She could not believe what he was saying.

Sterling lifted the reed from where it sat on the boulder and speared it into the pond. "So that is why we are here—to be redeemed." He looked to her and laughed somewhat nervously. "Think it can be done, lass?"

"I do not see a man who needs redeeming—I see a man who needs to be loved."

Sterling seemed to tremble as he leaned in to kiss her. He rose and then scooped her up, and together they tumbled onto the soft, verdant lawn. "Och, I knew there had to be something wrong with you. You were just too perfect for me. So beautiful, so passionate—but clearly no taste." He kissed her again, then leaned back until their noses were nearly touching. "But don't forget, lassie, my sin is greed, and I'll not let another have you. Ever."

"And, pray, my lord, how will you prevent that?" She shifted her weight and rolled atop him and smiled as she held his cheeks between her palms. "You must have a plan."

He chased her lips and kissed her. "Why, I'm going to marry you, of course."

As the hired carriage crossed Blackfriars Bridge for London, Isobel peered out the window at the gray water of the Thames and sighed with dismay. It had been another world, Beauchamp Grange, and she had experienced a day that, no matter what happened now that she and Sterling had returned to reality, would live on in her dreams both day and night.

She could scarce believe that Sterling had claimed to have a plan to marry her. Though she did not know whether he merely misspoke in the passion of the moment, or he truly meant what he said. Either way, for now, she chose to believe him.

They had crossed the bridge only a few short minutes ago, when something about her alerted Sterling of her discomposure.

He reached for her hand and squeezed. She turned from the window, creating the best smile she could, but she saw that he had already seen the sadness in her eyes.

"Lass, this is not the end. Don't look so forlorn. There will be many days like this in our future. I promise you." He angled his head to kiss her, when the carriage stopped suddenly.

Lurching back from her, Sterling opened the door of the cab and called out to the driver. "This isna our direction. Leicester Square, please."

The hackney driver dropped down off his perch, sending the carriage bouncing. He hurried to the door and opened it wide, his horselike teeth bared in an excited grin. "Thought you might want to stop here first, my lord." He winked broadly.

"Why, pray, would I wish to stop here—oh, God help us." Sterling leaned forward and peered out the open door. He clapped a hand over his eyes momentarily, then turned to Isobel and shook his head, with an amused yet slightly horrified expression on his face.

"Doctors' Commons." The hackney driver beckoned them out the cab.

Isobel flinched. "No. Oh no. We cannot step out here."

"Come on, my lord. Just pop on inside, quick like, and pick up a special license for you and Miss Carington, then you can marry anytime, anywhere."

Sterling laughed. "I appreciate your thoughts, sirrah, but we will continue on to Leicester Square, if you don't mind terribly." He glanced over his shoulder at Isobel. She covered her mouth to stifle a chuckle at the absurd helpfulness of the driver.

The hackney driver furrowed his thick brows. "This ain't a request, my lord."

Sterling glared at him. "I beg your pardon." He leaned forward to block the opening to the door, then reached a hand out behind him and pressed Isobel against the backrest. "Leicester Square, please."

"No, sir, I can't take you anywhere." He shook his head. "My wife'd have me hide if I let your lovely day end now."

"Y-your wife?" Isobel scooted around Sterling and peered out at the driver.

"Yes, miss. She is all caught up in the wager. Begs me to bring her the newspaper whenever I find one so she can read all the goings-on with the 'romance of the Season.' That's what she and the other hens at the market call it . . . I mean, what they call your relationship."

"You don't have to tell her you conveyed us anywhere," Sterling said, getting noticeably annoyed.

"I won't have to say a word." He stepped back and waved his hand to the crowd gathering behind him. "It will be all over London by nightfall." Hordes of people collected outside the hackney. A young girl squeezed between the driver and Sterling and passed a violet posy to Isobel.

"So I will have to ask you to step out here. This hackney ain't going anywhere else." He grinned. "Got a broken spoke, I reckon."

Sterling turned and looked to Isobel, appearing utterly astonished. "It seems we have no choice. Either we get out now, or the whole of London will be standing outside the cab within minutes." He raised a hand to Isobel. "Stay close to me."

Sterling stepped down from the hackney, then assisted Isobel down the steps to the pavers. Sterling reluctantly flipped the driver a few coins. They turned to depart, when the crowd divided, leaving only one path from the carriage to Doctor's Commons.

Sterling led Isobel forward, and the throng closed the space behind them as they walked.

"What are we going to do?" Isobel asked, huddling closer to Sterling.

"I have an idea. Stay with me." Sterling stopped walking. "Honestly, I have no coins left in my pocket. I cannot buy a special license today, so you might as well go about your afternoon."

Isobel opened her reticule, assisting Sterling with his ploy as best she could. Suddenly it was snatched from her hand. She lurched to grab it from the woman who had taken it, but it was gone from her sight in an instant. "Sterling!"

Then she heard it. The clinking of coins.

"Here, three shillings!"

"Six bob!"

"A sovereign, from me and my gel!"

Within a minute, the reticule was back in Isobel's hand, only now it was filled with coins.

"Oh, Sterling . . . what now?"

He shrugged and thrust his free hand toward Doctors' Commons. "Well, I suppose I ought to go inside for a special license, eh?" He took the reticule from her hand and held it in the air. The crowd roared, and applause filled the air around them.

Isobel clapped a hand over her lips as Sterling hurried her forward.

Gorblimey. He truly meant to marry her!

* * *

It was amazing what a modicum of notoriety and the backing of a hundred Londoners could do to aid in the acquisition of a special license to marry. Within an hour, Sterling and Isobel were at the pavers again, heading for the hackney stand to find a way to get Miss Carington home.

Isobel was giddy and skipped alongside Sterling, washed away in the romance of the day. Sterling was not. Legally his path was clear to marry Miss Carington, but there was still an impediment to a speedy union. Her father.

The hackney driver was still waiting at the edge of the pavers. "Now, see, it was a fine idea to stop here before Leicester Square, now wasn't it?" He walked to the rear left wheel and shook it. "And look here. Spokes are good as new—like there was never nothing wrong at all." He opened the door to the hackney. "Leicester Square, my lord?" He stood straight and tall, like a guard before St. James's Palace.

Sterling rose up on the toes of his boots and peered down the road. No other hackneys were in sight. He looked at Isobel, her face bright with hope. "My lady, your . . . ahem, carriage awaits."

She took his proffered arm and went inside. When the door closed and the wheels rolled over the cobbles, she knew it was time she must warn Sterling. "I do not know whether my father will agree to our marriage. There was a time, only days ago, when I was hard set against marrying anyone, and he had only you in his mind."

"But my discussion with Lord Elgin changed all of that."

"I honestly don't know." Her eyes grew watery. "He did not wish me anywhere near you last night at the musicale and had a notion that a Mr. Burke Leake, the staid yet well-connected member of the Society of Dilettanti, might be a politically more advantageous match for his wayward daughter."

Sterling reached out and took her into his arms. "What is it that you want, Isobel?"

She turned her head up to him. "I want to spend every day like today."

"Och, I did like the bit about crowds filling your bag with money." He grinned, then kissed the top of her head.

She gave him a playful push. "You know what I mean. Together. Happy. In love."

Sterling didn't say a word, but turned his head to peer out the window. Something seemed to concern him greatly. "I want those things too," he said, in a voice as soft as the breeze blowing through the window. "And I will have them, all." He shifted on the bench. "I will call upon your father tonight at nine of the clock to make an offer for you. I don't wish to wait any longer, for the newspaper to print some audacious column about the 'romance of the Season.'"

He waggled his brows at her, as if to break the tension stretched so tightly between them.

"I will make sure he is prepared . . . and knows of my feelings for you." She glanced down and felt the color rise in her cheeks. "Do you know, I have not told you the most important thing you should know about me."

"And what is that, my sweet lass?"

She raised her head, wanting to look into his eyes as she said it. "That I love you, Sterling. I love you."

"Och, Isobel." He pulled her close against his chest, then caught her chin and turned it up to kiss her mouth. "You don't know how happy you make me."

At the moment, the carriage arrived as Leicester Square, and the hackney opened the door for Isobel. "Please, do not see me to the door, Sterling."

"Why should I not?" He lifted his hand and caressed her cheek.

"Because an agent for an *on dit* columnist, at least that is what our maid Bluebell has said, has been crouched behind the hemlock for two days." She stepped out of the cab, then leaned back to touch his lips one last time. "I will see you this night," she whispered.

"Tonight," he replied.

Then she turned and raced on the toes of her slippers to the house. Her mind was giddy as she hurried inside to tell her father that Lord Blackburn was coming to make an offer for her . . . this very night.

Indeed, this day had been a dream. A dream of the very best sort.

Once inside, she flung her mantle and fichu to their hooks, then peered inside her father's library. He wasn't there. Probably still at the House of Commons, she thought, as she dashed up the staircase to her bedchamber.

She flung open her wardrobe, then sat down on her tester bed staring at the contents, wondering what she should wear on this grand occasion of her engagement. Tipping her head sideways, she considered her blue gown, but Father claimed she wore it too often.

Something suddenly started to unsettle Isobel, but she couldn't quite identify it.

She pushed up from the bed and walked up to the wardrobe and fingered the five dresses inside.

It couldn't be fear that her father would refuse the match. While she would greatly appreciate his consent, she was not a maid in her first Season. She did not truly require his permission at all to marry Lord Blackburn.

Lifting out her red walking dress, she carried it to her bed and spread it out. It was a lovely crimson, and its necklace was flattering—at least Christiana often told her so. It was suitable for the event. Not perfect, or grand by any means, but adequate.

Rather like her.

A moment of stillness crowded around her, as her mind circled her discontent on what should be the most glorious day of her life. Until it occurred to her exactly what bothered her so deeply that she sought to bury it.

Sterling had never told her that he loved her.

Chapter 16

The tighter you squeeze, the less you have.
Thomas Merton

The Sinclair residence
Grosvenor Square

I am asking for her hand tonight." Sterling waved at his trunk. "Go on, Grant. Choose something for me to wear. I haven't a valet any longer, and my mind is not in a place that would allow me to make a decision of such magnitude." He grinned at his brother, fully aware that Grant would not comprehend the jest.

"I think it's too soon." Grant pulled out a lawn

shirt and tossed it on the bed. "Oh, do *not* let Mrs.
Wimpole press this for you. She has scorched two
of mine already, and we cannot spare what few
garments we have to an overhot iron."

"So you will press it and my neck cloth then?"
Sterling asked, concealing the smile itching at
his lips.

Grant was too consumed by his search for the
perfect mix of garments for Sterling to pay his
brother's comment any notice. He gazed admir-
ingly at a fine blue silk waistcoat he had just withdrawn from the wooden cabinet that served, not
quite adequately, as Sterling's armoire. "*Ah*, this is
the one." He flung a waistcoat on Sterling's pallet.
"I always liked the way the sterling-silver threads
in this waistcoat bring out the sheen of the blue
silk. I tell you, Sterling, this should be your signature garment."

"Hold on now." Sterling disregarded his brother's comment on the waistcoat. "What do you
mean it's *too soon*, Grant?"

"Too soon to make an offer for her—you'll punch
a hole in the bet and sink us all." He looked up
at Sterling. "We're still exposed with the second
ten thousand. Your tactic right now should be to
appear completely lovelorn; make people believe
you haven't a chance with Miss Carington though
you wish nothing more."

"And that is precisely what I did at the musicale," Sterling huffed.

"What, one night? Do you think that will suffice?" Grant gave an exaggerated sigh. "The two of you have presented yourselves to anyone watching closely, and brother, there are many, that you are already lovers and that an offer for marriage is only a matter of time."

Sterling grumbled at Grant's depiction of him and Isobel, but he knew too that he could not deny it. "To what extent are we exposed—today?"

"Three thousand pounds on the margin of the first bet."

Sterling began to stalk the small garret in ever-widening circles. Why had he ever suggested such a wager—and then extended it? "What do you suggest?"

"A bluidy disaster, mate. One that makes it look like she will never marry you. But, certainly, one you can recover from before the end of the Season."

"Nay, I cannot do that to her. Damn it. Why did I ever even conceive of this wager?" He rubbed his temples hard.

Grant settled his hand on Sterling's shoulder. "Likely because . . . you never thought you would truly love her."

Sterling looked over his shoulder. If his feelings had been so visible to everyone for so long, why hadn't anyone thought to mention it to him? Had he realized it was love that set her in his mind day and night, made him yearn to be near her, made him race across crowded ballrooms to ask her to dance—maybe this wager would not have gotten so out of control. "I promised her I would speak with her father tonight and ask for her hand." He turned his pale eyes up at Grant. "I promised her."

"And suddenly you are a man of your word?" Grant said sarcastically.

"I have always been true to my word. That's why the hells and bettors always took my mark." Sterling snatched up the simple waistcoat he'd been wearing that day and withdrew from it a folded paper. "A special license. I bought a special license today if you can believe it."

"She's got you by the heartstrings, brother."

"Aye, she does. I love her, I only wish it had not taken me so long to know it." Sterling straightened his shoulders and exhaled. "I *will* marry her."

"Well, Christ, marry her then. A license like that gives you the freedom to choose when and where." Grant rubbed his chin in contemplation, but, seeming to come up with nothing, he looked back across at Sterling. "But . . . can't you wait a few days and make the bettors wonder if some-

thing went wrong between you and Miss Carington?"

"I promised her—*tonight*."

"But we need this money, Sterling. You know
how much we need it. The bills are mounting,
and Father's allowance is far from enough to
cover them."

Sterling shook his head. "We can make up the
deficit with the winnings from our bet on my fight
at Fives Court. There is still that."

"Aye, *if* you are the victor. But brother, your
competitor has killed two men in the ring already.
There is a resolution being discussed to prevent
him from fighting any more death battles."

"Death battles? Is that what the newspapers are
calling them? Bluidy hell."

"None would fault you if you withdrew now,
Sterling."

He shook his head. "I can't. I owe someone my
portion of the money."

"Well, I can't help you either if you don't listen
to my advice, Sterling. You need a disaster and
you need to drop the fight. It truly is simple."

"It's not quite as simple as you suggest." Sterling
shoved his fingers through his hair. "Believe me."

Grant spun around to leave, but stopped and
pointed at the trunk. "The buff breeches, right
there on top. Wear those. They'll accentuate your

thigh and calf muscles . . . and something else that ladies seem to value."

Sterling walked to window, leaned his hand on the sill, and peered out into the coming night. If only waiting a few days for the wager to come to a positive fruition were that simple.

But it was all too clear to Sterling that it wasn't.

The Carington residence
Leicester Square

Isobel heard the front door open and male voices in the passage. The carriage clock on her mantle proclaimed a quarter of an hour until nine of the clock. It was too early for the caller to be Sterling.

Still, she hurriedly finished pinning up the heavy golden locks of her hair, then crept down the stairs to see who had arrived. Whoever it was, his timing could not have been worse. She decided that she would make this clear to the visitor as politely as she could, because she needed this night to be perfect . . . and her father to be alone.

The door to her father's library was closed, but that would not dissuade her from entering.

She pinched her cheeks to impart a rosy glow to her countenance, then took in a deep breath and pressed down on the latch. When she saw who was sitting before her father's desk, the breath shot from her lungs, as surely as if she'd been punched.

Isobel's father remained seated, but Sir Richard Payne Knight and Mr. Burke Leake rose and dutifully bowed to her in greeting. She bobbed a hasty curtsy, then, utterly confused, directed her attention to her father.

"Sir, we have a special visitor about to arrive and he has requested a private audience with you." She walked around and stood beside his chair. "You have not forgotten, surely."

He tilted his head and looked sternly up at her. "I am not addled, Isobel. Nothing has slipped from my mind." He gestured for the two gentlemen to be seated. "I asked Payne Knight and Leake to join us for this interview with Lord Blackburn."

Payne Knight produced a smile that made her wonder if he was sucking the lemon from the tea on the desk before him. "We have a question for Lord Blackburn, the answer to which I am sure you would also be interested to hear."

Dread rose up inside Isobel. Something was wrong. "What is this about, Father? I demand to know. You know how important this night is to me."

"I do," he agreed. "But I think this question must be asked of Lord Blackburn before you start planning your wedding trousseau."

The knocker came down upon the door, and rather than waiting for Alton to answer it, Isobel spun around, raced into the entryway, and flung the door open.

A broad smile spread across Sterling's lips until he seemed to note the anxious twist of her features. "Isobel," he whispered, "is all well?"

She took his arm and brought him inside. "I do not know. Father has Sir Richard Payne Knight and Mr. Burke Leake in his library," she said on a half breath. "They mean to quiz you about . . . something." She looked up into his eyes and squeezed his hand briefly, before leading him in to face the British inquisition.

The gentlemen rose and greeted Sterling, before her father offered him a chair.

"I would prefer to stand, if you do not mind, Minister Carington." Sterling gestured to Isobel. "Miss Carington, please take the seat."

"Oh, for heaven's sake, Lord Blackburn," her father announced. "I can have another chair brought in."

Sterling stood straight and tall. "Not necessary, Minister Carington. I have come hoping to discuss a matter with you privately." He paused, but it was clear to all that no one was leaving the room. "As you must have guessed, I am here to request permission to marry your daughter, Isobel."

Isobel's focus went to her father's eyes. Instead of meeting her gaze, her father turned and exchanged some sort of secret communication with the pompous Payne Knight.

And then she knew why Payne Knight and Leake were here on the very evening Sterling had requested an audience with her father. This was an attack.

Her father looked back at Sterling. "Lord Blackburn," he began, speaking in his orator's tone, the affected way he did in Parliament or when he wanted to impress, "before we discuss a marriage contract, there is a question we would like to ask you. Your answer will determine my own."

Sterling shifted in his boots and then laced his fingers behind his back. "Very well, then. Ask it of me."

For the first time since he entered the house, Isobel saw a sudden nervousness in Sterling's eyes. The fingers of his clasped hands seemed to war with one another behind his back.

Isobel's corset suddenly felt oppressively tight, and her breaths became short and shallow. *What could Father know that Sterling fears so greatly?*

Sterling glanced behind himself, as if belatedly looking for a spare chair in which to sit. But there wasn't one, and he was forced to stand like a sol-

dier before a firing line. "Please, Minister Carington, ask your question. I am ready."

It was not her father, but rather Payne Knight
who spoke next. He removed a finger that had
been covering his pursed lips, but he paused for
several long moments before deigning to speak.
He did not stand, but eased back into his chair.
"Lord Blackburn, you are acquainted with the
wager on the books at White's?" He raised his
finger in the air as if to prevent Sterling from interrupting him. "Please, allow me to clarify," said
the former Parliamentarian. "The wager I speak
of is the one concerning you and Miss Carington
and the question as to whether or not the two of
you will marry before the end of the Season."

"I am aware of it." Sterling peered down quizzically at Payne Knight. "You've asked your question
and I have answered it. Now, if you do not mind, I
wish to ask Minister Carington my question."

"Do you not recognize preamble when you hear
it?" Payne Knight forced a short chuckle.

Sterling stiffened, but did not reply. Appearing
thunderstruck, he looked to Isobel's father, who
simply waved on Payne Knight.

"Did you, or someone of your acquaintance on
your behalf—*anonymously*, perhaps—place that
particular wager?" Payne Knight excitedly licked

his puckered full lips in anticipation of Sterling's reply.

Sterling stood silently.

"Sterling?" Isobel rose slowly from her chair. "Sterling, dear God, please answer him. Tell him you certainly did not! He is wrong. He only wishes to discredit you because you would have assisted Lord Elgin to save the marbles if you could have. He accuses you out of spite."

But Sterling said nothing. Finally he turned his head and looked straight at Isobel. The muscles in his throat worked, and she saw him swallow uncomfortably. He bowed his head, as if in shame.

"St-Sterling?" she stammered. "*Please*. Tell my father you are wrongly accused!"

"Darling," her father finally said, "he cannot answer, because he *is* responsible for the wager— the largest wager in White's history."

Isobel moved slowly from her chair and came to stand directly before Sterling. *No, this is impossible. I do not believe it.* Hot tears filled her eyes. Why would he not say something, anything, to defend himself from this accusation?

"Do you not understand, Miss Carington?" Payne Knight asked. "He does not wish to marry you. He doesn't love you. He *used* you to win the wager." He smirked at Sterling. "What did you expect? He is a Sinclair, after all."

"Sterling?" Her voice broke. "It's not true. It cannot be. Say it is not so!" Streams of tears coursed down her cheeks and dripped from her jaw as she pleaded with him. Droplets like rain speckled the lapels of her crimson walking dress.

Sterling grasped her shoulders. His eyes welled with emotion. "I am sorry, Isobel. It is true. I am the source of the anonymous wager at White's."

Isobel gasped, and her knees buckled beneath her.

Sterling caught her and held her, crumpled in his arms as she was, staring, pleading for another word that might redeem him. "After you slapped me at Almack's, I knew no one would ever believe that you would come to . . . love me. No one would ever believe that you would wish to marry a brute like me."

Her father gestured to Mr. Leake, who leaped from his chair and removed Isobel from Sterling's arms and settled her in his own chair beside Sir Richard Payne Knight. Sterling looked wholly stunned as her father then grabbed his muscular arm and led him into the passage. "Lord Blackburn, I beg you to leave now, before you cause my daughter any further distress."

Alton, the manservant, opened the front door and assisted the master of the house in escorting Sterling outside and down to the pavers.

"But I must explain myself! Isobel, you must listen!" came Sterling's voice from the front walk. "Isobel, please!" The front door slammed closed, and she heard the metallic click of the lock moving into place.

Her father entered the library looking all too pleased with himself.

Isobel pushed up from the chair in which Leake had placed her and started from the library. Her limbs felt weighted and her heart pounded in her ears.

Her father followed her into the passageway, and when her hand reached the newel post at the bottom of the stairs, he reached a hand out to her. "Isobel, please understand. He would only bring us more embarrassment. I have my career to consider."

She pulled away from him, dislodging the last remaining tear from her lashes, dispatching it down her cheek. "Why do you hate me so much, Father?" she asked. His features suddenly went lax, but he did not say a word to dispel her notion.

Without looking back, Isobel ascended the dark stairs. Her heart was void of happiness, filled instead with an unbearable level of despair.

For the first time, Isobel understood the existence of a sadness so great that her mother might have wished to take her own life rather than live with the horrible pain of loss.

But Isobel was not her mother.

And it was not as though she had not learned to live without love. She had. A long time ago.

And she would do it again.

Chapter 17

All earthly joy begins pleasantly, but at the end it gnaws and kills.

Thomas à Kempis

The next morning
The Sinclair residence
Grosvenor Square

The door of Sterling's garret crashed open, waking him from a whisky-induced sleep. Then he heard the pound of boots stalking heavily across the room toward him. The breaking of glass, the spin of a bottle on the bare floor.

"Damn it to Hades!" came Grant's voice.

He whisked the curtains wide, and bolts of

white light seemed to cut into Sterling's brain.

"Get up, Sterling! Get up and tell me what the hell you've done." Grant tore the threadbare coverlet off Sterling's back and thrust his boot to the pallet support, knocking Sterling from the bed to the floor.

Sterling crawled up onto his hands and knees, and growled. "Get out of here, Grant, before I make you regret ever being born."

Grant slapped Sterling's chest with his palms. "Do you think you are in any shape to take me on, Sterling? Well, come on. I would welcome a good reason to knock some sense into you."

Sterling reached out for the pallet and pulled up to sit upon it. He ran his hands over his throbbing head, then rubbed an index finger and a thumb over his eyes. Opening his lids, he looked at the broken glass on the floor, and the empty bottle. "We're down to six short glasses now. Since you broke the glass, Grant, you will be the one forced to wait until the rest of us have finished our drinks before taking a nip yourself."

"And are *you* finished drinking now, Sterling?" Grant snapped. "Or are you going to be like Father and hunt down another bottle to see you through the day?"

Rage boiled up inside Sterling. He lunged toward Grant, but his brother simply stepped out of the way. Sterling stumbled, just managing to catch himself by snagging the open door of the clothing cabinet.

"Look, man, I don't know exactly what happened last evening, but the newspaper column is reporting"—Grant pulled a folded newspaper from inside his coat— "that 'Mr. Cornelius C. of Leicester Square has announced that his daughter, Miss C., will not marry, and has never truthfully considered marrying, the Scottish marquess, Lord B.'"

"That's a damned lie." He pushed himself to a wobbly stand.

Grant raised a quieting hand. "There is more. 'Furthermore, Lord B. has confided to a member of the Society of Dilettanti that an agent, acting in his stead and under his expressed order, is in truth the originating source of the popular wager concerning a late summer wedding between himself and Miss C.'"

Sterling coughed up a laugh. "Well, they got that part right, except the bit about confiding in that pompous Sir Richard Payne Knight. He just happened to be one who was given the pleasure of revealing my involvement in the wager—while Isobel was in the room."

"Well, that's it then." Grant sighed. "It's all

over now. It is only a matter of time until White's closes the betting on the marriage wager, and allows those already made to be withdrawn if the bettor requests it. Hell, the money we escrowed to secure the wager will likely have to be forfeited. And we'd have no way to pay our bills. Face the morn, Sterling. We are as good as paupers."

Sterling looked up. "I never said I would forfeit the battle at Fives Court. There is still the victor's purse if I win."

"And one less mouth to feed if you are killed during the prizefight. Aye, it's win, win, all right." Grant clapped his hands to his head and shoved his hands through his hair in utter frustration. "Are you still completely foxed, Sterling? You cannot fight that man. He's already killed two people, and you are hardly more than a lucky amateur."

"I need the money." A cool stillness draped over Sterling, and his skin began to feel a little clammy. "I am going to fight."

"Sterling, we *all* need the money, but it's not worth risking your bluidy life. We'll find another way." Grant walked over to Sterling and shook him, but Sterling crumpled to the floor, and there he sat, knees bent beneath him.

"Nay, there isn't."

"Christ, there is no talking sense into you." Grant stared down at Sterling in disgust, then turned around and stomped out of the garret.

When the sound of Grant's footfall all but disappeared from his ears, Sterling crawled to the loose floorboard and pried it up with his fingernails. He reached deep inside the opening, fumbling around until he felt the crumpled pamphlet between his fingers. He slowly withdrew it from the hiding place, then peered down at it earnestly.

"I *need* the money," he said softly to himself. "And I will get it . . . for her."

At the same morning hour
Isobel's bedchamber

Isobel lay curled on her side on the tester bed, her arms wrapped around her feather pillow as Bluebell sat on the edge of mattress, patting her back, trying to soothe and calm her. But her efforts did no good.

She still wore her crimson walking dress, not having moved from the bed to which she had retreated last night. Her tears had long since run dry, but her heart still ached miserably.

"How could I have been so entirely wrong about him?" she asked more of herself than of Bluebell.

"Were you wrong? About what, may I ask,

miss?" Bluebell grasped Isobel's shoulder and abruptly pulled her over to face her. "About the wager?"

"Well, yes. He was responsible for placing the wager; he admitted as much." She covered her eyes with her hands. "He was only using me to win an obscene wager. How blind I was."

Bluebell scoffed at that. "I—I don't quite understand, miss. Does admitting to one convict him of the other?"

Isobel whisked her hands away. "Shouldn't it?"

"Not the way I see it." She took Isobel's nearer hand and squeezed it. "Miss Isobel, you always see the good in people. Didn't you see it in the Scotsman?"

"Certainly I did," she said. "Why else would I have given my heart to him?" Isobel's question was sincere; already she was beginning to understand her error in judging Sterling's heart when it was only the wager at White's he had admitted.

"Forgive me for saying so, miss, but the talk from the above stairs ladies is that he looked at you with love in his eyes."

Isobel sat up and stared at Bluebell.

"But I never listen much to gossip that makes its way to the kitchens." Bluebell's countenance suddenly appeared very serious. "I would believe you, though, Miss Isobel. So, please, tell me what your heart knows for certain. Was it love you saw when you looked into his eyes—or deceit?"

"It was . . . love." Isobel was thoroughly stunned by what she knew now to be the truth.

"I knew it." Bluebell smiled and reached down and pinched Isobel's cheek. "I just wanted to be sure you did too!"

Isobel rubbed her cheek. "That doesn't excuse the fact that he placed the wager that has been the bane of my life for weeks now."

Bluebell rose from the edge of the tester bed and headed for the door. "Miss Isobel, that he was to blame for all the excitement of the wager don't really matter. The wager wasn't what brought the tears on—was it?"

"N-no." Isobel swallowed the tears that had drained into her throat all night long. "It was . . . that I thought he didn't love me."

The maid pressed down the latch and opened the door. "Well, that was just silliness, wasn't it?"

Isobel nodded. It was. How could she have been such a fool? He loved her. She was sure of it.

Bluebell stepped into the passageway. "So what are you still doing in bed?" She gave a parting smile, then closed the bedchamber door behind her.

What indeed? A whisper of a smile touched Isobel's mouth, for now she had the one thing she did not own an hour before. Hope.

Three days later
Wenton Inn Square

Isobel's father had not ventured out of the house in days. She supposed his purpose was to guard her, more or less, in the event Lord Blackburn attempted to call upon her. But he didn't. Why would he, when she had been so willing to believe the worst of him? This seemed to imbue her father with enough confidence to believe Isobel's heart no longer lay with Blackburn. So this morning he had returned to his duties in the House of Commons.

But he had been wrong. Isobel's plan was to simply lie low until London Society grew weary of waiting for reports that either Sterling or she had tried to reach the other, to reconcile, perhaps. It would be difficult. She risked Sterling believing that she no longer loved him. But she knew too that if he only listened to his own heart, he would know that her love for him was far too substantial to be doused by a wager. Still, this was her only option. If she sent him a message, it might be intercepted by a greedy member of the Sinclair house staff, eager to collect a few coins from gossipmongers. If she tried to seek him out, an *on dit* columnist might report it, and her father, and Society, would quickly learn of it.

All she could do was hold on until the time was right, then go to him and hope that he understood why she had delayed in reassuring him of her love.

In the meanwhile, she had matters of her charity to occupy her time.

This morning, after her father left the house, Isobel had sent a card to Christiana requesting that her friend call as soon as she might and join her in taking a walk to escape the confinement of the house.

Their stroll took them down the usual streets and through the usual parks, until they reached Weston Inn Square, where Isobel's dream for the widows and orphans of Corunna had lain for some months.

Isobel stood peering up at the old inn wistfully. "It is going to be sold."

"You've known that for weeks," Christiana said. "Give up your hopes on this place. You haven't near enough to buy it, and I am sorry to say it, but you likely never will."

"I only thought I had more time to raise the money. It would have been the perfect lodging for the widows and orphans, until they find their own way."

"No one has purchased the old inn yet," Christiana countered. "There may still be time. You managed to interest several ladies of the Quality in supporting your charity already. Perhaps you can convince others."

"I doubt that very much," Isobel said sadly. "The swirl about the wager is over, and so now too is my ability to draw sizable donations."

"What are you talking about, Issy? The wager is not finished. In fact, I heard my father tell Lord Buntree that the column that reported your refusal to marry the likes of Lord Blackburn has *revived* the interest of the men in London. When the two of you seemed smitten, the wager lost interest for them. Now that it seems that you are infuriated with Lord Blackburn for using you in a gambling plot, their interest in betting against Lord Blackburn is at an all-time high. Isn't that diverting?"

"Not in the least," Isobel muttered. "All that matters is acquiring this inn for the widows and children."

And being with Sterling . . . forever.

Chapter 18

Love is all give.
Unknown

A sennight later

It was not yet dawn when Sterling rose from bed and packed the last of his personal belongings in his trunk . . . just in case he did not return from Fives Court.

His brothers and sisters had all tried to dissuade him from the battle, to no avail. Sterling simply did not care anymore whether he lived or died. The simple fact that the woman he loved believed he had used her solely as a pawn in his gamble pained him.

He didn't quite understand his feeling so. It was not as if he had never used someone to assuage his own greed. He had. But this was not one of those times. This time he was innocent, for since the moment he had contrived the idea of the wager, he had fully intended on marrying Miss Carington. True, he might not have loved her then, but he was not even convinced of this. He just had not yet named the swirl of emotion he felt from the moment he had first met her.

He glanced around the bare garret, and then, after ensuring nothing had been left lying about, he knelt down and pried up the loose floorboard. Sinking his hand down until the floor pressed against his armpit, Sterling reached the small leather bag and the crumpled pamphlet Isobel had been waving at the Pugilistic Club the night they first met. He lifted the two items from the opening in the floor, then replaced the board and stood.

His eyes began to burn and he rubbed his hand over his mouth, as the hard reality that he might never see Isobel again wrapped him like a shroud.

"Poplin," he called out softly, not wanting to wake anyone or let them hear the ragged emotion in his voice.

"Coming, my lord," the old man called quietly up the staircase.

While Sterling was waiting, he folded and rolled

up the old pamphlet and slipped it into the leather pouch. He twisted the Sinclair diamond ring from his finger and added that to the bag.

Poplin shuffled into the room just then. "Gentleman Jackson's carriage has arrived. Shall I wake your family to let them know you are leaving, my lord?"

Sterling shook his head. He looked at the leather pouch in his palm, then, with a sad smile stinging his lips, pressed it into Poplin's hand. "I want you, in the event anything happens to me, to see that Miss Isobel Carington receives this donation for her charity . . . I would like for her to purchase Wenton Inn if possible." He swallowed deeply. "Do you understand?"

"Not quite, my lord," Poplin admitted. "I do not know what you mean by 'in the event anything happens to me.'"

Sterling just shook his head. "Just please see that she receives this."

Poplin nodded his head. "Would you like assistance carrying anything to the carriage?"

Sterling started for the door to the stairway. He raised his fists and conjured a smile. "Nay, I believe all I shall require are these this day."

"What do you mean he has already gone?" Lachlan yelled at Poplin. "He hadn't spoken about the prizefight with Dooney for several days. I assumed he had finally given up the notion of fighting the Irishman."

Ivy, who sat upon the settee, burst into tears. "Grant was supposed to stop him, and if he couldn't, you and Killian were supposed to restrain him."

"He'll be killed." Siusan wrung her hands frantically as she paced the parlor floor. "One death-blow, that's all it takes the Irishman. And we will be wholly to blame!"

Priscilla sat in a gilt chair beside the cold hearth. She was shaking. Killian walked over to his twin and eased his hands over her shoulders.

"Lord Grant left only an hour after Lord Sterling," Poplin told them hopefully. "He will reach him in time, will he not?"

Killian nodded. "He should. God, I hope he does."

"We *made* him do this," Siusan suddenly interjected. "He's always felt responsible for us all. We could have existed on the small portion Father provided, but we didn't. We insisted on maintaining the appearance that we were rich. That money meant nothing to us."

"It was our pride," Priscilla said.

Ivy nodded and sniffed back her tears. "The battle is madness. Is he *trying* to kill himself?"

Lachlan shook his head, and though the hour was yet early, he poured himself a sip of whisky. "He would never give himself over to death, but for the right wager he might risk his life."

"He's lost Miss Carington. He doesn't care about anything anymore," Priscilla said.

"That isn't true," Siusan said, setting her hands on her hips. "He cares about us and our future."

Her comment propelled Killian across the parlor toward the passage.

"Where are you going?" Priscilla called out to him. She leaped from her chair and ran after him.

"If we find a hackney willing to trek to Tethersley, we may make the start of the fight. We may stop him yet." Killian raced out the front door and into the square, followed by Priscilla.

Siusan glanced up at Ivy and Lachlan, and then they too rushed from the parlor into the passage, and then out the door to the square.

The Carington Residence
No. 9 Leicester Square

Isobel had just finished taking her afternoon tea when her father came into the parlor seeking her out. The look on his face was confused. He was clearly disturbed. "What is it, Father? Are you unwell?"

He shook his head, but she could see that he was growing pale when he sat down at the table next to her.

"Isobel, I have been troubled since the night you learned about Lord Blackburn's involvement in the wager."

She peered uneasily down into her empty cup. No conversation that ever began in this fashion turned out to be a happy one.

"You accused me of hating you." She felt his eyes upon her and knew she must meet his gaze.

Tilting her empty teacup to her mouth, she pretended to drink, if only to gain purchase on a few more moments before being required to speak.

How many times over the years had she rehearsed such a reply in her head? How many instances, when he cursed her vexing existence in this world, had she wished to tell him that if she could have been the one who had died, instead of her brother and mother, she would have chosen that fate rather than live as nothing more than a disappointment to her father? But when the moment was now upon her, the words she wished she could say would not come. "You do. You do not love me, Father, and haven't for years." She raised her eyes. "More than that, you've made it plain that you wish me out of your life. So why, when Lord Blackburn came to request my hand—to offer to relieve you of your responsibility for me—did you not just forget about what you knew about the wager? Why didn't you just let me go . . . and be happy?"

"I have failed you, daughter." He reached out and, urging her hand from the teacup, took it into his own. "When your brother was killed at Corunna, a piece of me died with him. I was so broken and consumed with my own grief that I failed to see how your mother was foundering in her deep despair until she drowned in it."

Isobel's eyes were swimming in unshed tears. "We needed each other then, Father. I needed you, needed your support and love then more than ever. I had lost my brother, my mother, and the man I thought I would marry. But you pushed me away, making it clear to me that had you been able to choose which of your children would live, you would not have chosen me."

"Oh, Isobel, you so misunderstand." She wished he would hug her to him and tell her how she was wrong, had been wrong all these years. Instead he brought his other hand atop hers, cupping it between his palms. "For weeks, I could not make it through the day without falling to my knees in tears—me, the minister known as the Rock in Parliament. It was all I could do to hide my sadness from those around me. And then I would look at you—a young girl who had lost more than I—but who was able to turn her loss into something good. The charity to support others whose husband, brother, father, or son had died in the battle. You were so strong. And I was weak."

Isobel's mouth fell open, and yet she could not utter a single word. She had never heard her father speak of her this way or the charity she had founded and felt passionately about.

His eyes began to well. "I never wanted you to leave. You are all I have left. And I never thought you would go, after the ladies of the *ton* sullied your young reputation. I did not believe that a gentleman would ever offer for you, and, to be truthful, I think I relished the security that belief brought me."

"But why then did you practically force me into Lord Blackburn's arms if you did not wish me to marry and leave?" Isobel asked.

"That perhaps was my most selfish moment. A time when I so underestimated you and the Scotsman as well. When I learned the reputation of the Sinclairs, the Seven Deadly Sins, I at first sought to protect you and your own name from being associated with the wild Scots. But I saw too that the harder I strove to keep Lord Blackburn away from you, the more passionately he pursued you. And then I heard of the wager, and I knew I had nothing truly to fear. He was a gamester, consumed with greed, and you were naught but a means to winning an enormous bet."

"And yet that was when you threatened to send me to Great-aunt Gertrude's pig farm if I didn't marry. I don't understand. Why?"

Her father released her hands then and stood. He began to pace across the carpet, keeping his eyes averted from hers. "Because I knew you would eventually see that you were being used. You would believe that no man would honestly choose you, and you would finally give up any hold on your dream of marrying one day." He turned and faced her then. "And for that, I am greatly ashamed. Not only for trying to make you remain living at home with me, but for not caring that I was hurting you to do it."

"But Sterling was in love me, and I with him. That is what you never believed or understood."

He shook his head. "I did see it, eventually, and I knew you would marry him if the offer was presented. That is why I sought to pair you with Mr. Burke Leake."

"Why Mr. Leake, Father?" Isobel turned her cup around and around on its saucer. "His interest in me was clear. Mightn't he have offered for me?"

He nodded. "But he would stay here in London . . . and not whisk you away to Scotland." He sighed. "Isobel, I have failed you completely as a father. I only hope that someday you can forgive me, though I know after today, I fear that you will find it nearly impossible.

Isobel peered up at him as he neared the tea table again. Her chest tightened. "Why are you telling me this now?"

His skin grew paler, and his lips trembled, but he said nothing. "Father?" She was growing increasingly anxious.

Something was terribly wrong. She had seen her father look this way only once before . . . and that was when he had had to tell her that her mother had taken her own life. The day her life changed forever.

His hands trembled as he lifted something from his waistcoat pocket. Isobel peered down at the small leather pouch, which he slid slowly across the table to her.

She peered down at it, not sure if she should open it. No knowing if she wanted to.

"This arrived for you a short while ago." He nodded to it. "The man who delivered it said he was Poplin, Lord Blackburn's manservant."

"What?" Isobel untied the leather cord that

cinched the bag shut, pulled it open, and then emptied its contents on the linen tablecloth.

Out fell Sterling's ancestral diamond ring, the Sinclair diamond, and a wrinkled charity pamphlet for the benefit of the widows and orphans of Corunna. One of those, of her own making, that she had flashed about at the Pugilistic Club. The backs of her eyes pricked. "I—I don't understand." She looked up at her father.

"I don't quite either," he admitted, "not completely. Poplin said that Lord Blackburn wished you to have this . . . *in the event something happened to him.*"

A chill like a freezing rain swept over Isobel. "My God, has something happened to him? Where is he?"

"I asked the manservant that very question, and he reluctantly told me that Lord Blackburn had gone to Fives Court to battle the Irishman Dooney this evening."

"So Sterling is well. Nothing has happened to him at all. The battle has not yet even begun." The edges of her mouth twitched in the beginnings of a hopeful smile.

Her father's lips turned downward, and he shook his head. "You do not understand, Isobel. Lord Blackburn cannot win this battle. The Irishman's right is so powerful that his last two competitors were killed by his blow."

Tears began to collect in Isobel's lashes. "What are you saying to me, Father? Tell me plainly."

"Lord Blackburn is a fair fighter, a good fighter . . . for a marquess—but he cannot win."

"Cannot win . . . you mean he will—die?"

Her father said nothing until he lowered his head and was not meeting her gaze. "I am sorry, Isobel. I know that in some way, by revealing his wager, by destroying Lord Blackburn's hopes of marrying you, I am responsible for this." He lowered his head. "I fear what he plans to do is naught but suicide."

Isobel leaped to her feet, toppling her tea onto the linen cloth beneath it. "Then help me, Father, *please*. If you do love me as you claim, then help me stop this fight *now*."

"Fives Court is in Tethersley, hours from London," he confessed. "We may not arrive in time."

"We have to try." Isobel grabbed his hand and pulled him into the passage toward the door. "Because I love him."

Chapter 19

Reduce the complexities of life by eliminating the needless wants of life, and the labors of life will reduce themselves.

Teale

Fives Court
Tethersley

Isobel looked out the window with confusion at the scene before them. Carriages, donkey carts, and phaetons alike packed the road. Nothing was moving. Isobel whimpered in frustration. As she peered up the road, she saw that gentlemen and commoners, likely worried they might miss a single punch by the world champion, Dooney, were abandoning their vehicles in the road and heading on foot to the court still at least a mile distant.

"How long until the bout begins?" she asked her father. Her hand was already on the carriage door latch.

"None at all. It has begun."

In the distance, a great roar rose into the air. Isobel did not wait a moment longer. She flung open the carriage door and leaped down into the dusty road. Lifting her skirts to her knees, she ran toward the court.

Sterling stood in the roped ring facing Liam Dooney, the world champion of bare-knuckle battles. Their seconds led them to the lines and waited as their positions were checked.

"Please don't do this, Sterling," Grant said into his ear so Sterling could hear him over the roar of the crowd.

Unlike the usual gloved matches held at Fives Court, true enthusiasts preferred a bare-knuckle fight. The possibility that one of the fighters might be killed only increased the draw of spectators.

More than one thousand men stood around the ring, a few more in shuttered boxes, and still others in the rafter stands above.

Sterling surveyed the hordes of cheering gentlemen, eating, drinking, and smoking pipes as they would at any other Society event. This seemed odd to him, for this particular spectacular might end in the death of one man. Him.

Even if he had wished to forfeit the bout, his honor would not allow him to do so now.

He looked across at Grant, who had arrived an hour ago to claim the honor of second, along with Dooney's man, who was now being led a pace back from the chalked square on the stage so that the battle could begin. Grant beckoned for Sterling to come with him, but Sterling shook his head. Suddenly a surge in the crowd drew Sterling's attention and he turned his head, and to his great surprise, he saw Lachlan and Killian fighting their way to the edge of the stage.

"Sterling, this is madness," Killian yelled to him, before being pushed back by the heaving masses of spectators.

Lachlan made it to the ropes before one of the umpires yanked him down. "Leave the damned gold on the table, Sterling," he cried out as he was being dragged toward the rear of the court. "We don't need it!"

He wasn't leaving.

Sterling turned his head back and looked across at the Irishman. Dooney was a huge man, the very rare sort that made Sterling look average-sized in comparison. He was hailed as the most skilled fighter alive, with unmatched boxing skills and fast hands that could levy blows that could permanently maim or even kill—and had.

Sterling, on the other hand, was the product of Edinburgh sparring schools. He was quick on his feet, hard-hitting, athletic, and a natural pugilist ... who had only entered the prize ring when, at a young age, he had learned money was to be easily had from a few solid punches.

Attention was called. Sterling and Dooney were set legally at the lines, and at Gentleman John Jackson's signal, the battle commenced.

Sterling feinted and sparred with Dooney, who threw a few punches his way, but committed to none of them.

Most certainly the Irishman was waiting for Sterling to make the real first move. And so, being a gentleman, Sterling complied with his left fist. Dooney's head jerked, and he fell to his back on the stage.

The crowd rushed forward, likely not expecting Sterling to have landed such a tremendous blow so early in the bout.

Crawling back to his feet, Dooney wiped a smear of blood from his lip and returned to the chalk lines, which were being freshly set for the next round.

Sterling felt it then. His usual confidence in the

ring reemerged and surged into his throbbing fists. He rushed at Dooney, landing yet another vicious punch, while shrugging off several stinging counterblows. Dooney fell forward to his knees, wincing in pain and bleeding heavily from his left eye and his mouth. He staggered to his feet and raised his fists defensively before his face.

A calmness came over Sterling. He knew Dooney was hurt and exhausted. It would only take him one solid punch to floor the giant once and for all. The volume of the crowd swelled, making his ear throb from the noise.

Gauging his moment, he drew back his right fist. Suddenly there was a flash of movement at the ropes. He held his focus.

"Sterling, *no!*"

Isobel? He turned his head in time to see Isobel crawling under the ropes onto the stage, kicking at the umpires who were trying to stop her. "Isobel!"

There was a horrid flash of pain in his jaw. His head flung backward and his body slammed back against the stage.

He blinked, and suddenly Isobel was kneeling beside him, peering down. Tears were in her eyes.

"Christ, woman, you are going to be the death of me," he groaned.

"As long as it's me, and no one else." Isobel

glared up at Dooney, who was staring at her in astonishment.

"And that I die of exhaustion . . . from exploring Elgin's marbles." Pink embarrassment flooded Isobel's cheeks, and Sterling coughed a chuckle.

Grant looked worriedly down at him. "Good God, someone get a physician. I believe the blow has caused delirium."

The Sinclair residence
Grosvenor Square

"What do you think of *FOOL*?" Siusan asked Sterling as she threaded her finest embroidery needle with silk. "Nay, the split on your chin will require more letters than that. What say you to . . . *ISOBEL*, hmm?"

"I think I should like a simple cross-stitch if you can manage that, Su," Sterling snapped.

"Oh, do hurry and finish; now that you've removed the bandage he is dripping blood again," Priscilla said, settling the tea service on the marble table before the cold fireplace. "I should not wish to be required to scrub blood out of the settee's silk covering."

"I know . . . *MARBLES*." Siusan smiled wryly. "Grant told me what you said before you fell unconscious. What did you mean by that?"

Sterling shrugged. "I don't seem to recall."

Ivy giggled. "I think we should ask Miss Carington what he said. I daresay she would remember. After all, Grant said Sterling's words made her color fiercely."

The brass door knocker sounded, and Ivy and Priscilla rose.

"She's arrived," Ivy said excitedly.

Sterling tried to sit up, but Siusan flattened her palm on his forehead and held him in place, then resumed stitching—what felt to Sterling to be an M.

"Stay still," Siusan scolded. "Not one word either until I have finished."

Poplin led Isobel into the fore-parlor, forgetting to announce her.

After greeting each of his sisters, Isobel smiled brightly at Sterling. "How are you feeling?"

Sterling started to answer, but Siusan thumped him on the forehead with the flat of her palm.

"Almost finished . . ." Siusan said, to no one in particular. "There." She smiled at her handiwork and then looked up at Isobel. "By chance, do you sew, Miss Carington?"

Isobel's expression went blank. "Y-yes."

"I am so glad." Siusan rose from the edge of the settee. "Because I am giving it up. I find it too taxing." She caught Sterling's long legs, swung them off the settee, and then beckoned Isobel to be seated.

Isobel gazed into Sterling's eyes, and he into hers for several moments, saying nothing, until his sisters suddenly remembered they had promised to assist Mrs. Wimpole with soup making in the kitchen and scurried from the fore-parlor.

Isobel wrinkled her nose. "They had invited me for tea." She glanced at the tea service on the table, then at the empty doorway to the passage before turning her attention back to Sterling. "They . . . are returning, are they not?"

Sterling shrugged. "Soon enough, I expect."

Isobel seemed uneasy. "Just as well. I wished to speak to you privately anyway . . . to apologize for causing you to lose the battle." She fumbled with her reticule. "I had no notion you were about to become victor." Slowly she raised her eyes. "I heard about the Irishman's blows." She swallowed hard. "I was worried you would be badly hurt, and . . . oh Sterling, I could not have endured it if you were killed when I had it within my power to prevent it."

"By stepping between us."

"By doing anything I could to stop the battle." Though she had claimed to be sorry for her actions, it was clear she was not. Her gaze was firm and her features were set.

"Isobel, I do not fault you for your good-hearted intentions"—he shook his head slowly—"only your method of stopping the bout. *You* might have been killed. Why would you risk your own life after the pain I caused you over the wager?"

She averted her gaze and let it drift through the window to the square beyond. "You know the answer to that, Sterling." A golden coil of hair dangling at her brow suddenly required her undivided attention. She lifted the thick curl and peered upward at it, as if to ascertain to which side of her head it belonged. In her prolonged attempt to delay speaking, Isobel's eyes had nearly crossed by the time she finally made her determination and shoved the hair back into place. Only then, as Sterling waited in silence, did she speak. Her words were low and tremulous. "Because . . . I love you." She shifted her gaze back to him. "Don't you realize this?"

"I think it is more than that, lass. You knew in your heart, even when I could not deny that I had orchestrated the wager at White's, that I loved you too. That, while my actions might have been questionable, my feelings for you were pure. I loved you, I think, from the evening you first stepped into the ring at the Pugilistic Club, and from that moment, that feeling has grown each day."

"Then why did you contrive such an audacious wager?" she asked.

Sterling didn't know the answer to that, finding the advantage in any situation had always come naturally for him, but when he replied he was shaken with the raw truth of his answer. "The bet made what I was feeling for you seem safe. I'd convinced myself that I wasn't really risking my heart and rejection. It was just a wager, and the emotional investment I had made in you was only to reach a successful outcome to the bet. But the more time I spent with you, the more I realized that the risk was not my family's ten-thousand-pound portion. The true wager was my heart—I risked vulnerability when I gave you my love, hoping that for *once* that love would be returned."

Isobel sighed. "And it was."

"Aye, ten to one." Sterling exhaled the half breath he'd reserved in his lungs. "White's may nullify the wager and keep the money I escrowed to place the bet. My brothers and sisters may be forced to stomach Mrs. Wimpole's soup every day. But I won the wager . . . the real treasure—*you*."

"You are not a pauper, Sterling."

"Oh, but close to it at the moment," he said.

"No, Sterling, you still have this." She reached

into her reticule and withdrew a leather pouch and held it out to him.

"A pouch? Och, lass, I have several." He pushed it back to her. "You may keep this one."

Isobel looked as though she was growing frustrated with his levity. She emptied the ring out onto her palm. The Sinclair diamond fitted into the ring's center sparkled brilliantly in the fingers of afternoon light reaching through the front window. "I cannot keep this ring or sell it for the charity—ever. It belongs to your family. It is for you to give your son someday." When he did not take it from her, she set it on the marble table.

"If you will not take this ring, then please, will you allow me to give you something, lass?" He stood and extended his hand to her.

She took it and had started to come to her feet when she saw him kneel on one knee before her.

From his waistcoat he withdrew another ring—smaller than the Sinclair diamond, but its mate in every way. "You told me once that you don't need your father's consent to marry me. If I ask you, instead of him this time, would you be my wife?"

Isobel's eyes rounded in apparent surprise, but then her expression softened. "You will have to ask me to know that for certain, Lord Blackburn."

She tried to conceal a smile of joy, and he knew he had his answer already. Still, Sterling needed to hear it for himself.

"I do not deserve a woman so giving and so noble as you, but if you will have me, Isobel, if you will marry me, I will do everything in my power to become a man worthy of your love."

"Did you say . . . *noble*?" Isobel looked at him then as though for the first time. She cast her gaze down and ran her thumb along the lint bandage wrapped around his knuckles. "Sterling. My God, it was *you*—you are the one who has been leaving the donations for my charity. It wasn't some stranger—or even Leake as I had nearly convinced myself. It was *you* all the while." She clapped her hands over her eyes. "What a fool I have been not to realize it. Why didn't you tell me?"

"It is a noble cause, one I wanted to support, but I didn't wish anyone to know—might have ruined my sterling reputation, you know."

He had thought his quip would bring a quick smile to Isobel's lips again. Instead, tears caught like brilliant spangles in her lashes. Her chin began to quiver and her lower lip pouted.

Sterling wondered if he had read her intentions incorrectly and if she would deny him.

Truly, he did not deserve her, but he had always

found a way to obtain what he'd desired by whatever means necessary. Could it be what he wanted most in this world was atonement for his sins to earn his soul's redemption?

His heart hammered in his chest and throbbed in his ears as he impatiently awaited her reply, whatever it might be. "Isobel, will you marry me?"

"Yes." It was as if the wind had been stolen from her lungs, and he questioned himself as to whether she spoke or merely coughed.

Blinking, he leaned closer. "I apologize, dear Isobel, but I did not quite hear that."

She leaned toward him and rested her palm on his cheek. "I said yes, I will marry you." Isobel's lips hovered above his own, until they brushed his mouth ever so lightly. "Nothing would make me more proud than to be your wife, Sterling. I love you."

He ached upon hearing her words, and his throat threatened to close in upon itself.

No one had joined the words *proud* and *Sterling*. Ever. He closed his eyes for a moment and swallowed deeply, not wishing for the great emotion he felt to well over.

"Sterling?"

When he opened his eyes, it was concern coupled with great caring that he saw in Isobel's eyes. And, aye, *love*.

"I love you, Isobel. Each day I know you, my love for you grows greater still. My heart has never been so full. I have never felt more loved than when I am with you. Knowing you, feeling your love, I could no sooner live without you than without air."

Isobel smiled through her wet lashes as he raised his mother's ring and fitted it onto her finger.

"A symbol of my troth . . . and enduring love for you, my sweet Isobel."

Her gaze dropped. "I h-have nothing to give you . . . but my heart." Her voice was thickened with emotion, and she dropped her gaze to the ring.

"Then I will be a rich man indeed, for there is nothing more precious to me in this world." Sterling cupped her chin with this left hand and turned her face so that she had to look directly at him. "I have one more question for you."

"Anything, Sterling." Her breath came quick with anticipation.

He turned his chin up to her. "What did Siusan stitch on my chin?"

Isobel laughed, and suddenly her cheeks glowed like a setting sun. "It just says . . . Oh, I am too embarrassed to tell you." She brought her fingertips to her lips, but her grin peeked out from either side of her hand.

"Tell me." *Bluidy hell.* If it caused such a blush, he was sure his wicked sister had stitched *MARBLES*.

"It says . . . *MARRY HIM.*" She lowered her hand and angled her head to kiss his lips. "And so I shall."

Chapter 20

That man is richest whose pleasures are cheapest.
Thoreau

The Carington residence
Leicester Square

You are an honorable man, Lord Blackburn,"
Mr. Carington said, "though I do admit
there was a time when I was greatly doubtful and feared for my daughter's reputation."

Sterling accepted a crystal of brandy from Isobel's father, wondering all the while if he had just
received a compliment or an undercut. "I am relieved that I have assuaged your concerns, sir."

Carington tapped his index finger in the air. "I

admit, though my gift for seeing through a gentleman to his true thoughts and nature is, dare I say it . . . much lauded in the House of Commons, I confess that I sorely misread your intentions, Lord Blackburn."

"In what regard, sir?"

"Why, in every regard, it seems!" Mr. Carington walked toward his desk, crooking a finger over his shoulder at Sterling, then wordlessly touching a chair as an invitation for his guest to be seated. "I am certain Raggett will remove your wager from White's betting book promptly, for there is no other just outcome." He moved his glass to his lips, but withdrew it before sipping. "You have nothing to gain by marrying Isobel, so I must conclude that you do possess a true fondness for her."

"You are correct in your assessment. I love her."

"It is still rather extraordinary to me. After my great error in judgment of you, you still approach me to request Isobel's hand when she is not in need of my consent. The gesture is completely unnecessary."

"Except to show my respect for the man who, under difficult circumstances, raised such an extraordinary daughter, so passionate in her convictions," Sterling said.

"She is that." For the first time, Sterling saw Mr. Carington smile. "Had it not been for her expression of impassioned beliefs concerning Elgin's marbles, I would have never gone to view the marbles myself. I would have never seen their exquisite quality and come to agree with my daughter that the marbles must be preserved at any cost."

"So Lord Elgin's price was met, the cost of transport and storage?" Sterling asked. That sum had been very high, and if the government agreed to the price, Isobel's oration must have indeed been awe-inspiring.

"Lord Elgin may still fall into financial ruin—his price was not fully met—but he will have immortalized himself, as several have stated, for bringing the Parthenon marbles here for our people." He rolled his glass around in his palms, swirling the contents. "Had it not been for Isobel, I might have folded to the jealousies of Sir Richard Payne Knight and his society and convinced the British government to punish Lord Elgin's selfish actions by permitting his great collection to dissolve in the London rain."

Sterling straightened in his chair. "I had not heard. So the British Museum will acquire the marbles—all of them?"

"They are being moved to the museum for storage within a sennight. We hope to display the collection very soon."

Sterling rose. "Well, it seems two momentous events will take place then—the installation of the marbles and our wedding."

"Indeed . . ." Carington scratched his nose. "Mayhap you will allow me to make your wedding even more memorable—by way of a little surprise for Isobel."

Sterling set his glass down and leaned toward Mr. Carington. He'd seen that look before, in his own eyes many times. "What have you in mind, sir?"

Mr. Carington chuckled and beckoned for Sterling to draw closer still so Isobel, who was meant to be waiting in her bedchamber—but might have been lurking on the staircase—could not hear.

Ten of the clock in the evening
The Sinclair residence
Grosvenor Square

"Sterling told me that the wedding would be kept a secret from all but our families. We wanted a very private ceremony," Isobel said, but even she could hear the distress in own voice.

She stood in Siusan's bedchamber dressing for the event, but outside the stir and chatter of a great crowd made her nerves rattle.

"Och, what did you expect, dear? All of London

has been following your romance," Siusan replied. "Why, you would think Princess Charlotte herself was getting married, judging by the size of the crowd behind the wall."

Isobel peeked between the curtains. The entire back garden was curiously covered with huge swaths of billowing white linen. She opened the curtains wider and leaned her forehead against the windowpane for a better look, but the crowd, seeing her, roared and cheered, chasing her back into the interior of the chamber.

"Siusan, why is the garden tented with linen? Has Sterling mentioned anything to you?"

"Nay, but I am sure he saw the people collecting behind the house earlier and decided to take measures to ensure your privacy. You didn't notice there are no bed coverings or table linens anywhere in the house?" She laughed. "Nay, I expect not. You have more important things to think about this night." Siusan grinned.

Christiana cracked open the door, "Are you dressed? Might I come in now?"

Isobel giggled.

"Don't move," Siusan said, as her fingers worked a belt of white satin and crepe tightly below Isobel's bodice and then pinned it with a clasp of whitest pearls. "There, now you may turn around and look into the glass."

Isobel turned and stood before the cheval mirror and fairly gasped at her image. She wore a rose blossom-hued crepe gown with a short train over a white satin slip, cinched with a frock back and satin stomacher front.

She caught up the train and whirled around in front of the looking glass. Her back and neckline scooped low, cut purposely so for an evening wedding. The sleeves were short and, like the hem of the gown, were edged with white puckered satin embellished with tiny freshwater pearls.

Ivy rushed into the room with a convent cross of diamonds. "This belonged to our mother. Will you wear it today?"

Isobel felt overwhelmed by sentiment, but had willed herself not to shed a single tear on this day.

But then Christiana opened her reticule and withdrew a small box of white leather. "Your father asked me to give this to you." She lifted her palm for Isobel to take it. "These earrings were your mother's, and now they belong to you."

Isobel opened the leather and peered inside at the diamond studs ringed by tiny pearls. It was as if they had always been meant for this gown, for this day.

Priscilla leaned in through the doorway. "The vicar is ready. Come with me." She smiled excitedly, glancing back repeatedly over her shoulder at Isobel as they all descended the staircase and walked down the dark passage to the French windows leading to the walled garden beyond.

Isobel tugged nervously at her French kid gloves, moving them up and over her elbows. Christiana walked behind her, weaving the pearl-headed pins and brilliants tighter into Isobel's hair. She seemed every bit as tangled in nerves as Isobel herself.

When they turned the corner, she saw that the doors too had been draped to prevent her from peering out into the garden until they opened for her. Lachlan and Killian stood to the left and right of the windows, each waiting to press the latch and swing the doors wide for Isobel and her ladies to enter.

She glanced at Christiana, and a missish laugh wriggled from her lips. Sterling's sisters moved up behind her, and just then, the French windows were thrown wide.

Isobel stepped forward, and all of a sudden the white swaths covering the walled garden were torn back.

Isobel gasped. The moon and stars illuminated the garden as if a thousand candles had been set into a sky of black velvet.

The sweet smell of roses teased her senses as she lifted her satin slipper and stepped onto a trail of white blossoms.

As she passed the tall hedges of roses, the reason for Sterling's secrecy suddenly became clear.

He stood at the far end of the garden, the path of blossoms leading to him and the white-haired vicar beside him. Grant stood behind his brother, glancing at the high stone wall behind them topped with the bobbling heads and smiling faces of those in the crowd who had boosted themselves up to see over the wall and to watch the wedding of the year. The moment the crowd saw her, a great cheer rose up into the night sky.

But most incredible was that twelve of Elgin's marbles lined the trail, six gleaming exquisitely in the moonlight on either side of her.

The scene before her was drawn from a dream so grand that she would never have even imagined it.

As she passed through the column of marbles, she glimpsed three gray-haired gentlemen on her left. Her heart leaped into her throat when she realized they were her father, Lord Elgin, and a third man who looked so like Sterling that, without a doubt, she knew he could be none other than his father, the Duke of Sinclair, come down from Scotland.

She smiled at them all as she passed, but her sole focus now was only Sterling.

Drawing to his side, she looked up into his eyes, and in them saw so much love that she could not stop the tears of joy from welling in her eyes.

He took her hand, smiled at her as he turned her to face the vicar, and within a clutch of minutes Isobel's dream became reality as the clergyman proclaimed Sterling and her to be husband and wife.

In place of a wedding breakfast, theirs was a grand midnight feast. The gates to the walled garden were opened, and anyone who had stayed beyond the taking of vows was welcomed inside to join the celebration and to view the marbles.

"Your father has come," Isobel said softly to Sterling as together they bit into spice cake topped with orange blossom icing. "And he is coming this way."

"Other than a brief greeting, he hasn't told any of us why he has come." Sterling quickly wiped his mouth with a linen. "I suspect he heard about the wager and is here to cast me from the house." Sterling came to his feet to await his father, when Grant burst forth with Mr. Raggett from White's.

Sterling stiffened. *Damn it all. The timing of this could not be any worse.*

Isobel stood and wrapped her arm around Sterling's, supporting him for whatever might come.

Grant looked excited. "You will not believe it, Sterling. You simply will not, but it's true."

Sterling looked from Grant to Mr. Raggett, wanting to conclude this conversation momentarily so his father, the duke, would hear as little as possible.

"You are a very rich man, Lord Blackburn," Raggett said. "You have won your wager, Lord Blackburn. You may come to White's next week to collect your winnings. There are far too many bettors to require you to collect individually."

Sterling stared at Raggett, and then at Grant. "It was my understanding that the wager was stricken from the betting book."

"No, we could find no fault with the wager, though when we heard of your involvement, we did study the proceedings very carefully. White's business thrived, the shops of St. James's Street and Piccadilly gained from the additional patrons in the area come to place a bet." He shook his head as if he did not wish to say it. "You won your position. I congratulate you."

Sterling's father stood behind Raggett, and likely had heard almost every single word about the wager. Raggett turned to leave, pausing only to tip his hat to them all.

"Sterling," the duke said, making no attempt to keep what he was about to say private. "I have been kept informed about your doings since you have been in London. I was very distressed . . . until of late, when I learned of clandestine donations to the widows and orphans of Corunna—"

Sterling's gaze flew to Isobel, who shrugged her shoulders. Clearly she had not said anything; she had only learned of it herself belatedly.

"Oh, your wager at White's concerned me greatly, until I heard that your feelings for Miss Carington were authentic, and though you placed the wager, you were not using her for ill gains." He set his hand on Sterling's shoulder. "Your brothers and sisters, however, have not earned the name Sinclair and will be given no more than one thousand pounds each of the winnings—unless they wish to waive their possible future inheritance completely."

Sterling heard Ivy, who shamelessly lingered for the lone reason of overhearing the conversation, whine at their father's ruling, but he knew she would accept his decision.

"The wager you made risked my money, so I will make the decision concerning the rest of the winnings as well—unless you have some objection, Sterling."

Sterling shook his head. He gazed lovingly at

Isobel. He had already won the wager and had the greatest treasure imaginable at this side. "I will abide by your wishes, Father."

"The rest of the winnings will be given to you, Sterling. What will you do with them?" In the moonlight, it was difficult for Sterling to tell whether his father was studying him, testing him. And so he replied with what his heart told him was right. "The money will be used to purchase Wenton Inn for the widows and orphans of Corunna."

His father laughed and then clasped his arms around Sterling, pulling Isobel into the embrace as well. "You have made me very proud, Sterling. You have at last earned the right to bear the Sinclair name."

He turned to look at his other wayward spawn. "As for the rest of you, my agent in London will be watching, and reporting the findings to me. Your time to redeem yourselves is not endless. Your money will be depleted unless you learn to live frugally, or heaven forbid, become employed. There will be no more money coming from me until each of you proves yourself worthy of the Sinclair name."

When the last of the wedding guests had departed, Sterling and Isobel stood in each other's arms in the middle of the garden. The moon had lost its bright luster and night had crept in among the roses.

Isobel tilted her head back, and Sterling kissed the column of her throat. She lowered her head and turned to glance at the two rows of marbles. "They are so beautiful," she said. Then her eyes seemed to sparkle. "Pity my favorite, the reclining male, is not here." She laughed saucily.

"Ah, Dionysus."

"Alas, he was too large to fit through the gates. Poor chap, he had to be returned to the shed."

Isobel feigned a pout. "Too bad, I quite like that particular marble."

Sterling grinned then.

"What?"

"Well, if you truly wish to see it . . . tonight"— Sterling reached into his pocket—"I still have the key to the shed."

Isobel laughed, but even in the moonlight he could see her face flush with color.

"Let me collect my wrap," she said with a glint in her eye.

Following is a sneak peek of Kathryn Caskie's

THE MOST WICKED OF SINS

The second book in her exciting new series
The Seven Deadly Sins

Coming 2009
From

Avon Books

ady Ivy Sinclair's moss-hued eyes were flecked with gold, and quite honestly closer to hazel in color, but she felt the green-eyed monster rising within her just the same.

She narrowed her gaze at the ebony-haired Irish beauty who had been delayed at the assembly room door by a rush of gentlemen. The same doting cluster that had been lavishing *her* with admiration only a moment ago. But worse still, Ivy's own Viscount Tinsdale had also hastened to her side and was at that very moment looking quite captivated.

"I can't bear it, Siusan," she said to her sister, who stood beside her futilely swiping her cutwork fan through the thick, still air. "What say you, do you think the patronesses would hear of it if I took Miss Feeney into the withdrawing room and throttled her? I believe I have just cause."

"If you are serious about accepting the viscount's offer—*should he actually make one*—then for God's sake do something about it, instead of allowing her to steal Tinsdale's affections away." A sprinkling of perspiration beaded along Siusan's brow, and she drew as deep a breath as she could. "I can't endure this heat. My chemise is positively sticking to my skin." She gripped Ivy's wrist and tugged until she had retrieved her attention. "Let us away. I own, not a single lady or gentleman of consequence would notice our departure. It doesn't seem to matter a tick that we are Sinclairs—now that *she* has arrived."

Ivy glanced across the assembly room, managing to snare their brother Grant's eye. She lifted her chin, silently summoning him, before returning her gaze to Siusan. "You go. Grant will escort you home. I cannot leave just yet. Not until I know Lord Tinsdale's heart is still mine to claim."

Grant sidled up to his sisters. "I cannot tell you how relieved I am that you have come to your senses and wish to leave. I have been basting in my waistcoat and coat for more than an hour, and I am certain I am tender through and through. Come, let us away."

Siusan waved her fan before Grant, urging a swish of heat over his face. "Can't."

"Why the hell not?" Grant nudged Siusan's fan away.

Siusan fashioned an overwrought sigh. "Because Ivy will not leave until she is certain of the viscount's affections." She nodded toward the doorway where Viscount Tinsdale stood fawning over the enchanting Miss Fiona Feeney.

"Of all the bleeding nonsense, Ivy," Grant huffed. "We shall be here *forever*, because even I can see that Tinsdale's attentions have strayed from you. He's entirely taken with *her*."

Ivy twisted a tendril of her copper hair in her agitation. Grant had the right of it. How could she possibly compete with Miss Feeney? Her own hair was practically the color of an orange, while the Irish lass's was like the sky at midnight. Ivy was as tall as most Englishmen, and though she possessed the sort of curves that drew gentlemen's eyes, she was not a fragile bird of a creature, like Miss Feeney, built to fit perfectly into a man's embrace.

"You're right." Ivy's eyes began to well. "I can't compete with her for Tinsdale's affections."

Grant offered up an arm to each of his sisters. "Well, then, perhaps you should find a gentleman to compete with Tinsdale for *hers*." He laughed, glancing at her and Siusan in clear expectation of their joining him.

Suddenly a jolt coursed through the entirety of Ivy's body and her eyes widened, the tears inside them seeming to recede instantly. Why had she not considered this before? It was so simple!

Siusan finally relented and began to chuckle along with Grant as she took his arm to leave.

"Aren't you coming, Ivy?"

"No, I'm not." She whirled around, scanning the assembly room most earnestly.

"Ivy, what are you doing?" Grant lowered his head as if sensing defeat already. "Come, let us leave. *Please*."

"You two go on." Ivy rose up on the tips of her toes and surveyed the shifting sea of dark coats. "I think I would rather stay a bit longer."

Siusan groaned. "Now you've done it, Grant."

"What are you going on about?" he protested. "I've done nothing."

"Aye, you have. You've given me the answer." Ivy set her hand on Grant's shoulder and leaned up to press a grateful kiss upon his cheek.

"What do you mean?" he asked.

"If I can't compete with Miss Feeney, then I will simply find the perfect gentleman to compete with Lord Tinsdale—*for her*."

One week later
Berkeley Square

Ivy peered out of the carriage door at the regal town house on the corner of Berkeley Square. "Are you sure this is the one, Poplin? It doesn't look quite as grand as I had imagined. I mean, I am paying a hundred pounds for one short month." She turned and looked at him for justification.

The elderly manservant, whose dubious services were included with the rent the Duke of Sinclair paid for his children's temporary lodgings in Grosvenor Square, nodded his head warily. "When I inquired, the carpenter . . . umm . . . butler, Mr. Cheatlin, informed me that renovations are being undertaken both inside and out in preparation for the new earl's arrival just before Christmastide. As long as your impostor is gone within thirty days, you've naught to fear. But the cost of your ruse is one hundred pounds."

"A month? I shouldn't think it will take that long," Ivy said confidently. "Shall we have a look inside and meet the staff?"

Poplin looked suddenly worried. "The staff . . . well, they'll be costing you a bit extra."

Ivy was incensed. "Their services were to be included! I might be a Sinclair, but I have only a thousand pounds for the rest of the year."

When the hackney drew to a halt before the house, Poplin did not wait for the driver to open the door. Instead he shakily stepped down the stairs to the pavers and then reached a gloved hand up to Ivy. "Their . . . services, cooking, cleaning, gardening . . . yes, all included—God help you—but keeping their mouths closed about your impostor . . . allow me to rephrase . . . *your* Earl of Counterton, and supporting your efforts when they can—well, that will cost you a clean guinea each . . . five total."

Ivy was aghast at this new development. She hadn't yet found her perfect gentleman to win Miss Feeney away from Tinsdale and already she was out one hundred and five pounds and five shillings for a house and a full staff. Robbery.

Poplin led her up the walk and rapped upon the door with his knobby knuckles. "Will you be sure the door knocker is replaced?" Ivy asked, leaning down to polish the door latch with a bit of her skirt. "All appearances must support that the new Earl of Counterton is unexpectedly at home. He is unknown in London, so there should be no problem."

"Lady Ivy," Poplin asked quietly as they waited for the door to be answered, "dare I ask what happens if *your* Earl of Counterton is exposed as an impostor?"

"Oh, I am sure he will be . . . eventually. It will be my task to delay that eventuality for as long as possible." Ivy smiled at the worried little manservant. "By then, if all goes well, Miss Feeney will have jilted Tinsdale and I will have a ring upon my finger. It will be too late for anyone to do anything about it."

Poplin groaned softly.

The latch depressed, and Ivy could hear grunting noises on the other side, but a moment later the door came unstuck and swung wide. A tall, burly man stood before them, blocking entry. "So, is this her, Poplin?" He peered down at Ivy.

Lud, Ivy thought, he didn't look the least like a butler.

" 'Tis." Poplin, seeming unnerved by the man, took a step backward.

"Has she got the coin?" The man did not remove his hard gaze from Ivy.

"I do, so if you do not mind, I am coming inside so I am not spied from the street." Ivy charged toward him, and when he did not move, she squeezed between him and the door and then beckoned for Poplin to follow. "You don't look at all like a butler, you know. Are you sure you can carry off this ruse?"

"My da was a manservant, so I have a clue about what is required. I'm the master carpenter, hired to oversee the renovation on the new Lord Counterton's town house. But don't you worry none, my lady, me and crew have the skills you're looking for, and we can and will do whatever is required as long as your guineas gleam."

Ivy dug inside her reticule, counted out five guineas, then pressed them into Mr. Cheatlin's outstretched hand. Then she whisked off her bonnet and thrust it at him. "Well, then, shall we get started?"

Cheatlin took her hat from her, chuckling as he set it to a hook alongside the door. "You can sure tell she's a Scot, can't you?" he said to Poplin, "but I think we'll all get along just fine." Pressing the door firmly closed behind them all, he bade Ivy to follow him on a tour of the house.

"God help us all," Poplin muttered, as he turned to follow his mistress.

The following evening
Drury Lane

Lady Ivy Sinclair silently lowered the carriage window and then pressed back against the seat cushion, concealing herself from passersby in the inky shadows of the cab. Outside, the carriage lanterns glowed in the darkness, their soft halos of light just reaching the stage door of the Drury Lane Theatre.

Come now, I know you are in there. Show yourself.

Ivy shifted anxiously. The play had ended nearly an hour past, and since tonight marked the final show, the actors were only now beginning to quit the theater.

Small clusters of boisterous merrymakers exited through the stage door and passed by the carriage. Ivy leaned forward and studied each of the actors as they emerged, watching, waiting for *him* to appear.

She felt confident that she would know *her* Earl of Counterton the moment her eyes fell upon him. She knew this with the same surety that he would be found here tonight. Her sister Siusan had glimpsed him just last evening, after all.

She'd said he would stand out from the others. His height would set him head and shoulders apart from the other men. And his shoulders, well, Ivy was sure they would be impossibly broad and as hard-muscled as his chest and his capable arms. She smiled at the handsome image she had pinned in her mind. He would be the sort who would make a woman's gloved hand tingle when he took it and guided her through a dance.

The earl's hair would be dark, and wavy, with rakish wisps fringing his entirely too handsome face. His eyes would be the color of a moonlit sea. And when he gazed at a woman, she would feel completely under his masculine control.

He would need to do nothing more than raise a single ebony eyebrow or lift the edges of his lips seductively, and she would be utterly powerless to refuse him.

Aye, she would know him by sight, though they'd never met—but it would be his kiss that would identify him beyond all doubt. The touch of his lips would be firm, and a claiming sort of kiss, that would reduce a woman's knees to melted wax, making her collapse into his embrace. Making her never want to leave his arms. She sighed again and leaned closer to the open window.

Ivy's pulse quickened inside her veins as the flow of actors and patrons grew more frequent. The stage door flung open again and again. He was coming, she knew it . . . it was only a matter of moments now. She bit into her lower lip in anticipation.

But then the stage door closed and, to her dismay, remained that way for several minutes.

As the moments passed, Ivy's stomach muscles began to tense, and after a minute more, the backs of her eyes began to sting. *No, no. He has to be here.* She knew it with every fiber of her being. He must be. He must.

Lud, she didn't have time to look anywhere else! The play closed tonight. She had to find the perfect actor, the perfect foil, willing to accept her coin to woo the Irish beauty away from the man she might still marry.

Precious time was slipping away. Her future was evaporating. Ivy's heart double-thudded in her chest, and she felt faint. She set an unsteady hand on the latch and flung the carriage door open. Lifting her silk skirts to her knees, she leaped down to the pavers and ran toward the stage door.

She lunged for the door, just as it opened. Suddenly her skull exploded with pain. Flashes of light blotted out her vision. And then everything became black.

"Damn it all, answer me!" A deep voice cut into her consciousness, rousing her from the cocoon of darkness blanketing her. She could feel herself being lifted, and then someone shouting something about summoning a physician.

She managed to flutter her lids open just as she felt her back skim the seat cushion inside the carriage.

Blinking, she peered up at the dark silhouette of a large man leaning over her.

"Oh, thank God, you are awake. I thought I killed you when I coshed your head with the door." He leaned back then, just enough that a flicker of light touched his visage.

Ivy gasped at the sight of him.

He shoved his black hair back away from his eyes that looked almost silver in the dimness. A cleft marked the center of his chin, and his angular jaw was defined by a dark sprinkling of stubble. His full lips parted in a relieved smile.

There was a distinct fluttering in Ivy's middle. It was *he*. The perfect man . . . for the position. "It's *you*," she whispered softly.

"I apologize, miss, but I didn't hear what you said." He leaned toward her. "Is there something more I can do to assist you?"

Ivy nodded and feebly beckoned him forward. He moved back inside the cab and sat next to her as she lay across the bench.

She gestured for him to come closer still.

It was wicked, what she was about to do, but she had to be sure.

He turned his head so that his ear was just above her mouth. "Yes?"

"I assure you that I am quite well, sir," she whispered into his ear, "but there is indeed something you can do for me." She didn't wait for him to respond. Ivy shoved her fingers through his thick hair and turned his face to her. Peering deeply into his eyes, she pressed her mouth to his, startling him. She immediately felt his fingers curl around her wrist, and yet he didn't pull away.

Instead his lips moved over hers, making her yield to his own kiss. His mouth was warm and tasted of brandy, and his lips parted slightly as he masterfully claimed her with his kiss.

Her heart pounded and her sudden breathlessness blocked out the sounds of carriages, whinnying horses, and theater patrons calling to their drivers on the street.

His tongue slid slowly along her top lip, somehow making her feel impossible things lower down. Then he nipped at her throbbing bottom lip, before urging her mouth wider and exploring the soft flesh inside with his probing tongue. Hesitantly she moved her tongue forward until it slid along his. At the moment their tongues touched, a soft groan welled up from the back of his throat, and a surge of excitement shot through her body.

Already she felt the tug of surrender. Of wanting to give herself over to the passion he somehow tapped within her.

And then it was as if he knew what he made her feel, made her want—and he suddenly pulled back from her.

She peered up at him through drowsy eyes.

"I fear, my lady, that you mistake me for someone else," he said, not looking the least bit disappointed or astounded by what she had done.

"No," Ivy replied, "no mistake." She wriggled, pulling herself to sit upright. "You are exactly who I thought you were."

"I beg your pardon, but I know we have never met. I am quite certain I would remember meeting *you*."

Ivy smiled at him. How perfect he was. How absolutely perfect. "I am Lady Ivy Sinclair." She watched for any recognition.

How curious. He didn't seem to react to the mention of the Sinclair name. Could it be he truly did not know she was one of the Seven Deadly Sins? Oh, he was perfect.

"And I am—" he began, but Ivy raised her hand, silencing him. He raised a quizzical eyebrow.

Ivy straightened her back and looked quite earnestly into his eyes. "You are the Earl of Counterton . . . or rather you will be, if you accept my offer."

**Warm up the winter nights
with a sizzling hot read!
With four upcoming
Romance Superleaders
from bestsellers
Elizabeth Boyle, Laura Lee Guhrke,
Kerrelyn Sparks, and Kathryn Caskie,
you won't even feel the cold . . .**

Coming September 2008

Tempted By the Night

**An exciting new paranormal romance
by *New York Times* bestselling author**

ELIZABETH BOYLE

*Lady Hermione Marlowe has loved the rakish Earl of
Rockhurst from afar forever, defending his scandalous
ways at every turn. One of her greatest desires is to follow
after him, completely unseen, so as to reveal his true noble
nature . . . and then, much to her shock, Hermione finds herself fading from sight as the sun sets, until she is completely
invisible! Freed of the confines of Society, she recklessly
follows the earl into the temptations of the night and shock-
ingly discovers that his disreputable veneer is merely a cover
for his real duty: safeguarding London as the Paratus, the
Protector of the Realm.*

❋

Thomasin appeared in the same state of shock. "Oh. My.
Goodness," she managed to gasp, her eyes wide with
amazement as she gazed somewhere over Hermione's shoulder. "You are never going to believe this, Minny."

India blinked and tried again to speak, her mouth waver-
ing open and shut as if she couldn't quite find the words to
describe the sight before her.

"What is it?" Hermione asked, glancing over her shoulder
and only seeing the narrow, tall figure of Lord Battersby
behind her. Certainly his arrival wouldn't have India looking like she'd swallowed her aunt's parrot.

"Oh, let me tell her," Thomasin was saying, rising up on her toes.

"No, let me," India said as she finally found her voice. "I saw *him* first."

Him. Hermione shivered. There was only one *him* in the *ton* as far as she was concerned.

Rockhurst.

Oh, but her friends had to be jesting, for the earl would never make an appearance at Almack's. She glanced at both their faces, fully expecting to find some telltale sign of mirth, some twitch of the lips that would give way to a full-blown giggle.

But there were none. Just the same, wide-eyed gaping expression that she now noticed several other guests wore.

Turning around slowly, Hermione's jaw dropped as well.

Nothing in all her years out could have prepared her for the sight of the Earl of Rockhurst arriving at Almack's.

"Jiminy!" she gasped, her hand going immediately to her quaking stomach. Oh, heavens, she shouldn't have had that extra helping of pudding at supper, for now she feared the worst.

And here she thought she'd be safe at Almack's.

"I didn't believe you," she whispered to India.

"I still don't believe it myself," India shot back. "Whatever is he doing here?"

"I don't know, and I don't care," Thomasin replied, "but I'm just glad Mother insisted we come tonight, if only for the crowing rights we will have tomorrow over everyone who isn't here."

"Oh, this is hardly the gown to catch his eye," Hermione groaned. "It is entirely the wrong shade of capucine," she declared, running her hands over the perfectly fashionable, perfectly pretty gown she'd chosen.

Thomasin laughed. "Minny, stop fussing. The three of us could be stark naked and posed like a trio of wood nymphs, and he wouldn't notice us."

"True enough," India agreed. "You have to see that you are too respectable to garner his fancy."

"He fancied Charlotte," Hermione shot back, trying to ignore the little bit of jealousy that niggled in her heart as she said it.

"Oh, I suppose he did for about an hour," India conceded, "but you have to admit, Charlotte was a bit odd the last few weeks. Not herself at all."

Hermione nodded in agreement. There had been something different about Charlotte. Ever since . . . ever since her Great-Aunt Ursula had died and she'd inherited . . . Hermione glanced down at her gloved hand. Inherited the very ring she'd found yesterday . . .

Beneath her glove, she swore the ring warmed, even quivered on her finger, like a trembling bell that foretold of something ominous just out of reach.

"Did you hear of his latest escapade?" Lady Thomasin was whispering. There was no one around them to hear, but some things just couldn't be spoken in anything less than the awed tone of a conspiratorial hush.

India nodded. "About his wager with Lord Kramer—"

"Oh, hardly that," Thomasin scoffed. "Everyone has heard about that. No, I am speaking of his renewed interest in Mrs. Fornett. Apparently she was seen with him at Tattersall's when everyone knows she is under Lord Saunderton's protection." The girl paused, then heaved a sigh. "Of course there will be a duel. There always is in these cases." Lady Thomasin's cousin had once fought a duel, and so she considered herself quite the expert on the subject.

"Pish posh," Hermione declared. "He isn't interested in her."

"I heard Mother telling Lady Gidding, that she'd heard it from Lady Owston, who'd had it directly from Lord Filton that he was at Tatt's with Mrs. Fornett." Thomasin rocked back on her heels, her brows arched and her mouth set as if that was the final word on the subject.

"That may be so, but I heard Lord Delamere tell my brother that he'd seen Rockhurst going into a truly dreadful house in Seven Dials. The sort of place no gentleman would even frequent. With truly awful women inside."

Hermione wrinkled her nose. "And what was Lord Delamere doing outside this sinful den?"

"I daresay driving past it to get to the nearest gaming hell. He's gone quite dice mad and nearly run through his inheritance. Or so my brother likes to say."

"And probably squiffed, I'd wager," Hermione declared, forgetting her admonishment to Viola about using such phrases. "I don't believe any of it. Whatever is the matter with Society these days when all they can get on with is making up gossip about a man who doesn't deserve it?"

"Not deserve it?" Lady Thomasin gaped. "The Earl of Rockhurst is a terrible bounder. Everyone knows it."

"Well, I think differently." Hermione crossed her arms over her chest and stood firm, even as her stomach continued to twist and turn.

"Why you continue to defend him, I know not," India said, glancing over where the earl stood with his cousin, Miss Mary Kendell. "He's wicked and unrepentant."

"I disagree." Hermione straightened and took a measured glance at the man. "I don't believe a word of any of it. The Earl of Rockhurst is a man of honor."

Lady Thomasin snorted. "Oh, next you'll be telling us he spends his nights, spooning broth to sickly orphans and bestowing food baskets to poor war widows."

India laughed. "Oh, no, I think he's like the mad earl in that book your mother told us not to read." She shivered and leaned in closer to whisper. "You know the one . . . about the dreadful man who kidnapped all sorts of ladies and kept them in his attic? I'd wager if you were to venture into the earl's attics, you'd find an entire harem!"

"Oh, of all the utter nonsense! How can you say such dreadful things about a man's reputation?" Hermione argued. "The earl is a decent man, I just know it. And I'll not let the Lord Delameres and the Lord Filtons of the world tell me differently."

"Well, the only way to prove such a thing would be to follow him around all night—for apparently only seeing the truth with your own eyes will end this infatuation of yours, Hermione."

She crossed her arms over her chest and set her shoulders. "I just might."

"Yes, and you'd be ruined in the process," Thomasin pointed out. "And don't think he'll marry you to save your reputation, when he cares nothing of his own."

India snapped her fingers, her eyes alight with inspiration. "Too bad you aren't cursed like the poor heroine in that book we borrowed from my cousin. Remember it? *Zoe's Dilemma* . . . No, that's not it. *Zoe's Awful* . . . Oh, I don't remember the rest of the title."

"I do," Lady Thomasin jumped in. "*Zoe or the Moral Loss of a Soul Cursed.*"

India sighed. "Yes, yes, that was it."

Hermione gazed up at the ceiling. Only Thomasin and India would recall such a tale at a time like this. She glanced over at the earl, and then down at her gown. Oh, she should never have settled on this dress. It was too pumpkin and not enough capucine. How would he ever discover her now?

Thomasin continued, "You remember the story, Minny. At sunset, Zoe faded from sight so no one could see her. What I would give to have a night thusly."

"Whatever for?" India asked. "You already know the earl is a bounder."

Their friend got a devilish twinkle in her eye. "If I were unseen for a night, I'd make sure that Miss Lavinia Burke had the worst evening of her life. Why, the next day, every gossip in London would be discussing what a bad case of wind she had, not to mention how clumsy she's become, for I fear I'd be standing on her train every time she took a step."

Hermione chuckled, while India burst out laughing.

"I do think you've considered this before," Hermione said.

Thomasin grinned. "I might have." Then she laughed as well. "If you were so cursed, Hermione, you could follow Rockhurst from sunset to sunrise, and then you'd see everyone is right about him."

India made a more relevant point. "Then you could end this disastrous *tendré* you have for him and discover a more eligible *parti* before the Season ends."

And your chances of a good marriage with them, her statement implied, but being the bosom bow that India was, she wouldn't say such a thing.

Still, Hermione wasn't about to concede so easily. "More likely you would both have to take back every terrible thing you've ever said about him."

"Or listen to your sorry laments over how wretchedly you've been deceived," Thomasin shot back.

Hermione turned toward the earl. Truly no man could be so terribly wicked or so awful.

Oh, if only . . .

Coming October 2008

Secret Desires of a Gentleman

**The final book in the *Girl-Bachelor Chronicles*
by *USA Today* bestselling author**

LAURA LEE GUHRKE

*Phillip Hawthorne, Marquess of Kayne, has his life mapped
out before him. He is a responsible member of the peerage,
and rumor has it he may become the next prime minister. And
then he runs into Maria Martingale. Twelve years ago, Maria
was the cook's daughter, and she fancied herself in love with
Lawrence Hawthorne, the marquess's younger brother, but
Phillip quickly put an end to that romance. Now Phillip, still
as cold and ruthless as he had been all those years ago, is concerned Maria will ruin things for Lawrence and his impending
marriage, so he does the only thing he can think of to distract
her—seduction.*

Maria started down the street, still looking over her
shoulder at the shop. "Perfect," she breathed with rev-
erent appreciation. "It's absolutely perfect."

The collision brought her out of her daydreams with painful
force. She was knocked off her feet, her handbag went flying,
and she stumbled backward, stepping on the hem of her skirt
as she tried desperately to right herself. She would have fallen
to the pavement, but a pair of strong hands caught her by the
arms, and she was hauled upright, pulled hard against what
was definitely a man's chest. "Steady on, my girl," a deep

voice murmured, a voice that somehow seemed familiar. "Are you all right?"

She inhaled deeply, trying to catch her breath, and as she did, she caught the luscious scents of bay rum and fresh linen. She nodded, her cheek brushing the unmistakable silk of a fine necktie. "I think so, yes," she answered.

Her palms flattened against the soft, rich wool of a gentleman's coat and she pushed back, straightening away from him as she lifted her chin to look into his face. The moment she did, recognition hit her with more force than the collision had done.

Phillip Hawthorne. The Marquess of Kayne.

There was no mistaking those eyes, vivid cobalt blue framed by thick black lashes. Irish eyes, she'd always thought, though if any Irish blood tainted the purity of his oh-so-aristocratic British lineage, he'd never have acknowledged it. Phillip had always been such a dry stick, as unlike his brother, Lawrence, as chalk was from cheese.

Memories came over her like a flood, washing away ten years in the space of a heartbeat. Suddenly, she was no longer standing on a sidewalk in Mayfair, but in the library at Kayne Hall, and Phillip was standing across the desk from her, holding out a bank draft and looking at her as if she were nothing.

She glanced down, half-expecting to see a slip of pale pink paper in his hand—the bribe to make her leave and never come back, the payment for her promise to keep away from his brother for the rest of her life. The marquess had only been nineteen then, but he'd already managed to put a price on love. It was worth five hundred pounds.

That should be enough, since my brother assures me there is no possibility of a child.

His voice, so cold, echoed back to her from ten years ago, and shaken, she tried to gather her wits. She'd always expected she'd run into Phillip again one day, but she had not expected it to happen so literally, and she felt rather at sixes and sevens. Lawrence she'd never thought to see again, for she'd read in some scandal sheet years ago that he'd gone off to America.

His older brother was a different matter. Phillip was a marquess, he came to London for the season every year, sat in the House of Lords, and mingled with the finest society. Given all the balls and parties where she'd served hors d'oeuvres to aristocrats while working for Andre, Maria had resigned herself long ago to the inevitable night she would look up while offering a plate of canapés or a tray of champagne glasses and find his cool, haughty gaze on her, but it had never happened. Ten years of beating the odds only to cannon into him on a street corner. Of all the rotten luck.

Her gaze slid downward. Phillip had always been tall, but standing before her was not the lanky youth she remembered. This man's shoulders were wider, his chest broader, his entire physique exuding such masculine strength and vitality that Maria felt quite aggrieved. If there was any fairness in the world at all, Phillip Hawthorne would have gone to fat and gotten the gout by now. Instead, the Marquess of Kayne was even stronger and more powerful at thirty-one than he'd been at nineteen. How nauseating.

Still, she thought as she returned her gaze to his face, ten years had left their mark. There were tiny lines at the corners of his eyes and two faint parallel creases across his forehead. The determination and discipline in the line of his jaw was even more pronounced than it had been a dozen years ago, and his mouth, a grave, unsmiling curve that had always been surprisingly beautiful, was harsher now. His entire countenance, in fact, was harder than she remembered it, as if all those notions of duty and responsibility he'd been stuffed with as a boy weighed heavy on him as a man. Maria found some satisfaction in that.

Even more satisfying was the fact that she had changed, too. She was no longer the desperate, forsaken seventeen-year-old girl who'd thought being bought off for five hundred pounds was her only choice. These days, she wasn't without means and she wasn't without friends. Never again would she be intimidated by the likes of Phillip Hawthorne.

"What are you doing here?" she demanded, then grimaced at her lack of eloquence. Over the years, she'd invented an entire repertoire of cutting, clever things to say to him should they ever meet again, and that blunt, stupid query was the best she could do? Maria wanted to kick herself.

"An odd question," he murmured in the well-bred accent she remembered so clearly. "I live here."

"Here?" A knot of dread began forming in the pit of her stomach as his words sank in. "But this is an empty shop."

"Not the shop." He let go of her arms and gestured to the front door of the first town house on Half Moon Street, an elegant red door out of which he must have just come from when they'd collided. "I live there."

She stared at the door in disbelief. *You can't live here*, she wanted to shout. *Not you, not Phillip Hawthorne, not in this house right beside the lovely, perfect shop where I'm going to live.*

She looked at him again. "But that's impossible. Your London house is in Park Lane."

He stiffened, dark brows drawing together in a puzzled frown. "My home in Park Lane is presently being remodeled, though I don't see what business it is of yours."

Before she could reply, he glanced at the ground and spoke again. "You've spilled your things."

"I didn't spill them," she corrected, bristling a bit. "You did."

To her disappointment, he didn't argue the point. "My apologies," he murmured, and knelt on the pavement. "Allow me to retrieve them for you."

She watched him, still irritated and rather bemused, as he righted her handbag and began to pick up her scattered belongings. She watched his bent head as he gathered her tortoiseshell comb, her gloves, her cotton handkerchief, and her money purse, then began placing them in her handbag with careful precision. So like Phillip, she thought. God forbid one should just toss it all inside and get on with things.

After all her things had been returned to her bag, he closed the brass clasp and reached for his hat, a fine gray felt Bromburg, which had also gone flying during the collision. He donned his hat and stood up, holding her bag out to her.

She took it from his outstretched hand. "Thank you, Phillip," she murmured. "How—" She broke off, not knowing if she should inquire after his brother, but then she decided it was only right to ask. "How is Lawrence?"

Something flashed in his eyes, but when he spoke, his voice was politely indifferent. "Forgive me, miss," he said with a cool, impersonal smile, "but your use of Christian names indicates a familiarity with me of which I am unaware."

Miss? She blinked, stunned. "Unaware?" she echoed and started to laugh, not from humor, but from disbelief. "But Phillip, you've known me since I was five years—"

"I don't believe so," he cut her off, his voice still polite and pleasant, his gaze hard and implacable. "We do not know each other, miss. We do not know each other at all. I hope that's clear?"

Her eyes narrowed. He knew precisely who she was and he was pretending not to, the arrogant, toplofty snob. How dare he snub her? She wanted to reply, but before she could think of something sufficiently cutting to say, he spoke again. "Good day, miss," he said, then bowed and stepped around her to go on his way.

She turned, watching his back as he walked away. Outrage seethed within her, but when she spoke, her voice was sweet as honey. "It was delightful to see you again, *Phillip*," she called after him. "Give Lawrence my best regards, will you?"

His steps did not falter as he walked away.

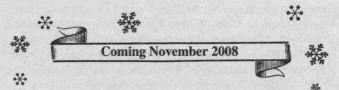

Coming November 2008

All I Want for Christmas Is a Vampire

The latest in the *Love at Stake* series by *New York Times* bestselling author

KERRELYN SPARKS

Vampire Ian MacPhie is on a mission—he's on the lookout for true love. He claims that all he wants is another vampire. . . . until Toni Duncan comes along. Toni's best friend is locked up in a psycho ward, deemed insane when she confesses that vampires attacked her. The only way to get her out is for Toni to prove that vampires exist. So Toni comes up with a plan: make Ian lose control and beg him to make her one of his kind . . .

Ian felt ten degrees hotter in spite of the cold December air that drifted through the open window and over his white undershirt. The lamp between the two wingback chairs was turned on low, and it cast a golden glow across the room to outline her form with a shimmering aura.

She made a stunning cat burglar, dressed entirely in black spandex that molded to her waist and sweetly curved hips. Her golden hair hung in a ponytail down her back. The ends swished gently across her shoulder blades, as she moved her head from side to side, scanning the bookshelf.

She stepped to the side, silent in her black socks. She must have left her shoes outside the window, thinking she'd move more quietly without them. He noted her slim ankles, then let his gaze wander back up to golden hair. He would have to be careful capturing her. Like any Vamp, he had super strength, and she looked a bit fragile.

He moved silently past the wingback chairs to the window. It made a swooshing sound as he shut it.

With a gasp, she turned toward him. Her eyes widened.

Eyes green as the hills surrounding his home in Scotland.

A surge of desire left him speechless for a moment. She seemed equally speechless. No doubt she was busily contemplating an escape route.

He moved slowly toward her. "Ye willna escape through the window. And ye canna reach the door before me."

She stepped back. "Who are you? Do you live here?"

"I'll be asking the questions, once I have ye restrained." He could hear her heart beating faster. Her face remained expressionless, except for her eyes. They flashed with defiance. They were beautiful.

She plucked a heavy book off a nearby shelf. "Did you come here to test my abilities?"

An odd question. Was he misinterpreting the situation? "Who—?" He dodged to the side when she suddenly hurled the book at his face. Bugger, he'd suffered too much to get his older, more manly face, and she'd nearly smacked it.

The book flew past him and knocked over the lamp. The light flickered and went out. With his superior vision, he could see her dark form running for the door.

He zoomed after her. Just before he could grab her, she spun and landed a kick against his chest. He stumbled back. Damn, she was stronger than he'd thought. And he'd suffered too much to get his broader, more manly chest.

She advanced with a series of punches and kicks, and he blocked them all. With a desperate move, she aimed a kick at his groin. Dammit, he'd suffered too much to get his bigger, more manly balls. He jumped back, but her toes caught the hem of his kilt. Without his sporran to weigh the kilt down, it flew up past his waist.

Her gaze flitted south and stuck. Her mouth fell open. Aye, those twelve years of growth had been kind. He lunged forward and slammed her onto the carpet. She punched at him, so he caught her wrists and pinned her to the floor.

She twisted, attempting to knee him. With a growl, he blocked her with his own knee. Then slowly, he lowered himself on top of her to keep her still. Her body was gloriously hot, flushed with blood and throbbing with a life force that made his body tremble with desire.

"Stop wiggling, lass." His bigger, more manly groin was reacting in an even bigger way. "Have mercy on me."

"Mercy?" She continued to wriggle beneath him. "I'm the one who's captured."

"Cease." He pressed more heavily on her.

Her eyes widened. He had no doubt she was feeling it.

Her gaze flickered down, then back to his face. "Get off. Now."

"I'm halfway there already," he muttered.

"Let me go!" She strained at his grip on her wrists.

"If I release you, ye'll knee me. And I'm rather fond of my balls."

"The feeling isn't mutual."

He smiled slowly. "Ye took a long look. Ye must have liked what ye saw."

"Ha! You made such a *small* impression on me, I can barely remember."

He chuckled. She was as quick mentally as she was physically.

She looked at him curiously. "You smell like beer."

"I've had a few." He noted her dubious expression. "Okay, more than a few, but I was still able to beat you."

"If you drink beer, then that means you're not . . ."

"No' what?"

She looked at him, her eyes wide. He had a sinking feeling that she thought he was mortal. She wanted him to be mortal. And that meant she knew about Vamps.

He studied her lovely face—the high cheekbones, delicate

jawline, and beguiling green eyes. Some Vamps claimed mortals had no power whatsoever. They were wrong.

Their eyes met, and he forgot to breathe. There was something hidden in those green depths. A loneliness. A wound that seemed too old for her tender age. For a moment, he felt like he was seeing a reflection of his own soul.

"Ye're no' a thief, are you?" he whispered.

She shook her head slightly, still trapped in his gaze. Or maybe it was he who was trapped in hers.

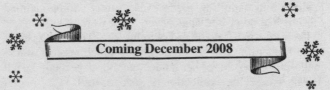

Coming December 2008

To Sin With a Stranger

The first in the new *Seven Deadly Sins* series by *USA Today* bestselling author

KATHRYN CASKIE

The Sinclairs are one of the oldest, wealthiest, and wildest noble families in all of Scotland. The seven brothers and sisters of the clan enjoy a good time, know no boundaries, and have scandal follow in their wake. They are known amongst the ton as The Seven Deadly Sins. But now their father has declared they must become respectable married members of proper Society . . . This is Sterling, Marquess of Blackburn's, story of how greed and a young beauty, Miss Isobel Carington, almost became his downfall.

"As the Sinclair children grew older, they seemed to embrace the sins Society had labeled them with. Sterling, Marquess of Blackburn, is cursed with greed." Christiana turned her eyes toward the fighter and Isobel followed her gaze. "Lady Siusan epitomizes sloth, and Lady Ivy, the copper-haired beauty, envy."

"This is nonsense."

"Is it?" Christiana continued. "Lord Lachlan is a wicked rake. No wonder his weakness is lust. Lord Grant, the one with the lace cuffs, is said to have a taste for luxury and indulgence. His sin is gluttony. The twins are said to be the worst of all." She raised her nose toward the Sinclair with a sheath of hair so dark that it almost appeared a deep blue. "Lord Killian's sin is wrath. Whispers suggest that he is the true fighter in the family, but his anger is too quick and fierce. Why, there is even one rumor that claims that he actually killed a man who merely looked at his twin sister! That's her, there. Lady Priscilla. Just look at her with her haughty chin turned toward the chandelier—here, in a room full of nobility! Her sin is, quite clearly, *pride*."

"Nonsense! I do not believe it," Isobel countered. "I do not believe any of the story. The tale is naught but idle gossip."

"I believe it." Christiana set one hand on her hip and waved the other in the air as she spoke. "Why else would they have come to London, if not to leave their sinful reputations behind in Scotland?"

"I am sure I do not know." Isobel saw Christiana's jaw drop, then felt the presence of someone behind her.

"Perhaps I have come to London to ask you to dance with me, lassie." His rich Scottish brogue resonated in her ears, making her vibrate with his every word.

Isobel whirled around and stared up into none other than Sterling's grinning face.

"I apologize. I would address you by name, but alas, I dinna know what it is. Only that you are easily the most beautiful woman in this assembly room." Before she could blink, he reached a hand, knuckles stitched with black threads, and brushed his fingers across her cheek—just as he'd done at the club. "English lasses dinna stir me the way you do. You must be a wee bit Scottish."

Isobel gasped, drew back her hand, and gave his cheek a stinging slap. "My lord, you humiliated me, made light of my charity and my attempts to help widows and orphans of war. Why would I ever agree to dance with an ill-mannered rogue like you?"

"Because I asked, and I saw the way you were lookin' at me." He lifted an eyebrow teasingly, bringing to the surface a rage Isobel could not rein in. She slapped his face with such force that his head wrenched to the left. He raised his hand to his cheek. "Not bad. Have you thought about pugilism as a profession?" He grinned at her again.

Isobel stepped around Sterling Sinclair and started for her father. But he was only two steps away. Staring at her. Aghast. She reached out for him, but he stepped back, out of her reach.

She glanced to her left, then her right. Everyone was staring. Everyone.

Isobel covered her face with her trembling hands and shoved her way through the crowd of amused onlookers. She dashed out the door and down the steps to the liveried footman who opened the outer door for her to the street.

She ran outside and rested her hands on her knees as she gasped for breath. Her father would cast her to the street for embarrassing him this night.

No matter what punishment he chose for her, Isobel was certain he would never allow her to show her face in Town again.

And Sterling, the wicked Marquess of Blackburn, was wholly to blame.

At Avon Books, we know your passion for romance—once you finish one of our novels, you find yourself wanting more.

May we tempt you with . . .

- **Excerpts** from our upcoming releases.
- Entertaining **extras**, including authors' personal photo albums and book lists.
- Behind-the-scenes **scoop** on your favorite characters and series.
- **Sweepstakes** for the chance to win free books, romantic getaways, and other fun prizes.
- Writing **tips** from our authors and editors.
- **Blog** with our authors and find out why they love to write romance.
- **Exclusive content** that's not contained within the pages of our novels.

Join us at
www.avonbooks.com

AVON

An Imprint of HarperCollins*Publishers*
www.avonromance.com